THE BOOK OF LAUGHTER AND FORGETTING

Milan Kundera was born in 1929 in Czechoslovakia and since 1975 has been living in France.

Milan Kundera

The Book of Laughter and Forgetting

Translated from the French by
Aaron Asher

faber and faber

This translation first published in the USA in 1996
by HarperCollins Publishers, Inc.
First published in Great Britain in 1996
by Faber and Faber Limited
3 Queen Square London WC1N 3AU

This edition first published in 2000

Printed in Great Britain by Mackays of Chatham PLC

Kniha Smichu a Zapomneni © Milan Kundera, 1978.
Le Livre du Rire et de L'oubli © Editions Gallimard, 1979.
English language translation first published in the USA in 1980
by Alfred A Knopf, Inc.
French translation revised by Milan Kundera
© Editions Gallimard, 1985.
Author's Note © Milan Kundera, 1996.
New English language translation © Aaron Asher, 1996.

Grateful acknowledgement is made to the following for permission to reprint
from previously unpublished material. Editions Gallimard: excerpts from
Rhinoceros by Eugene Ionesco, © Editions Gallimard, 1959; excerpts from *"Le
Visage de la Paix,"* taken from *Oeuvres Completes*, Volume 2, by Paul Eluard,
© Editions Gallimard, 1968. Editions Bernard Grasset: excerpts from *Parole de
Femme* (1976) by Annie Leclerc.

Arron Asher is hereby identified as translator of this work
in accordance with Section 77 of the Copyright,
Designs and Patents Act 1988.

A CIP record for this book is
available from the British Library

ISBN 0–571–20387–6

2 4 6 8 10 9 7 5 3

CONTENTS

AUTHOR'S NOTE

The Book of Laughter and Forgetting was written in Czech between 1976 and 1978. Between 1985 and 1987, I revised the French translations of all my novels (and stories) so deeply and completely that I was able to include, in the subsequent new editions, a note affirming that the French versions of these works "are equal in authenticity to the Czech texts." My intervention in these French versions did not result in variants of my original texts. I was led to it only by a wish for accuracy. The French translations have become, so to speak, more faithful to the Czech originals than the originals themselves.

Two years ago, when Aaron Asher and I reread the English language version of *The Book of Laughter and Forgetting,* we agreed on the need for a new translation. I suggested translating from the authentic French edition and urged Aaron to take it on himself. Following his work very closely, I had the pleasure of seeing my text emerge in his translation as from a miraculous bath. At last I recognized my book. I thank Aaron for that with all my heart.

Paris, December 1995

PART ONE

Lost Letters

1

In February 1948, the Communist leader Klement
Gottwald stepped out on the balcony of a Baroque
palace in Prague to harangue hundreds of thousands
of citizens massed in Old Town Square. That was a
great turning point in the history of Bohemia. A fateful moment of the kind that occurs only once or twice
a millennium.

Gottwald was flanked by his comrades, with
Clementis standing close to him. It was snowing and
cold, and Gottwald was bareheaded. Bursting with
solicitude, Clementis took off his fur hat and set it on
Gottwald's head.

The propaganda section made hundreds of thousands of copies of the photograph taken on the balcony
where Gottwald, in a fur hat and surrounded by his
comrades, spoke to the people. On that balcony the
history of Communist Bohemia began. Every child
knew that photograph, from seeing it on posters and in
schoolbooks and museums.

Four years later, Clementis was charged with trea-
son and hanged. The propaganda section immediately
made him vanish from history and, of course, from all
photographs. Ever since, Gottwald has been alone on

the balcony. Where Clementis stood, there is only the bare palace wall. Nothing remains of Clementis but the fur hat on Gottwald's head.

2

It is 1971, and Mirek says: The struggle of man against power is the struggle of memory against forgetting.

With this he is trying to justify what his friends call carelessness: meticulously keeping a diary, preserving his correspondence, compiling the minutes of all the meetings where they discuss the situation and ponder what to do. He says to them: We're not doing anything that violates the constitution. To hide and feel guilty would be the beginning of defeat.

A week before, at work with his crew on the roof of a building under construction, he looked down and was overcome by vertigo. He lost his balance, and his fall was broken by a badly joined beam that came loose; then they had to extricate him from under it. At first sight, the injury seemed serious, but a little later, when it turned out to be only an ordinary fracture of the forearm, he was pleased by the prospect of some weeks of vacation and the opportunity finally to take care of things he had never found the time for.

He ended up agreeing with his more prudent

friends. The constitution did indeed guarantee freedom of speech, but the laws punished anything that could be considered an attack on state security. One never knew when the state would start screaming that this word or that was an attempt on its security. So he decided to put his compromising papers in a safe place.

But first he wanted to settle the Zdena business. He had phoned her in the town where she lived, but was unable to reach her. That cost him four days. He got through to her only yesterday. She had agreed to see him this afternoon.

Mirek's seventeen-year-old son protested: Mirek would be unable to drive with his arm in a cast. And he did have trouble driving. Powerless and useless in its sling, the injured arm swayed on his chest. To shift gears, Mirek had to let go of the steering wheel.

3

He had had an affair with Zdena twenty-five years earlier, and all that remained from that time were some memories.

One day, she had appeared for a date wiping her eyes with a handkerchief and sniffling. He asked her what was wrong. She told him that a Russian statesman had died the day before. A certain Zhdanov, Arbuzov, or Masturbov. Judging by the abundance of her tears, the death of Masturbov had moved her more strongly than the death of her own father.

Could that really have happened? Isn't it merely his present-day hatred that has invented those tears over Masturbov's death? No, it had certainly happened. But of course it's true that the immediate circumstances which had made these tears real and believable baffled him now, and that the memory had become as implausible as a caricature.

All his memories of her were like that: They had come back together by streetcar from the apartment where they first made love. (Mirek noted with distinct satisfaction that he had completely forgotten their coitions, that he was unable to recall even a single moment of them.) She sat on a corner bench in the jolting streetcar, her face sullen, closed, surprisingly old. When he asked her why she was so silent, she told him she had not been satisfied with their lovemaking. She said he had made love to her like an intellectual.

In the political jargon of those days, the word "intellectual" was an insult. It indicated someone who did not understand life and was cut off from the people. All the Communists who were hanged at the time by other Communists were awarded such abuse. Unlike those who had their feet solidly on the ground, they were said to float in the air. So it was fair, in a way, that as punishment the ground was permanently pulled out from under their feet, that they remained suspended a little above the floor.

But what did Zdena mean by accusing him of making love like an intellectual?

For one reason or another, Zdena was displeased with him, and just as she was capable of imbuing the most abstract relationship (the relationship with Masturbov, whom she didn't know) with the most concrete feeling (embodied in a tear), so she was capable of giving the most concrete of acts an abstract significance and her own dissatisfaction a political name.

4

In the rearview mirror, he noticed a car persistently staying behind him. He had never doubted he was being followed, but up to now they had behaved with model discretion. Today a radical change had taken place: they wanted him to know they were there.

Out in the country, about twenty kilometers from Prague, there was a high fence with a service station and auto-repair shop behind it. He had a pal working there who could replace his defective starter. He stopped the car in front of a red-and-white-striped barrier blocking the entrance. Beside it stood a heavy woman. Mirek waited for her to raise the barrier, but she just stood there staring at him. He honked his horn, in vain. He stuck his head out of the open window. "Didn't they arrest you yet?" asked the woman.

"No, they haven't arrested me yet," answered Mirek. "Could you raise the barrier?"

She stared absently at him for some more long moments, then yawned and went back to her gatekeeper's shack. She sat down there behind a table, no longer looking his way.

So he got out of the car, walked around the barrier, and went into the repair shop to find the mechanic he knew. The mechanic came back with him and raised the barrier himself (the heavy woman was still sitting in the gatekeeper's shack, staring absently), allowing Mirek to drive in.

"You see, it's because you showed up too much on TV," said the mechanic. "All those dames know who you are."

"Who is she?" asked Mirek.

The mechanic told him that the invasion of Bohemia by the Russian army, whose occupation of the country had affected everything, had been for her a signal of a new life, out of the ordinary. She saw that people who ranked above her (and everyone ranked above her) were being deprived, on the slightest allegation, of their powers, their positions, their jobs, and their bread, and that excited her; she started to denounce people herself.

"So why is she still a gatekeeper? Why wasn't she promoted?"

The mechanic smiled. "She can't count to ten. They can't find another job for her. All they can do is let her go on denouncing people. For her, that's a promotion!"

He raised the hood and looked at the engine.

Mirek suddenly became aware of a man standing near him. He turned: the man was wearing a gray jacket, a white shirt with tie, and brown trousers. Above the thick neck and puffy face was a head of gray hair in a permanent wave. He had planted himself there to watch the mechanic leaning under the raised hood.

After a moment, the mechanic noticed him too, and he straightened up and said: "Looking for somebody?"

The thick-necked man with the permanent wave answered: "No. I'm not looking for anybody."

The mechanic leaned over the engine again and said: "In Wenceslaus Square, in Prague, a guy is throwing up. Another guy comes up to him, pulls a long face, shakes his head, and says: 'I know just what you mean.'"

5

The assassination of Allende quickly covered over the memory of the Russian invasion of Bohemia, the bloody massacre in Bangladesh caused Allende to be forgotten, the din of war in the Sinai Desert drowned out the groans of Bangladesh, the massacres in Cambodia caused the Sinai to be forgotten, and so on, and on and on, until everyone has completely forgotten everything.

At a time when history still made its way slowly, the few events were easily remembered and woven into a backdrop, known to everyone, before which private life unfolded the gripping show of its adventures. Nowadays, time moves forward at a rapid pace. Forgotten overnight, a historic event glistens the next day like the morning dew and thus is no longer the backdrop to a narrator's tale but rather an amazing *adventure* enacted against the background of the over-familiar banality of private life.

Since there is not a single historic event we can count on being commonly known, I must speak of events that took place a few years ago as if they were a thousand years old: In 1939, the German army entered Bohemia, and the Czech state ceased to exist. In 1945, the Russian army entered Bohemia, and the country once again was called an independent republic. The people were enthusiastic about the Russia that had driven out the Germans, and seeing in the Czech Communist Party its faithful arm, they became sympathetic to it. So the Communists took power in February 1948 with neither bloodshed nor violence, but greeted by the cheers of about half the nation. And now, please note: the half that did the cheering was the more dynamic, the more intelligent, the better.

Yes, say what you will, the Communists were more intelligent. They had an imposing program. A plan for an entirely new world where everyone would find a place. The opponents had no great dream, only some tiresome and threadbare moral principles, with which they tried to patch the torn trousers of the established order. So it's no surprise that the enthusiasts, the spirited ones, easily won out over the halfhearted and the cautious, and rapidly set about to realize their dream, that idyll of justice for all.

I emphasize: *idyll* and *for all*, because all human beings have always aspired to an idyll, to that garden where nightingales sing, to that realm of harmony where the world does not rise up as a stranger against man and man against other men, but rather where the world and all men are shaped from one and the same matter. There, everyone is a note in a sublime Bach fugue, and anyone who refuses to be one is a mere useless and meaningless black dot that need only be caught and crushed between thumb and finger like a flea.

There were people who immediately understood that they did not have the right temperament for the idyll and tried to go abroad. But since the idyll is in essence a world for all, those who tried to emigrate showed themselves to be deniers of the idyll, and instead of going abroad they went behind bars. Thousands and tens of thousands of others soon joined them, including many Communists like the foreign minister, Clementis, who had lent his fur hat to Gottwald. Timid lovers held hands on the movie screens, adultery was harshly suppressed by citizens' tribunals of honor, nightingales sang, and the body of Clementis swung like a bell ringing in the new dawn of humanity.

And then those young, intelligent, and radical people suddenly had the strange feeling of having sent out into the world an act that had begun to lead a life of its own, had ceased to resemble the idea it was based on, and did not care about those who had created it. Those young and intelligent people started to scold their act, they began to call to it, to rebuke it, to pursue it, to give chase to it. If I were to write a novel about that gifted and radical generation, I would call it *In Pursuit of an Errant Act*.

6

The mechanic lowered the hood, and Mirek asked how much he owed him.

"Forget it," said the mechanic.

Touched, Mirek got behind the wheel. He had no desire to go on with his trip. He would rather have stayed here with the mechanic and listened to his funny stories. The mechanic leaned into the car and threw him a friendly punch. Then he went over to the gatekeeper's shack to raise the barrier.

As Mirek drove past him, the mechanic nodded toward the car parked at the entrance to the service station.

The thick-necked man with the waved hair stood gazing at Mirek beside the open gate. The one behind the wheel was also looking at him. The two men stared at him insolently and shamelessly, and driving by, Mirek tried to look at them the same way.

In the rearview mirror, he saw the man get into the car, which made a U-turn to go on following him.

He thought he really should have gotten rid of his compromising papers earlier. If he had done it the first day after his accident, instead of waiting to reach Zdena on the phone, he might have been able to move them without danger. But all he could think about was this trip to see Zdena. Actually, he had been thinking about it for several years now. But in recent weeks he'd had the feeling he could not wait much longer, because his destiny was rapidly coming to its end and he must do everything to make it perfect and beautiful.

7

Breaking up with Zdena in those long-ago days (their affair had lasted nearly three years) gave him a tremendous feeling of immense freedom, and suddenly everything began to go well for him. He soon married a woman whose loveliness gave him self-confidence. Then his beautiful wife died, and he was left alone with his son in an alluring solitude that gained him the admiration, interest, and solicitude of many other women.

At the same time, he made a name for himself as a scientist, and that protected him. The state needed him, so he could allow himself to be caustic about it at a time when hardly anyone was daring to. Little by little, as those who were in pursuit of their own act gained influence, he appeared on television more and more, becoming well known. After the Russians arrived, he refused to renounce his convictions, was removed from his job and hounded by the secret police. That didn't break him. He was in love with his destiny, and even his march toward ruin seemed noble and beautiful to him.

Please understand me: I said he was in love with his destiny, not with himself. These are two entirely different things. It is as if his life had freed itself and suddenly had interests of its own, which did not correspond at all to Mirek's. This is how, I believe, life turns itself into destiny. Destiny has no intention of lifting a finger for Mirek (for his happiness, his security, his good spirits, his health), whereas Mirek is ready to do everything for his destiny (for its grandeur, its clarity, its beauty, its style, its intelligible meaning). He felt responsible for his destiny, but his destiny did not feel responsible for him.

His connection to his life was that of a sculptor to his statue or a novelist to his novel. It is an inviolable right of a novelist to rework his novel. If the opening does not please him, he can rewrite or delete it. But Zdena's existence denied Mirek that author's prerogative. Zdena insisted on remaining on the opening pages of the novel and did not let herself be crossed out.

8

But just why was he so horribly ashamed of her?

The easiest explanation is this: Mirek is among those who very soon joined in pursuit of their own act, whereas Zdena has always been loyal to the garden where nightingales sing. Lately she was among the two percent of the nation who joyfully welcomed the arrival of the Russian tanks.

Yes, that's true, but I don't consider this explanation convincing. If her rejoicing at the arrival of the Russian tanks were the only reason, he would have attacked her loudly and publicly, and not denied he knew her. No, Zdena was guilty of something differently serious. She was ugly.

But why did her ugliness matter, when he hadn't made love to her in twenty years?

It mattered: even from afar, Zdena's big nose cast a shadow on his life.

Some years earlier, he'd had a pretty mistress. Once, she returned from a visit to the town where Zdena lived and asked with annoyance: "Tell me, how could you possibly have gone to bed with that horror?"

He professed she was only an acquaintance and vehemently denied having had an affair with her.

For he was aware of the great secret of life: Women don't look for handsome men. Women look for men who have had beautiful women. Having an ugly mistress is therefore a fatal mistake. Mirek tried hard to sweep away all traces of Zdena, and since the nightingale-lovers hated him more with every passing day, he hoped that Zdena, busy making her career in the party, would swiftly and gladly forget him.

He was mistaken. She talked about him all the time, everywhere and every chance she got. Once by disastrous coincidence they met in public, and she was quick to speak of something that clearly showed they had formerly been very close.

He was furious.

Another time, one of his friends who knew her asked him: "If you hate that woman so, why were you with her in those days?"

Mirek began by explaining that he had been a foolish kid of twenty and she was seven years older. She was respected, admired, all-powerful! She knew everyone on the party Central Committee! She helped him, pushed him, introduced him to influential people!

"I was a climber, you idiot!" and he started shouting: "That's why I hung on to her, and I didn't give a damn about how ugly she was!"

9

Mirek was not telling the truth. Even though she had cried over Masturbov's death, Zdena had no great connections twenty-five years before and no means of making a career for herself or of easing the way to one for others.

Why then had he invented that? Why did he lie?

Driving with one hand, he saw the secret-police car in the rearview mirror and suddenly blushed. A completely unexpected memory had sprung to mind:

When she reproached him, the first time they made love, about his acting too intellectual, he had tried, starting the next day, to correct that impression by showing spontaneous, unbridled passion. No, it's not true that he had forgotten all their coitions! This one he remembered clearly: He moved on her with feigned fierceness, emitting a lengthy growl like a dog struggling with his master's slipper, at the same time observing (with mild astonishment) the very calm, silent, and nearly impassive woman stretched out under him.

The car resounded with that twenty-five-year-old growl, the unbearable sound of his submissiveness and servile zeal, the sound of his overattentiveness and subservience, of his ridiculousness and misery.

Yes, it was so: Mirek had gone so far as to proclaim himself a climber to avoid confessing the truth: he had made love to an ugly woman because he didn't dare approach pretty ones. He thought himself unworthy of anyone better than a Zdena. That weakness, that deprivation, was the secret he was hiding.

The car resounded with the frenzied growl of passion, and the sound proved to him that Zdena was merely an apparition he wanted to get to in order to destroy his own hated youth.

He parked in front of her apartment building. The car following parked right behind him.

10

Historical events mostly imitate one another without any talent, but it seems to me that in Bohemia history staged an unprecedented experiment. There, things did not go according to the old formula of one group of people (a class, a nation) set against another, but instead, people (a generation of men and women) rebelled against their own youth.

They tried hard to recapture and tame their own act, and for a while they nearly succeeded. In the sixties, they gained more and more influence, and at the beginning of 1968 their influence was almost complete. That is the period commonly referred to as the "Prague Spring": the guardians of the idyll saw themselves forced to remove microphones from private apartments, the borders were opened, and the notes were escaping from the enormous Bach score for everyone to sing in his own way. It was an unbelievable gaiety, it was a carnival!

Russia, which had composed the enormous fugue for the entire terrestrial globe, could not tolerate the scattering of the notes. On August 21, 1968, she sent an army of half a million men to Bohemia. Soon about one hundred twenty thousand Czechs had left the country, and of those who remained, about five hundred thousand had been forced to leave their jobs, for isolated workshops in the depths of the country, for distant factories, for the steering wheels of trucks—that is to say, for places where no one would ever hear their voices.

And because not even the shadow of a bad memory should distract the country from its restored idyll, both the Prague Spring and the arrival of the Russian tanks, that stain on a beautiful history, had to be reduced to nothing. That is why today in Bohemia the August 21 anniversary goes by silently and the names of those who rose up against their own youth are carefully erased from the country's memory, like mistakes in a schoolchild's homework.

They effaced Mirek's name too. And as he climbs the steps to Zdena's door, he is really only a white stain, a circumscribed fragment of the void going up the spiral staircase.

11

His arm swaying in its sling, he sits facing Zdena. Looking at him sideways, Zdena averts her eyes and speaks glibly:

"I don't know why you've come. But I'm glad you're here. I've been talking to some comrades. It's quite insane for you to end up as a construction worker. It's certain, I know it is, that the party still hasn't closed the door on you. There's still time."

He asks her what he should do.

"Ask for a hearing. You yourself. It's up to you to make the first move."

He saw what was going on. They were letting him know he still had five minutes, the last five minutes, to proclaim loudly that he renounces everything he said and did. He was familiar with this kind of deal. They were ready to sell people a future in exchange for their past. They wanted to force him to appear on television and explain in a choked voice that he had been in error when he spoke against Russia and against nightingales. They wanted to compel him to cast his life away and become a shadow, a man without a past, an actor without a role, and to turn even his castaway life, even the role the actor had abandoned, into a shadow. Having turned him into a shadow, they would let him live.

He looks at Zdena: Why is she talking so fast and in such an uncertain tone of voice? Why is she looking at him sideways, why is she averting her eyes?

It's only too obvious: She's set a trap for him. She's acting under instructions from the party or the police. Her task is to convince him to surrender.

12

But Mirek is mistaken! No one has assigned her to deal with him. Ah no! Nowadays, no one among the powerful would give Mirek a hearing, even if he were to beg. It's too late.

Zdena urges him to do something to save himself and pretends to be transmitting a message from high-ranking comrades only because she feels a confused and futile desire to help him as best she can. And she talks rapidly and averts her eyes not because she has a set trap in hand but because she is empty-handed.

Has Mirek ever understood her?

He always thought Zdena was so frenetically faithful to the party because she was a fanatic.

That was not true. She remained faithful to the party because she loved Mirek.

When he left her, her only desire was to show that faithfulness was a value superior to all others. She tried to show that he was unfaithful *in all* and that she was faithful *in all*. What looked like political fanaticism was merely a pretense, a parable, a demonstration of faithfulness, disappointed love's coded reproach.

I imagine her on a beautiful August morning awakening with a start to the terrible din of airplanes. She runs out into the street, where panic-stricken people tell her that the Russian army is occupying Bohemia. She breaks into hysterical laughter! Russian tanks have come to punish all the unfaithful! At last she'll see Mirek's downfall! At last she'll see him on his knees! At last she—the one who knows what faithfulness is—will be able to lean over him and come to his aid.

Mirek has decided to break off abruptly a conversation that is heading in the wrong direction.

"You know I used to write you a lot of letters. I want them back."

She raises her head in surprise. "Letters?"

"Yes, my letters. At the time, I must have written you at least a hundred."

"Yes, your letters, I know," she says, and suddenly ceasing to look away, she fixes her eyes on him. Mirek has the unpleasant impression that she can see into the depths of his soul, that she knows exactly what he wants and why he wants it.

"Your letters, yes, your letters," she repeats. "I reread them a little while ago. I wondered how you could have been capable of such an explosion of feelings."

She repeated the words "explosion of feelings" several times, uttering them not rapidly or with any kind of haste but slowly and reflectively, as though she were aiming at a target she did not want to miss, not taking her eyes off it, making sure that she hit the bull's-eye.

13

His arm in its cast is swaying on his chest and his face is flushed: he looks as if he has just been slapped.

Ah yes! undoubtedly his letters were terribly sentimental. He had needed at all costs to prove to himself that it was not his weakness and poverty that bound him to this woman, but love! And only a truly immense passion could justify an affair with such an ugly girl.

"Do you remember writing me that we were comrades in arms in the struggle?"

If possible, his blush deepens. What an infinitely ridiculous word, this word "struggle"! What was that struggle of theirs? The interminable meetings they went to put blisters on their buttocks, but the moment they stood up to utter some extreme opinions (it was necessary to castigate the class enemy ever more harshly, to formulate this or that idea in ever more categorical terms), they felt like the figures in heroic paintings: he, gun in hand, falling to the ground with a bleeding wound in his shoulder, and she, clutching a pistol, going forward, ahead to where he can no longer go.

At that time, his skin was still covered with youthful acne, and to keep it from showing he wore a mask of rebellion. He told everyone that he had broken permanently with his father, a well-off farmer. He spat, he said, on the age-old rural tradition of attachment to the land and to property. He described the scene of the quarrel and his dramatic departure from the parental home. There was not an ounce of truth to any of this. When he looks back nowadays, he sees only legends and lies.

"At that time, you were a different man," said Zdena.

He imagines taking the parcel of letters away with him. Stopping at the first garbage can, he carefully holds the parcel between two fingers, as if it were besmirched with shit, and drops it in among the filth.

14

"What would you do with these letters?" she asks. "Just why do you want them?"

He couldn't tell her he wanted to throw them in the garbage can. So he put on a melancholy tone of voice and began to tell her he had reached the age when you start to look back at the past.

(He felt uncomfortable saying this, having the impression that his fairy tale was unconvincing, and he was ashamed.)

Yes, he was looking back, because nowadays he had forgotten who he had been when he was young. He knew he had failed. That is why he wanted to know where he had come from, to understand where he had gone wrong. That is why he wanted to go back to his correspondence with Zdena, to find there the secret of his youth, of his beginnings and of his roots.

She shook her head: "I'll never give them to you."

He lied: "I only want to borrow them."

She shook her head again.

He reflected that somewhere in this apartment were letters of his, which at any time she could give to anyone at all to read. That a piece of his life remained in Zdena's hands was unbearable, and he longed to hit her over the head with the big glass ashtray on the coffee table between them and take away his letters.

Instead, he again began to tell her he was looking back to find out where he had come from.

She raised her eyes, silencing him with a look: "I'll never give them to you. Never."

15

When they came out of Zdena's apartment building together, the two cars were still parked, one behind the other, right in front of the door. The secret-police men were pacing up and down the opposite sidewalk. They stopped now to look.

He pointed at them: "These two gentlemen followed me the whole way."

"Really?" she said incredulously, with forced irony. "Is everyone persecuting you?"

How could she be so cynical as to maintain that the two men opposite, who were conspicuously and insolently looking them over, were only chance passersby?

There was only one explanation. She was playing their game. The game that consisted of pretending the secret police did not exist and no one was being persecuted.

Now the secret-police men crossed the street and, in full view of Mirek and Zdena, entered their car.

"Goodbye," said Mirek, not even looking at her. He

got behind the wheel of his car. In the rearview mirror, he saw the secret-police car pulling out behind him. He did not see Zdena. He did not want to see her. He never wanted to see her again.

And so he did not know she stood on the sidewalk, following him with her eyes, for a long while. She looked terrified.

No, it was not cynicism on Zdena's part to refuse to see secret police in the two men who were pacing up and down on the opposite sidewalk. She was panic-stricken by things that were beyond her. She had wanted to hide the truth from him, and to hide it from herself.

16

A speeding red sports car suddenly cut in between Mirek and the secret-police car. Mirek stepped on the gas. They were entering a built-up area. Then there was a curve in the road. Realizing that his pursuers were momentarily unable to see him, Mirek turned off into a small street. His tires squealed, and a kid start-ing to cross the street jumped back just in time. In the rearview mirror, Mirek saw the red car going by on the main road. But the secret-police car had not yet appeared. A moment later, he managed to turn into another street and disappeared for good from their field of vision.

He left the town by a road going in an entirely different direction. He looked in the rearview mirror. No one was following him, the road was empty.

He imagined the unlucky secret-police men looking for him, afraid of being lambasted by their superior. He burst out laughing. Slowing down, he started to look at the scenery. Actually, he had never before looked at the scenery. He had always driven toward a goal, to arrange or discuss something, and for him the world's space had become a negative, a waste of time, an obstacle slowing down his activity.

Not far ahead, two red-and-white-striped crossing barriers were slowly coming down. He came to a stop.

All at once, he felt immensely tired. Why had he gone to see her? Why did he want the letters back?

He felt assailed by everything absurd, ridiculous, and childish about his trip. It was not reasoning or a plan that had led him to this trip but an irresistible desire. The desire to extend his arm far back to the past and hit it with his fist. The desire to slash the painting portraying his youth. A passionate desire he could not control and that was going to remain unsatisfied.

He felt immensely tired. Now he could probably no longer remove the compromising papers from his apartment. The secret police were on his heels and would not let him go. It was too late. Yes, it was too late for everything.

He heard the distant chugging of a train. A woman wearing a red kerchief on her head stood in front of the crossing keeper's house. The slow local train came by, with a sturdy countryman, pipe in hand, leaning out a window to spit. Then a bell rang and the woman in the red kerchief walked over to the grade crossing and turned a crank. The barriers rose up, and Mirek moved forward. He came to a village that was just a long street ending at the railroad station: a small, white, one-story house with a wooden fence through which you could see the platform and the rails.

17

The railroad station's windows are decorated with flowerpots filled with begonias. Mirek has stopped the car. He sits behind the wheel, looking at the house with red flowers at its windows. From a long-forgotten time the image comes to him of another white house with the red glow of begonia petals on its windowsills. It is a small hotel in a mountain village where he spends his summer vacations. At the window, among the flowers, a very big nose appears. Mirek is twenty; he looks up at that nose and feels immense love.

He wants to step quickly on the gas so as to escape

that memory. But this time I am not going to let myself be fooled, and I call on that memory to linger awhile. And so I repeat: at the window, among the begonias, there is Zdena's face, with its gigantic nose, and Mirek feels immense love.

Is that possible?

Yes. And why not? Can't a weak boy feel true love for an ugly girl?

He told her he was in rebellion against his reactionary father, she inveighed against intellectuals, they got blisters on their buttocks, and held hands. They went to meetings, denounced their fellow citizens, told lies, and were in love. She cried over Masturbov's death, he growled over her body like a dog, and neither one could live without the other.

He wanted to efface her from the photograph of his life not because he had not loved her but because he had. He had erased her, her and his love for her, he had scratched out her image until he had made it disappear as the party propaganda section had made Clementis disappear from the balcony where Gottwald had given his historic speech. Mirek rewrote history just like the Communist Party, like all political parties, like all peoples, like mankind. They shout that they want to shape a better future, but it's not true. The future is only an indifferent void no one cares about, but the past is filled with life, and its countenance is irritating, repellent, wounding, to the point that we want to destroy or repaint it. We want to be masters of the future only for the power to change the past. We fight for access to the labs where we can retouch photos and rewrite biographies and history.

How long did he stay in front of the railroad station?

And what did this stop mean?

It meant nothing.

He immediately wiped it from his mind, so that now he no longer remembers the small white house with the begonias. Again the world's space was merely an obstacle slowing down his activity.

18

The car he had succeeded in shaking off was parked in front of his house. The two men were a short distance away from it.

He pulled up behind their car and got out. They smiled at him almost cheerfully, as though his escape were a prank that had greatly amused them. As he passed in front of them, the man with the thick neck and waved hair started laughing and nodded at him. Mirek was gripped by anguish at this familiarity, which meant that now they were going to be still more intimately connected.

Not batting an eye, Mirek entered the house. He opened the door to the apartment with his key. First he saw his son, a look of suppressed emotion on his face.

A stranger wearing glasses approached Mirek and identified himself. "Do you want to see the prosecutor's search warrant?"

"Yes," said Mirek.

There were two more strangers in the apartment. One was standing at the worktable, on which papers, notebooks, and books were piled. He was picking up items from it one after the other. Sitting at the desk, the second man was taking dictation from the first man.

The man with the glasses took a folded piece of paper out of his breast pocket and offered it to Mirek. "Here, this is the search warrant, and over there"—he indicated the two men—"they're making a list for you of the items we're seizing."

Papers and books were scattered all over the floor, the cupboard doors were open, the furniture had been pushed away from the walls.

His son leaned over toward Mirek and said: "They came five minutes after you left."

At the worktable, the two men drew up the list of seized items: letters from Mirek's friends, documents from the earliest days of the Russian occupation, analyses of the political situation, minutes of meetings, and some books.

"You don't have much consideration for your friends," said the man with the glasses, nodding toward the seized items.

"There's nothing here that violates the constitution,"

said his son, and Mirek recognized his own words.

The man with the glasses replied that it was up to the court to decide what does or does not violate the constitution.

19

Those who have emigrated (one hundred twenty thousand people) and those who were reduced to silence and driven from their jobs (half a million people) are disappearing like a procession moving away into the fog, invisible and forgotten.

But a prison, even though entirely surrounded by walls, is a splendidly illuminated scene of history.

Mirek had known this for a long time. For all of the past year, he had been drawn irresistibly to the idea of prison. It was probably the way Flaubert was drawn to Madame Bovary's suicide. No, Mirek could not imagine a better ending for the novel of his life.

They wanted to efface hundreds of thousands of lives from memory and leave nothing but an unstained age of unstained idyll. But Mirek is going to land his whole body on that idyll, like a stain. He'll stay there just as Clementis's hat stayed on Gottwald's head.

They made Mirek sign the list of seized items and then asked him and his son to come along with them. The trial took place after a year of preventive detention. Mirek was sentenced to six years, his son to two years, and ten of their friends to one to six years in prison.

PART TWO

Mama

1

There was a time when Marketa disliked her mother-in-law. That was when she and Karel were living with her in-laws (her father-in-law was still alive) and Marketa was exposed daily to the woman's resentment and touchiness. They couldn't bear it for long and moved out. Their motto at the time was "as far from Mama as possible." They had gone to live in a town at the other end of the country and thus could see Karel's parents only once a year.

Then one day Karel's father died and Mama was alone. They saw her at the funeral; she was subdued and miserable and seemed smaller to them than before. The same words ran through both their heads: "Mama, you can't stay here alone, come live with us."

The words resounded in both their heads, but neither one could say them. Especially because, on a sad walk together the day after the funeral, Mama, thoroughly miserable and diminished as she was, reproached them with misplaced vehemence for all the wrongs they had done her. "Nothing will ever change her," Karel said to Marketa later, once they were on the train. "It's sad, but I think it'll always have to be 'far from Mama.'"

Though as the years passed Mama did indeed stay the same, Marketa probably changed, because she suddenly had the impression that whatever her mother-in-law had done to them was actually innocuous and that it was she, Marketa, who had committed the real offense in giving such importance to her grumbling. She had seen Mama at the time the way a child sees an adult, but now the roles were reversed: Marketa was the adult and, from that great distance, Mama appeared to her small and defenseless as a child. Marketa felt an indulgent patience toward her, and had even started to write to her regularly. The old woman very swiftly became used to this, replying conscientiously and demanding more and more letters from Marketa, for these letters, she maintained, were the only thing that enabled her to bear her loneliness.

Some time ago, the words that had taken shape at Karel's father's funeral had begun to run through their heads again. And again it was the son who suppressed the daughter-in-law's kindness, so that instead of saying "Mama, come live with us," they invited her to stay for a week.

It was the Easter holiday, and their ten-year-old son was away. Eva was expected on the following weekend. They were willing to spend all week with Mama, all but Sunday. "Come and spend a week with us," they said to her. "From this Saturday to next Saturday. We're busy next Sunday. We have to go somewhere."

So as not to have to talk about Eva, they told her nothing more precise. On the telephone, Karel said it twice more: "From this Saturday to next Saturday. We're busy next Sunday, going somewhere." And Mama said: "Yes, children, you're very nice, and I'll certainly leave whenever you want me to. All I ask is to get away a bit from my loneliness."

But on Saturday evening, when Marketa asked her what time tomorrow morning she wanted to be taken to the railroad station, Mama unhesitatingly and bluntly announced that she would not be leaving until Monday. When Marketa looked at her, surprised, Mama went on: "Karel told me you'll be busy on Monday, going somewhere, and I should leave on Monday morning."

Of course, Marketa could have replied: "Mama, you're mistaken, it's tomorrow that we're going," but she lacked the courage. She was unable, on the spur of the moment, to invent the place where they were going. Realizing they had been very careless in preparing their lie, she said nothing and resigned herself to the idea that her mother-in-law would stay with them through Sunday. She reassured herself that since the boy's room, where her mother-in-law was sleeping, was at the other end of the apartment, Mama wouldn't be disturbing them. And she said to Karel reproachfully:

"Please, don't be nasty to her. Look at the poor woman. Just looking at her breaks my heart."

2

Karel shrugged his shoulders in resignation. Marketa was right: Mama had really changed. She was pleased with everything, grateful for everything. Karel had been expecting in vain a quarrel over some little thing.

On a walk a day or two before, she had gazed into the distance and asked: "What is that pretty little white village over there?" It wasn't a village, just boundary stones. Karel took pity on his mother, whose sight was dimming.

But her faulty vision seemed to express something more basic: what appeared large to them, she found small; what they took for boundary stones, for her were distant houses.

To tell the truth, that was not an entirely new trait of hers. The difference was that at one time it had annoyed them. One night, for instance, their country was invaded by the tanks of a gigantic neighboring country. That had been such a shock and brought such terror that for a long time no one could think of anything else. It was August, and the pears in their garden were ripe. A week earlier, Mama had invited the pharmacist to come and pick them. But the pharmacist neither came nor even apologized. Mama was unable to forgive him, which infuriated Karel and Marketa. They reproached her: Everyone else is thinking about tanks, and you're thinking about pears. Then they moved out, taking the memory of her pettiness with them.

But are tanks really more important than pears? As time went by, Karel realized that the answer to this question was not as obvious as he had always thought, and he began to feel a secret sympathy for Mama's perspective, which had a big pear tree in the foreground and somewhere in the distance a tank no bigger than a ladybug, ready at any moment to fly away out of sight. Ah yes! In reality it's Mama who is right: tanks are perishable, pears are eternal.

In the past, Mama wanted to know everything about her son and became angry when he hid anything about his life. And so now, to please her, they talked about what they were doing, what was happening to them, about their plans. But they soon noticed that Mama was listening to them mainly out of politeness, breaking into their account by talking about her poodle, which she had left with a neighbor while she was away.

Before, Karel would have considered that behavior self-centered or petty; but now he knew that it was nothing of the kind. More time had passed than he had realized. Mama had relinquished the marshal's baton of her motherhood and gone into a different world. On another walk with her, they had been caught in a storm. They held her by the arm, one on either side, literally carrying her to keep the wind from sweeping her away. Karel was moved by the pathetic lightness of the burden in his hand, and he realized that his mother belonged to a realm of other creatures: smaller, lighter, more easily blown away.

3

Eva arrived after lunch. Marketa had gone to pick her up at the railroad station, because she thought of her as her friend. She didn't like Karel's girlfriends. But things were different with Eva. Actually, Marketa had met her first.

That was about six years before. She and Karel were at a spa. Every other day, she went to the sauna. Bathed in sweat, she was sitting in the cabin on a wooden bench along with other women when a tall, naked girl came in. Though strangers to each other, they exchanged smiles, and in a moment the young woman began talking to Marketa. Because she was so straightforward and Marketa so grateful for that expression of affinity, they quickly became friends.

Marketa was captivated by the charm of Eva's singularity: That way of speaking to her immediately! As if they had made a date to meet there! And she didn't waste time starting the conversation with conventional remarks about how healthy the sauna is and how good for the appetite, but instead began right away to talk about herself, a bit like people becoming acquainted through a personal ad trying hard to compress into the very first letter to their future partner who and what they are.

Who then is Eva, in Eva's own words? Eva is a cheerful man-chaser. But she doesn't chase them to marry them. She chases them the way men chase women. Not love but only friendship and sensuality exist for her. So she has many friends: men are not afraid she wants to marry them, and women have no fear she is seeking to deprive them of a husband. Besides, if she ever married, her husband would be a friend she would allow everything to and demand nothing from.

Having explained all this to Marketa, she announced that Marketa was beautifully "built" and that this was very rare, because few women, Eva thought, had really beautiful bodies. Her praise slipped out so naturally that Marketa took more pleasure in it than in a compliment from a man. The girl had turned her head. She felt she had entered the realm of sincerity, and made a date to meet Eva in the sauna at the same time the day after next. Later, she introduced her to Karel, but in this friendship he was always in third place.

"My mother-in-law is staying with us," Marketa told her guiltily as they left the railroad station. "I'm going to introduce you as my cousin. I hope it doesn't bother you."

"On the contrary," said Eva, and then asked Marketa to brief her on her family.

4

Mama had never been much interested in her daughter-in-law's family, but the words "cousin," "niece," "aunt," and "granddaughter" warmed her heart: they were in the comfortable sphere of familiar notions.

What she had long known was being confirmed: her son was an incorrigible eccentric. As if her being here at the same time as a visiting relative could disturb them! She realized they would want to chat by themselves. But that was no reason to send her away a day early. Fortunately, she knew how to deal with them. She simply decided she had been mistaken about the day of departure, and had chuckled a bit over that nice Marketa's inability to tell her to leave on Sunday morning.

Yes, she had to admit they were nicer than before. A few years earlier, Karel pitilessly would have told her to leave. Her little ruse of the day before had actually done them a great service. This time, at least, they wouldn't have to blame themselves for having sent their mother, for no reason at all, back to her loneliness a day early.

Besides, Mama was very glad to have met this new relative. She was a very nice girl. (And it was incredible how she reminded her of someone, but who?) For a good two hours, Mama had answered her questions. How did Mama wear her hair as a girl? She had a braid. Of course, it was still in the old days of Austria-

Hungary. Vienna was the capital. Mama went to a Czech high school, and Mama was a patriot. And all of a sudden she had longed to sing them some of the patriotic songs they sang at that time. Or to recite the poems! She surely still knew many of them by heart. Right after the war (yes, of course, after the 1914 war, in 1918, when the Czechoslovak Republic was established, my God, the cousin didn't even know when the republic was proclaimed!), Mama had recited a poem at a school ceremony. They were celebrating the end of the Austrian Empire. They were celebrating independence! And would you believe it, all of a sudden, having come to the last stanza, her mind went blank; she couldn't remember what followed. She fell silent, sweat ran down her brow, she thought she would die of shame. And then all at once, unexpectedly, there was a great burst of applause! Everybody thought the poem was over, nobody noticed the last stanza was missing! Even so, Mama was in despair, and, ashamed, she ran and locked herself in the toilet and the principal himself rushed to find her and kept banging on the door, begging her not to cry and to come out, because she had been a great success.

The cousin laughed, and Mama stared at her for a long time: "My God, you remind me of someone, who is it you remind me of . . . ?"

"But you weren't still going to high school after the war," Karel remarked.

"I should know, it seems to me, when I went to high school!"

"But you graduated in the last year of the war. It was still under Austria-Hungary."

"I know very well when I graduated," she answered with irritation. But even as she said it, she knew Karel was not mistaken. It was true, she had graduated during the war. Where then did the memory of that post-war school ceremony come from? Suddenly Mama hesitated and fell silent.

Marketa broke the brief silence. She spoke to Eva, and what she said concerned neither Mama's recitation nor 1918.

Mama felt abandoned among her recollections, betrayed by the sudden lack of interest and by the failure of her memory.

"Have a good time, children, you're young and have a lot of things to talk about." Abruptly a victim of discontent, she went off to her grandson's room.

5

While Eva was plying Mama with questions, Karel looked at her with tender affection. In the ten years he had known her, she had always been like that. Straightforward and dauntless. He had become acquainted with her (he and Marketa were still living with his parents) nearly as quickly as his wife had some years later. One day, he received a letter at his office from a woman unknown to him. She said she knew him by sight and had decided to write to him because social conventions meant nothing to her when she was attracted to a man. She was attracted to Karel, and she was a man-chaser. A chaser of unforgettable experiences. She did not allow love. Only friendship and sensuality. Enclosed with the letter was a photo of a naked girl in a provocative pose.

Suspecting a practical joke, Karel at first hesitated to answer. But finally he was unable to resist. He wrote to the young woman and invited her to a friend's studio apartment. Eva arrived, tall, thin, and badly dressed. She looked like an oversized adolescent who had put on her grandmother's clothes. Seated across from him, she explained that social conventions meant nothing to her when she was attracted to a man. That she allowed only friendship and sensuality. Signs of embarrassment and effort showed on her face, and Karel felt a kind of fraternal compassion for her rather than desire. But then he told himself that no opportunity should be missed:

"That's wonderful," he said to reassure her, "a meeting of two chasers."

These were the first words with which he finally interrupted the young woman's voluble confession, and Eva immediately regained her courage, relieved of the burden of a situation she had heroically borne all alone for nearly a quarter of an hour.

He told her she was beautiful in the photo she had

sent and asked (with a chaser's provocativeness) if it aroused her to show herself naked.

"I'm an exhibitionist," she said in all innocence, as if she were avowing that she was an Anabaptist.

He told her he wanted to see her naked.

Relieved, she asked if there was a record player in the studio.

Yes, there was a record player, but Karel's friend liked only classical music—Bach, Vivaldi, and Wagner operas. Karel would have found it odd for the young woman to undress to Isolde's singing. Eva too was displeased with the records. "Isn't there any pop music here?" No, there wasn't any pop. Finding no other solution, he ended up putting a Bach suite on the record player. He sat down in a corner of the room for a panoramic view.

Eva tried to move rhythmically, but soon said that you couldn't with such music.

Raising his voice, he responded harshly: "Shut up and strip!"

Bach's celestial music filled the room, and Eva continued to move obediently. That music, everything but danceable, made her performance especially painful, and Karel thought that from the moment she pulled off her sweater to the moment she removed her underpants, the distance she had to cover must have seemed endless to her. The music played on, and Eva writhed in syncopated dance movements, throwing one piece of clothing off after the other. She didn't look at Karel, concentrating entirely on herself and on her gestures like a violinist playing a difficult piece by heart and afraid of being distracted by seeing the audience. When she was entirely naked, she turned to face the wall and grabbed herself between her legs. Karel had already undressed and was ecstatically watching the masturbating young woman's back. It was glorious, and so it is easily understandable that ever since he has always taken Eva's side.

Besides, she was the only woman who wasn't annoyed by Karel's love for Marketa. "Your wife should understand that you love her but you're a woman-chaser and your chasing is no threat to her. But no woman understands that. No, there isn't a woman who understands men," she added sadly, as if she herself were a misunderstood man.

Then she offered to do everything she could to help him.

6

The boy's room, where Mama had gone, was barely six meters away and separated from them by only two thin walls. Mama's shadow was still with them, and it oppressed Marketa.

Fortunately, Eva was talkative. It was a long time since she had seen them, and many things had happened: she had moved to another town and, most important, had married an older man, who had found an irreplaceable friend in her, for, as we know, Eva had a great gift for companionship and rejected love, with its selfishness and hysteria.

She also had a new job. It paid well enough, but it scarcely gave her time to breathe. She had to be back at work tomorrow.

Marketa was appalled. "What! But when do you want to go?"

"There's an express at five."

"My God, Eva, you'll have to get up at four! That's horrible!" And just then she felt, if not anger, at least a kind of bitterness at the idea that Karel's mother had stayed with them. Living far away and with little time at her disposal, Eva had nonetheless reserved this Sunday for Marketa, who was unable to devote herself to her as she wished because of the phantom mother-in-law who was always with them.

Marketa's good mood had now been spoiled, and as it never rains but it pours, the telephone started ringing. Karel picked up the receiver. His voice was hesitant, there was something suspect and equivocal about his terse replies, giving Marketa the impression he was choosing his words carefully, to hide their meaning. She was certain he was making a date with a woman.

"Who was that?" she asked. Karel said it was a colleague, a woman in a nearby town who was coming that week to discuss something with him. From then on, Marketa did not say a word.

Was she that jealous?

When they were first in love, she unquestionably had been. But years had passed and what she experienced now as jealousy was probably only a habit.

Putting it another way: every love relationship rests on an unwritten agreement unthinkingly concluded by the lovers in the first weeks of their love. They are still in a kind of dream but at the same time, without knowing it, are drawing up, like uncompromising lawyers, the detailed clauses of their contract. O lovers! Be careful in those dangerous first days! Once you've brought breakfast in bed you'll have to bring it forever, unless you want to be accused of lovelessness and betrayal.

In the first weeks of their love, it was decided between Karel and Marketa that Karel would be unfaithful and Marketa would accept it, but that Marketa would have the right to be the better of the two and Karel would feel guilty toward her. No one knew better than Marketa how sad it is to be better. She was better, but only for lack of anything better.

Deep down, of course, Marketa knew full well that in itself the telephone conversation meant nothing. The important thing was not what the conversation *was* but what it *represented*. With eloquent concision, it expressed the entire situation of her life: everything Marketa did she did for Karel and because of Karel. She took care of his mother. She introduced him to her best friend. She gave her to him as a gift. Solely for him and for his pleasure. And why did she do all that?

Why did she give herself pain? Why like Sisyphus did she keep pushing her boulder uphill? Whatever she did, Karel was mentally absent. He made a date with someone else and always eluded her.

In high school, she had been untamable, rebellious, almost too full of life. Her old math teacher liked to tease her: "Marketa, no one will be able to rein you in! I already feel sorry for the man you marry!" She laughed proudly, his words seeming to be a happy omen. And all at once, without knowing how, she ended up in an entirely other role, contrary to her expectations, contrary to her wishes and her taste. And all this because she hadn't been on her guard during the week when she had unwittingly drawn up the contract.

She no longer enjoyed being better. Suddenly all the years of her marriage landed on her like a heavy sack.

7

Marketa was increasingly sullen, and Karel's face showed signs of anger. Eva was panic-stricken. She felt responsible for their marital happiness and talked all the more to disperse the clouds gathering in the room.

But the task was beyond her strength. Outraged by

what, this time, was an all too obvious injustice, Karel obstinately kept silent. Because she was unable to control her bitterness or tolerate her husband's anger, Marketa got up and went into the kitchen.

Eva meanwhile tried to persuade Karel not to spoil an evening they had been looking forward to for so long. But Karel was inflexible: "The time comes when you can't go on anymore. I'm getting tired of this! I'm always being accused of something or other. I'm not interested anymore in always being made to feel guilty! And guilty of such trivia! Trivia! No, no. I can't stand the sight of her anymore. I can't stand it!" Going around in circles, he repeated that again and again, and refused to listen to Eva's imploring intercessions.

So she finally left him alone and went off to join Marketa, who, hiding in the kitchen, knew that what had happened need not have happened. Eva tried to show her that the telephone call in no way justified her suspicions. Marketa, who deep down knew full well that this time she had no grounds for them, replied: "But I can't go on anymore. It's always the same. Year after year, month after month, nothing but women and lies. I'm getting tired of it. Tired. I've had enough of it."

Eva realized that husband and wife were equally stubborn. And she decided that the vague idea she had had in coming here, and whose decency had at first appeared questionable, was a good one after all. If she wanted to help them, she should not be afraid to act on her own initiative. They loved each other, but they needed someone to relieve them of their burden. Someone to free them. So the project she had come here with was not only in her own interest (yes, undeniably it served her own interest above all, and that was just what worried her a bit, since she never wanted to behave selfishly toward her friends) but also in Marketa and Karel's interest.

"What should I do?" asked Marketa.

"Go find him. Tell him to stop sulking."

"I can't stand it. I can't stand the sight of him anymore!"

"Then lower your eyes. That'll be all the more touching."

8

The evening was saved. Marketa ceremoniously took out a bottle and handed it to Karel, who opened it with a grandiose gesture, like a starter at the Olympics setting off the final race. Wine was poured into three glasses, and Eva went swaying to the record player, chose a record, and continued swiveling through the room to the music (not Bach this time but Duke Ellington).

"Do you think Mama's already asleep?" asked Marketa.

"It might make sense to go and say good night to her," Karel advised.

"If you go and say good night to her, she'll start up again with her chatter and we'll lose still another hour. You know Eva has to get up early."

Marketa thought they had already lost too much time; she took her friend by the hand and, instead of going to say good night to Mama, went into the bathroom with Eva.

Karel stayed in the room, alone with Ellington. He was happy the clouds had dispersed but was expecting nothing more this evening. That bit of an incident over the telephone call had suddenly revealed something he had refused to acknowledge: he was tired and no longer desired anything.

Some years ago, Marketa had urged him to make love in a threesome with her and a mistress of his she was jealous of. Her proposal made him dizzy with arousal! But the evening scarcely gave him any pleasure. On the contrary, it was a horrible effort! The two women were kissing and embracing each other in front of him but never for a moment ceased to be rivals vigilantly watching to see which one he was more attentive to, which one he was more tender with. He carefully weighed his every word, measured his every caress, and behaved more like a scrupulously considerate, solicitous, courteous, and impartial diplomat than like a lover. At any rate, he failed. First his mistress burst into tears right in the midst of the lovemaking, and then Marketa shut herself into a deep silence.

If he could have believed that Marketa needed their

little orgies out of pure sensuality—she as the worse one of the couple—they would certainly have given him pleasure. But as it had been agreed upon from the beginning that he was the worse one, all he could see in her debauchery was a painful self-sacrifice, a generous effort to anticipate his polygamous inclinations and turn them into the gears of a happy marriage. He had been marked forever by the sight of Marketa's jealousy, that wound he himself had inflicted in the earliest days of their love. When he saw her in another woman's arms, he wanted to go down on his knees and ask her forgiveness.

But are such debauchery games really an exercise in penitence?

The thought then occurred to him that for their three-way lovemaking to become something joyous, Marketa shouldn't be feeling she was up against a rival. She should bring a friend of her own, a woman who doesn't know Karel and isn't interested in him. That is why he contrived Marketa and Eva's meeting at the sauna. The trick succeeded: the two women became friends, allies, accomplices who raped him, played with him, amused themselves at his expense, and desired him together. Karel hoped Eva would manage to drive away Marketa's anxiety about love, so he could finally be both free and guiltless.

But now he saw that there was no way to change what had been decided years earlier. Marketa was still the same, and he was still the accused.

But why then had he brought about the meeting of

Marketa and Eva? Why had he made love to the two women? On whose behalf had he done all that? For a long time now, anyone else could turn Marketa into a cheerful, sensual, and happy girl. Anyone but Karel. He saw himself as Sisyphus.

Really as Sisyphus? Wasn't it Sisyphus Marketa had compared herself to?

Yes, as the years went by, man and wife became twins, with the same vocabulary, the same ideas, the same destiny. Each had given the gift of Eva to the other, each to make the other happy. Each had the impression of having to push a boulder uphill. Each one was tired.

Karel heard water gurgling and the two women laughing in the bathroom, and he reflected that he had never been able to live the way he wanted, to have the women he wanted and to have them the way he wanted them. He longed to run away to a place where he could weave his own story, weave it by himself to his own taste and out of the reach of loving eyes.

And deep down he did not even care about weaving himself a story, he simply wanted to be alone.

9

Her clear-sightedness clouded by impatience, Marketa wasn't reasonable in believing Mama had fallen asleep and thus in not going to say good night to her. During this visit at her son's, Mama's thoughts had taken to turning over more rapidly in her mind, and that evening they were particularly agitated. It was all because of that likable relative of Marketa's, who kept reminding her of someone from her youth. But who was it she reminded her of?

At last she remembered: Nora! Yes, exactly the same figure, the same carriage, going through the world on beautiful long legs.

Nora lacked kindness and modesty, and Mama had often been wounded by her behavior. But she wasn't thinking about that now. What mattered more to her was that she had suddenly found a bit of her youth here, a greeting reaching her from the distance of half a century. She was thrilled by the thought that everything she long ago experienced was still with her, surrounding her in her loneliness and speaking to her. Although she had never liked Nora, she was glad to meet her here, all the more because she was thoroughly tamed and embodied in someone who appeared to be filled with respect for Mama.

When that thought came to her, she wanted to rush to rejoin them. But she controlled herself. She knew full well she was here today only by trickery and that those silly children wanted to be alone with their cousin. Well, let them tell each other their secrets! She wasn't at all bored in her grandson's room. She had her knitting, she had something to read, and most of all, she always had something to occupy her mind. Karel had shaken up her thoughts. Yes, he was entirely right, of course she had graduated from high school during the war. She had been mistaken. The incident of the recitation with its forgotten last stanza had taken place at least five years earlier. True, the principal had pounded on the door of the toilet where she had locked herself in to weep. But that year she had been barely thirteen years old, and it had all happened at a school ceremony just before Christmas vacation. There had been a decorated Christmas tree on the platform, the children had sung Christmas carols, and then she had recited a little poem. Just before the last stanza her mind went blank and she couldn't go on.

Mama was ashamed of her poor memory. What should she say to Karel? Should she admit she had been mistaken? As it was, they took her for an old woman. They were nice to her, all right, but she noticed they treated her like a child, with a kind of indulgence that annoyed her. If she now agreed that Karel had been entirely right and she really had confused a children's Christmas performance with a political ceremony, they would rise still higher and she would feel still smaller. No, no, she wouldn't give them the pleasure.

She would tell them it was really true that she had recited a poem at that ceremony after the war. Yes, she had already graduated, but the principal remembered her because she had been the best at recitation and had asked his former pupil to come and recite a poem.

It was a great honor! But Mama deserved it! She was a patriot! They had no idea what it had been like after the war, the collapse of Austria-Hungary! What joy! Those songs, those flags! And again she had a great longing to rush in to tell her son and daughter-in-law about the world of her youth.

Besides, she now almost felt it her duty to go to them. Though she had promised not to disturb them, that was only half the truth. The other half was that Karel didn't understand how she could have participated in a school ceremony after the war. Mama was an old lady and her memory sometimes failed her. She had not known right away how to explain it to her son, but now that she had at last recalled how it had really happened, she couldn't just pretend to have forgotten his question. That wouldn't be nice. She would go to them (in any case, they had nothing so important to say to one another) and apologize: she didn't mean to disturb them, and she certainly wouldn't go back if Karel hadn't asked her how she could have recited at a school ceremony after she had already graduated.

Then she heard a door opening and closing. She heard two women's voices and again a door opening. Then laughter and the sound of running water. She thought that the two young women were already washing up for the night. So it was high time she got there, if she still wanted to chat a bit with the three of them.

10

Mama's return was a hand extended to Karel with a
smile by a playful god. The more her timing was off,
the more timely her arrival. She didn't have to look for
excuses, for Karel immediately bombarded her with
cordial questions: what had she done all afternoon,
wasn't she feeling a bit sad, why hadn't she come earlier?

Mama pointed out that young people always had
much to say to one another and that old people should
know enough to avoid disturbing them.

By now the two girls, shrieking with laughter, could
be heard rushing toward the door. Eva came in first, in
a dark-blue T-shirt that ended just where her black
pubic thatch began. Catching sight of Mama, she took
fright but, no longer able to retreat, could only give her
a smile and head farther into the room toward an armchair, in which she very swiftly hid her poorly concealed nakedness.

Karel knew Marketa was close behind and expected
her to be in an evening gown, which in their private
language meant that she would be wearing only a
string of beads around her neck and a scarlet velvet
sash around her waist. He knew he should intervene to
stop her from coming in and spare Mama a fright. But
what could he do? Could he shout "Don't come in!" or

"Get dressed quick, Mama's here!"? There might have been another, more clever way to hold Marketa back, but in the one or two seconds he had for thought nothing came to him. To the contrary, he was overcome by a kind of euphoric torpor that robbed him of all presence of mind. He did nothing, and Marketa headed for the room's threshold stark naked except for a necklace and a sash around her waist.

Just then, Mama had turned to Eva and said with an affable smile: "Surely you want to go to bed, and I don't want to keep you." Eva, who had seen Marketa from the corner of her eye, answered with a no, not at all, actually nearly shouting it as though she were trying with her voice to cover the body of her friend, who understood at last and retreated into the corridor.

When Marketa returned moments later, wrapped in a long bathrobe, Mama repeated what she had said to Eva: "Marketa, I don't want to keep you. Surely you want to go to bed."

Marketa was ready to agree, but Karel cheerily shook his head: "No, Mama, we're glad to have you with us." And Mama was finally able to tell them the story of the recitation at the school ceremony after the end of the 1914 war, when Austria-Hungary collapsed and the principal asked his former pupil to recite a patriotic poem.

The two young women weren't paying any attention to Mama, but Karel listened to her with interest. I want to be more exact: The story of the forgotten stanza didn't interest him much. He had heard it many times and forgotten it many times. What interested him wasn't the story told by Mama but Mama telling the story. Mama and her world that looked like a huge pear on which a tiny Russian tank had alighted like a ladybird. The toilet door on which the principal pounded his fist was in the foreground, and very much beyond that door, the eager impatience of the two young women was barely visible.

That's what pleased Karel greatly. He gazed at Eva and Marketa with delight. Their nakedness quivered impatiently under T-shirt and bathrobe. All the more assiduously, he brought up further questions about the principal, the school, and the 1914 war, and finally he asked Mama to recite the patriotic poem whose last stanza she had forgotten.

Mama thought for a moment and then with utter concentration began to recite the poem she had recited at the school ceremony when she was thirteen. Instead of a patriotic poem, they were some lines about a Christmas tree and the star of Bethlehem, but none of them noticed that detail. Not even Mama. She had only one thing on her mind: would she recall the lines of the last stanza? And she did remember them. The star of Bethlehem shines and the three kings come to the manger. Moved by her success, she laughed and shook her head.

Eva applauded. Looking at her, Mama remembered the most important thing she had come to tell them: "Karel, do you know who your cousin reminds me of? Nora!"

11

Karel looked at Eva, not believing what he had heard: "Nora? Mrs. Nora?"

He clearly recalled Mama's friend from his childhood. She was a dazzling beauty, tall and with the magnificent face of an empress. Karel did not like her, since she was haughty and inaccessible, and yet he could never take his eyes off her. My God, what resemblance could there be between her and warmhearted Eva?

"Yes," replied Mama. "Nora! All it takes is to look at her. That height. That walk. And that face!"

"Stand up, Eva!" said Karel.

Eva was afraid to stand up, because she wasn't sure her short T-shirt would cover her crotch. But Karel was so insistent she finally had to obey. She stood up and, arms pressed against her sides, discreetly tugged down on her T-shirt. Karel watched her intently and, all of a sudden, really did have the impression she looked like Nora. It was a distant resemblance and difficult to grasp, appearing only in swift flashes that Karel tried to hold on to, for through Eva he wished, in a long-lasting way, again to see the beautiful Mrs. Nora.

"Turn around!" he ordered her.

Eva hesitated to make an about-face, because she had not stopped thinking about being naked under her

T-shirt. But Karel kept insisting, even though Mama too started to protest: "The young lady isn't about to drill like in the army!"

Karel persisted: "No, no, I want her to turn around." And Eva ended up obeying him.

Let's not forget that Mama's vision was poor. She took boundary stones for a village, she confused Eva with Mrs. Nora. But with eyes half closed, Karel too could take boundary stones for houses. Hadn't he, for an entire week, envied Mama her perspective? With eyelids half shut, he saw before him a beauty of long ago.

He had retained an unforgettable secret memory of it. Once when he was about four, he and Mama and Mrs. Nora were at a spa (where was it? he had no idea), and he had to wait for them in the deserted changing room. He waited there patiently, alone among all the forsaken feminine clothes. Then a tall, splendid-looking naked woman entered the changing room, turned her back to the child, and reached for the peg on the wall where her bathrobe was hanging. It was Nora.

The image of that naked body, standing up and seen from behind, had never been effaced from his memory. He was very little and was seeing that body from below, from the perspective of an ant, and if he at his present height were to look up at her today, it would be as if she were a statue five meters high. He was close to the body, yet infinitely distant from it. Doubly distant. In space and in time. It rose very high above him and was separated from him by countless years. That double distance made the little four-year-old boy dizzy. Now he was again feeling the same dizziness, with immense intensity.

He looked at Eva (she still had her back to him), and he saw Mrs. Nora. He was separated from her by two meters and one or two minutes.

"Mama," he said, "it was really nice of you to come out and chat with us. But now the ladies want to go to sleep."

Humble and docile, Mama left the room, and he immediately told the two women about his memory of Mrs. Nora. He crouched down in front of Eva and again made her turn her back to him, to let his eyes retrace the gaze of the child of long ago.

His fatigue was swept away all at once. He threw her to the floor. She lay on her stomach, and he crouched at her feet and let his gaze glide up along her legs to her rump, then threw himself on her and took her.

He had the impression that this leap onto her body was a leap across an immense period of time, the leap of a little boy hurling himself from childhood to manhood. And then, while he was moving back and forth on her, he seemed incessantly to be describing the same movement, from childhood to adulthood and then in reverse, and once again from the little boy miserably gazing at the gigantic body of a woman to the man clasping that body and taming it. That movement, usually measuring fifteen centimeters at most, was as long as three decades.

The two women yielded to his frenzy, and he went from Mrs. Nora to Marketa, then returned to Mrs. Nora, and so on. That lasted a very long time, and then he needed a bit of respite. He felt marvelously well, felt stronger than ever. Stretched out on an armchair, he contemplated the two women lying before him on the wide daybed. During that brief rest period, it wasn't Mrs. Nora he was seeing but his old girlfriends, his life's witnesses Marketa and Eva, and he felt like a great chess player who has conquered opponents simultaneously on two chessboards. The comparison pleased him enormously, and he couldn't help laughing and shouting: "I'm Bobby Fischer! I'm Bobby Fischer!"

12

While Karel was yelling that he was Bobby Fischer (who not long before had won the world chess championship in Iceland), Eva whispered in Marketa's ear as they lay snuggled on the daybed: "All right?"

Marketa nodded and pressed her lips against Eva's.

An hour earlier, when they were in the bathroom together, Eva had asked Marketa (it was the idea she had arrived here with and whose decency had seemed questionable to her) to come visit someday in return.

She would gladly invite Karel as well, but Karel and Eva's husband were each too jealous to tolerate the presence of another man.

At the moment, Marketa had thought it impossible to accept, and she merely laughed. Still, some minutes later, in the room where Mama and Karel's babble skimmed past their ears, she became all the more obsessed with Eva's proposition, just because it had at first seemed unacceptable. The specter of Eva's husband was here with them.

And then when Karel began to yell he was four years old and crouched down to gaze at Eva standing up, she thought it was as if he really were a four-year-old, as if he were fleeing to his childhood, leaving the two women alone except for his extraordinarily efficient body, so mechanically robust that it seemed impersonal and empty, and imaginable with anyone else's soul. Even, if need be, the soul of Eva's husband, that perfect stranger, a man without face or form.

Marketa let herself be made love to by this mechanical male body, then watched that body flinging itself between Eva's legs, but she tried not to see the face, so as to think of it as a stranger's body. It was a masked ball. Karel had put a mask of Nora on Eva and put a child's mask on himself, and Marketa had removed the head from his body. He was a man's body without a head. Karel disappeared and a miracle occurred: Marketa was free and joyous!

Am I trying in this way to confirm Karel's suspicion, his belief that for Marketa their little domestic orgies had up until now amounted only to self-sacrifice and suffering?

No, that would be an oversimplification. Marketa really desired, with both her body and her senses, the women she considered Karel's mistresses. And she also desired them with her head: fulfilling the prophecy of her old math teacher, she wanted—at least to the limits of the disastrous contract—to show herself enterprising and playful, and to astonish Karel.

But as soon as she found herself naked with them on the wide daybed, the sensual wanderings immediately vanished from her mind, and seeing her husband was enough to return her to her role, the role of the better one, the one who is wronged. Even when she was with Eva, whom she loved very much and of whom she was not jealous, the presence of the man she loved too well weighed heavy on her, stifling the pleasure of the senses.

The moment she removed his head from the body, she felt the strange and intoxicating touch of freedom. That anonymity of the body was a suddenly discovered paradise. With an odd delight, she expelled her wounded and too vigilant soul and was transformed into a simple body without past or memory, but all the more eager and receptive. She tenderly caressed Eva's face, while the headless body moved vigorously on top of her.

But here the headless body interrupted his movements and, in a voice that reminded her unpleasantly of Karel's, uttered unbelievably idiotic words: "I'm Bobby Fischer! I'm Bobby Fischer!"

It was like being awakened from a dream. And just then, as she lay snuggled against Eva (as the awakening sleeper snuggles against his pillow to hide from the dim first light of day), Eva had asked her, "All right?" and she had consented with a sign, pressing her lips against Eva's. She had always loved her, but today for the first time she loved her with all her senses, for herself, for her body, and for her skin, becoming intoxicated with this fleshly love as with a sudden revelation.

Afterward, while they lay side by side on their stomachs, with their buttocks slightly raised, Marketa could feel on her skin that the infinitely efficient body was again fixing its eyes on hers and at any moment was going to start again making love to them. She tried to ignore the voice talking about seeing beautiful Mrs. Nora, tried simply to be a body hearing nothing while lying pressed between a very soft-skinned girlfriend and some headless man.

When it was all over, her girlfriend fell asleep in a moment. Marketa envied her animal sleep, wanting to inhale that sleep from her lips, to doze off to its rhythm. She pressed herself against Eva and closed her eyes to fool Karel, who, thinking both women had fallen asleep, soon went to bed in the next room.

At four-thirty in the morning, she opened the door to his room. He looked up at her sleepily.

"Go back to sleep, I'll take care of Eva," she said, kissing him tenderly. He turned over and immediately was asleep again.

In the car, Eva again asked: "Is it all right?"

Marketa was no longer as determined as she had been the evening before. Yes, she would be quite willing to trespass against their old unwritten agreements. But how to do it without destroying love? How to do it when she continued to love Karel so much?

"Don't worry," said Eva. "He won't notice anything. Between the two of you, it's been established once and for all that it's you and not he who has the suspicions. You really have no reason to fear he suspects anything."

13

Eva dozes in the jolting compartment. Marketa has returned from the railroad station and is already back asleep (she will have to get up again in an hour to prepare for work), and now it is Karel's turn to take Mama to the station. It's train day. Some hours later (by then both husband and wife will already be at work), their son will step onto the station platform to bring this story to an end.

Karel is still filled with the night's beauty. He knows full well that of his two or three thousand acts of love (how many times had he made love in his life?), no more than two or three are really essential and unforgettable, while the others are merely recurrences, imitations, repetitions, or evocations. And Karel knows that yesterday's lovemaking is one of those two or three important acts of love, and he has a feeling of immense gratitude.

As he is driving her to the railroad station, Mama does not stop talking.

What does she say?

First she thanks him: she's had a very good time at her son and daughter-in-law's.

Then she reproaches him: they had done her many wrongs. When he and Marketa were still living with her, he had been impatient with Mama, often even rude and inconsiderate, and she had suffered greatly because of it. Yes, she admits, this time they'd been very nice, different from before. Yes, they had changed. But why had they waited so long?

Karel listens to this long litany of blame (he knows it by heart) but is not in the least irritated. He looks at Mama out of the corner of his eye, again surprised by how little she is. As if all of her life has been a slow process of shrinkage.

But just what is that shrinkage?

Is it the real shrinkage of a person abandoning his adult dimensions and starting on the long journey through old age and death toward distances where there is only a nothingness without dimensions?

Or is that shrinkage only an optical illusion, owing to the fact that Mama is going away, that she is elsewhere, that he is seeing her from afar, that she looks to him like a lamb, a doll, a butterfly?

When Mama pauses for a moment in her litany of

blame, Karel asks her: "What's become of Mrs. Nora?"

"She's an old woman now, you know. She's nearly blind."

"Do you ever see her?"

"Don't you know?" says Mama, offended. The two women had stopped seeing each other a long time ago, falling out with a bitter quarrel and never reconciling. Karel should have remembered that.

"Do you know where we went on vacation with her when I was little?"

"Of course I do!" says Mama, naming a spa in Bohemia. Karel knows it well but never realized the women's changing room there was where he had seen Mrs. Nora naked.

Now he pictured the gently rolling landscape surrounding the town, the spa building with its peristyle of carved wooden columns, the hilly meadows where grazing sheep made themselves heard by the tinkling of their little bells. He imagined putting into this landscape (like a collage artist sticking into a print a piece of another one) Mrs. Nora's naked body, and the thought then came to him that beauty is a spark that flashes when, suddenly, across the distance of years, two ages meet. That beauty is an abolition of chronology and a rebellion against time.

And he is overflowing with beauty and with gratitude for it. Then he says, point-blank: "Mama, we're wondering, Marketa and I, whether you might want to come live with us. It wouldn't be hard for us to get a slightly bigger apartment."

Mama caresses his hand. "You're very nice, Karel. Very nice. I'm glad to hear you say that. But you know, my poodle is used to things at home. And I've become friends with women in the neighborhood."

Then they board the train and Karel is trying to find a compartment for Mama. They are all crowded and uncomfortable. Finally he seats her in a first-class compartment and runs off to look for the conductor and pay the additional fare. And his wallet still in his hand, he takes out a hundred-crown bill and puts it in Mama's hand as if Mama were a little girl being sent off far away into the world, and Mama accepts the bill without surprise, quite naturally, like a schoolgirl used to adults now and then slipping her a bit of money.

And later, Mama is at the window as the train starts up, and Karel on the platform waves at her for a long, long time, until the very last moment.

PART THREE

The Angels

1

Rhinoceros is a play by Eugène Ionesco in which the characters, possessed by a desire to be similar to one another, one by one turn into rhinoceroses. Gabrielle and Michelle, two American girls, were studying the play at a summer course for foreign students in a small French town on the Mediterranean coast. They were the favorite students of Madame Raphael, their teacher, because they always gazed attentively at her and carefully wrote down every one of her remarks. Today she had asked the two of them to prepare a talk together on the play for the next class session.

"I don't really get what it means, that they all turn into rhinoceroses," said Gabrielle.

"You have to see it as a symbol," Michelle explained.

"That's right," said Gabrielle. "Literature is made up of signs."

"The rhinoceros is mainly a sign," said Michelle.

"Yes, but even if you assume they don't really turn into rhinoceroses, but only into signs, why do they become just that sign and not another one?"

"Yes, it's obviously a problem," said Michelle sadly, and the two girls, who were on their way back to their student residence hall, walked for a long while in silence.

It was Gabrielle who broke it: "Don't you think it's a phallic symbol?"

"What?" asked Michelle.

"The horn," said Gabrielle.

"That's right!" Michelle cried out, but then she hesitated. "Only, why does everybody turn into phallic symbols? Women just as well as men?"

The two girls heading rapidly toward the student residence hall were silent again.

"I've got an idea," Michelle said suddenly.

"What is it?" Gabrielle asked with interest.

"Besides, it's something Madame Raphael sort of implied," said Michelle, piquing Gabrielle's curiosity.

"So what is it? Tell me," Gabrielle insisted impatiently.

"The author wanted to create a comic effect!"

Her friend's idea so captivated Gabrielle that, concentrating entirely on what was going on in her head, she disregarded her legs and slowed her pace. The two girls came to a halt.

"Do you think the symbol of the rhinoceros is there to create a comic effect?" Gabrielle asked.

"Yes," said Michelle, smiling the proud smile of someone who has found the truth.

"You're right," said Gabrielle.

Pleased with their own boldness, the two girls looked at each other, and the corners of their mouths quivered with pride. Then, all of a sudden, they emitted short, shrill, spasmodic sounds very difficult to describe in words.

2

"Laughter? Do people ever care about laughter? I mean real laughter, beyond joking, mockery, ridicule. Laughter, an immense and delicious sensual pleasure, wholly sensual pleasure . . .

"I said to my sister, or she said to me, come over, shall we play laughter? We stretched out side by side on a bed and began. By pretending, of course. Forced laughter. Laughable laughter. Laughter so laughable it made us laugh. Then it came, real laughter, total laughter, taking us into its immense tide. Bursts of repeated, rushing, unleashed laughter, magnificent laughter, sumptuous and mad. . . . And we laugh our laughter to the infinity of laughter. . . . O laughter! Laughter of sensual pleasure, sensual pleasure of laughter; to laugh is to live profoundly."

This quotation is from a book called *Parole de femme* (Woman's Word). It was published in 1976 by one of the passionate feminists who have made a distinctive mark on the climate of our time. It is a mystical manifesto of joy. To oppose male sexual desire, which is devoted to the fleeting moments of erection and thus fatally engaged with violence, annihilation, and extinction, the author exalts, as its antipode, female *jouissance*—gentle, pervasive, and continuing sensual pleasure. For a woman who is not alienated from her own essence, "eating, drinking, urinating,

defecating, touching, hearing, or even just being here"
are all sensual pleasures. Such enumeration of pleasures extends through the book like a beautiful litany.
"Living is being happy: seeing, hearing, touching,
drinking, eating, urinating, defecating, diving into the
water and gazing at the sky, laughing and crying."
And coition is beautiful because it is the sum of "all of
life's possible sensual pleasures: touching, seeing,
hearing, talking, feeling, as well as drinking, eating,
defecating, knowing, dancing." Breast-feeding too is a
joy, even giving birth a sensual pleasure and menstru-
ating a delight, with that "warm saliva, that dark
milk, that warm, syrupy blood flow, that pain with the
scalding taste of happiness."

Only a fool could laugh at this manifesto of joy. All
mysticism is excessive. The mystic must not be afraid
of ridicule if he wants to go to the limits, the limits of
humility or the limits of sensual pleasure. Just as Saint
Theresa smiled in her agony, so Saint Annie Leclerc
(the author of the book I have been quoting) maintains
that death is a part of joy and dreaded only by the
male, who is wretchedly attached "to his petty self and
petty power."

Up above, as the vault of this temple of pleasure, is
the sound of laughter, "that delightful trance of happiness, that utmost height of sensual pleasure. Laughter
of sensual pleasure, sensual pleasure of laughter."
Unquestionably, such laughter is "beyond joking,
mockery, ridicule." The two sisters stretched out on
their bed are not laughing about anything in particular,

their laughter has no object, it is the expression of being rejoicing in being. Just as someone in pain is linked by his groans to the present moment (and is entirely outside past and future), so someone bursting out in such ecstatic laughter is without memory and without desire, for he is emitting his shout into the world's present moment and wishes to know only that.

You certainly remember this scene from dozens of bad films: a boy and a girl are running hand in hand in a beautiful spring (or summer) landscape. Running, running, running, and laughing. By laughing the two runners are proclaiming to the whole world, to audiences in all the movie theaters: "We're happy, we're glad to be in the world, we're in agreement with being!" It's a silly scene, a cliché, but it expresses a basic human attitude: serious laughter, laughter "beyond joking."

All churches, all underwear manufacturers, all generals, all political parties, are in agreement about that kind of laughter, and all of them rush to put the image of the two laughing runners on the billboards advertising their religion, their products, their ideology, their nation, their sex, their dishwashing powder.

Michelle and Gabrielle's laughter is precisely that kind of laughter. Hand in hand, they are emerging from a stationery store, and in her free hand each one is swinging a small bag of colored paper, glue, and rubber bands.

"You'll see, Madame Raphael will be just wild about it," says Gabrielle, and emits shrill, spasmodic sounds.

Michelle nods in agreement and then makes just about
the same noise.

3

Soon after the Russians occupied my country in 1968,
I was driven from my job (like thousands upon thousands of other Czechs), and no one had the right to
give me another. Some young friends too young to be
on the Russians' lists and thus still working in editorial
offices, schools, and film studios would come to see
me. Hoping to help me earn a living, these good young
friends, whom I will never betray, proposed plays,
radio and television dramas, articles, reportage, film
scripts, for me to write under their names. I did accept
a few such offers, but more often I rejected them,
because I could not have managed to handle everything that was proposed, and also because it was dangerous. Not for me, but for them. The secret police
wanted to starve us, reduce us to poverty, force us to
capitulate and make public retractions. And so they
vigilantly kept an eye on the pitiful emergency exits we
used in our attempts to avoid encirclement, and harshly
punished those who donated their names.

Among those generous donors was a young woman
named R. (Everything has since been laid bare, so in this

case I have little to hide.) Shy, subtle, and intelligent, she was an editor at a mass-circulation magazine for young people. Since the magazine at the time was obliged to publish an unbelievable number of indigestible political articles singing the praises of the fraternal Russian people, the editorial board was always looking for new ways to attract the readers' attention. So they decided to make an exception and depart from Marxist ideological purity by starting an astrology column.

During those years of exclusion, I had cast thousands of horoscopes. If the great Jaroslav Hasek could be a dog dealer (selling many stolen dogs and passing mutts off as pedigreed), why couldn't I be an astrologer? Friends in Paris had sent me all the astrological treatises of André Barbault, whose name on the title pages was proudly followed by *"Président du Centre international d'astrologie,"* to which, disguising my handwriting, I added in pen and ink: *"À Milan Kundera avec admiration, André Barbault."* I unobtrusively laid out these signed copies on a table, explaining to my surprised Prague clients that once for several months I had been the illustrious Barbault's assistant.

When R. asked me to write an astrology column for the weekly in secret, I of course reacted enthusiastically and advised her to tell the editorial board that the writer would be a brilliant nuclear physicist who did not want his name revealed for fear of being made fun of by his colleagues. Our undertaking seemed to me doubly shielded: by the nonexistent scientist and by his pseudonym.

And so, under an assumed name, I wrote a fine long article on astrology, then each month a brief and rather silly piece on each of the signs, with my own drawing of Taurus, Aries, Virgo, Pisces. The pay was pathetic and the task itself neither amusing nor remarkable. The only amusing thing about it all was my existence, the existence of a man erased from history, from literary histories, and from the telephone book, of a dead man now returned to life in an amazing reincarnation to preach the great truth of astrology to hundreds of thousands of young people in a socialist country.

One day, R. informed me that the editor in chief had been won over by the astrologer and wanted his horoscope cast. I was thrilled. This editor in chief, who had been put in charge of the magazine by the Russians, had spent half his life studying Marxism-Leninism in Prague and in Moscow!

"He was a bit ashamed to ask for this," R. told me with a smile. "He doesn't want it spread around that he believes in such medieval superstitions. But he's terribly tempted."

"That's great," I said with satisfaction. I knew the editor in chief. Besides being R.'s boss, he was a member of the party's supreme committee in charge of cadre and as such had ruined the lives of quite a few of my friends.

"He wants to remain totally anonymous. I have to give you his date of birth, but you must never know that it's his."

That amused me still more: "All the better!"

"He'll give you a hundred crowns for casting his horoscope."

"A hundred crowns? That's what he thinks, that tightwad."

He ended up sending me a thousand crowns. I filled ten pages depicting his character and describing his past (about which I was well enough informed) and future. I labored at it for a whole week, often consulting with R. With a horoscope we can indeed wonderfully influence, even direct, people's behavior. We can advise them to do certain things and warn them against doing others, and induce them into humility by acquainting them with the disasters in their future.

The next time I saw R., a while later, we had a good laugh. She claimed the editor in chief had improved since reading his horoscope. He shouted less. He had begun to guard against the harshness the horoscope warned him about, was setting great store by the bit of kindness he was capable of, and in his often vacant gaze you could recognize the sadness of a man who realizes that the stars merely promise him suffering.

4 *(On Two Kinds of Laughter)*

To see the devil as a partisan of Evil and an angel as a warrior on the side of Good is to accept the demagogy of the angels. Things are of course more complicated than that.

Angels are partisans not of Good but of divine creation. The devil, on the other hand, is the one who refuses to grant any rational meaning to that divinely created world.

Dominion over the world, as we know, is divided between angels and devils. The good of the world, however, implies not that the angels have the advantage over the devils (as I believed when I was a child) but that the powers of the two sides are nearly in equilibrium. If there were too much incontestable meaning in the world (the angels' power), man would succumb under its weight. If the world were to lose all its meaning (the devils' reign), we could not live either.

Things deprived suddenly of their supposed meaning, of the place assigned to them in the so-called order of things (a Moscow-trained Marxist believing in horoscopes), make us laugh. In origin, laughter is thus of the devil's domain. It has something malicious about it (things suddenly turning out different from what they pretended to be), but to some extent also a beneficent relief (things are less weighty than they appeared to be, letting us live more freely, no longer oppressing us with their austere seriousness).

The first time an angel heard the devil's laughter, he was dumbfounded. That happened at a feast in a crowded room, where the devil's laughter, which is terribly contagious, spread from one person to another.

The angel clearly understood that such laughter was directed against God and against the dignity of his works. He knew that he must react swiftly somehow, but felt weak and defenseless. Unable to come up with anything of his own, he aped his adversary. Opening his mouth, he emitted broken, spasmodic sounds in the higher reaches of his vocal range (a bit like the sound made on the street of a seaside town by Michelle and Gabrielle), but giving them an opposite meaning: whereas the devil's laughter denoted the absurdity of things, the angel on the contrary meant to rejoice over how well ordered, wisely conceived, good, and meaningful everything here below was.

Thus the angel and the devil faced each other and, mouths wide open, emitted nearly the same sounds, but each one's noise expressed the absolute opposite of the other's. And seeing the angel laugh, the devil laughed all the more, all the harder, and all the more blatantly, because the laughing angel was infinitely comical.

Laughable laughter is disastrous. Even so, the angels have gained something from it. They have tricked us with a semantic imposture. Their imitation of laughter and (the devil's) original laughter are both called by the same name. Nowadays we don't even realize that the same external display serves two absolutely opposed internal attitudes. There are two laughters, and we have no word to tell one from the other.

5

A magazine photograph: a row of men in uniform, bearing rifles and in helmets with protective plastic visors, watch a group of young people in jeans and T-shirts, hand in hand in a ring, dance in front of them.

It is clearly an interlude before a clash with police guarding a nuclear power plant, a military training camp, the offices of a political party, or the windows of an embassy. The young people have taken advantage of a lull to form a circle and, to a simple, well-known tune, take two steps in place, one step forward, raise first the left leg and then the right.

I think I understand them: they have the impression that the circle they are describing on the ground is a magical circle uniting them like a ring. And their chests swell with an intense feeling of innocence: they are united not by *marching*, like soldiers or fascist formations, but by *dancing*, like children. What they are trying to spit in the cops' faces is their innocence.

That is how the photographer saw them, and he brought out an eloquent contrast: on one side, the police in the *false* unity (imposed, commanded) of the row, on the other, the young people in the *true* unity (sincere and natural) of the circle; on this side, the police in the *sullen* posture of lying in wait, and on that one, those who are *delighting* in play.

Dancing in a ring is magic; a ring dance speaks to us

88

from the ancient depths of our memories. Madame Raphael, the teacher, clipped that photo from the magazine and gazed at it dreamily. She too wished to dance in a ring. All her life she had looked for a circle of men and women with whom she could hold hands in a ring dance, at first in the Methodist Church (her father was a religious fanatic), then in the Communist Party, then in the Trotskyist Party, then in a Trotskyist splinter party, then in the movement against abortion (a child has a right to life!), then in the movement to legalize abortion (a woman has a right to her body!), then she looked for it in Marxists, in psychoanalysts, in structuralists, looked for it in Lenin, in Zen Buddhism, in Mao Tse-tung, among the followers of yoga, in the school of the *nouveau roman,* and finally she wishes at least to be in perfect harmony with her students, to be at one with them, meaning that she always compels them to think and say the same things she does, to merge with her into a single body and a single soul in the same circle and the same dance.

Her students Gabrielle and Michelle are now bent over the Ionesco play in their room at the residence hall. Michelle is reading from it aloud:

"'Logician, to the old gentleman: Get a sheet of paper and work it out. If you take two paws from two cats, how many paws does each cat have left?

"'Old gentleman, to the logician: There are several possible solutions. One cat might have four paws, the other one, two. There might be one cat with five paws and the other cat with one paw. By taking two of the eight paws from the two cats we might have one cat with six paws. We might have one cat with no paws at all.'"

Michelle interrupts her own reading: "I don't get how you could take paws from a cat. Could he—would he—cut them off?"

"Michelle!" Gabrielle cries out.

"And I don't get how a cat can have six paws."

"Michelle!" Gabrielle again cries out.

"What?" asks Michelle.

"Did you forget? You're the one who said it!"

"What?" asks Michelle again.

"This dialogue is certainly intended to create a comic effect!"

"You're right," says Michelle, looking elatedly at Gabrielle. The two girls look into each other's eyes, their lips quiver with something like pride, and finally their mouths let out some short, spasmodic sounds in the higher reaches of their vocal range. Then the same sounds again and again. "A forced laugh. A laughable laugh. A laugh so laughable they can do nothing but laugh. Then comes real laughter. Bursts of repeated, rushing, unbridled laughter, explosions of magnificent laughter, sumptuous and mad. They laugh their laughter until the infinity of their laughter. . . . O laughter! Laughter of sensual pleasure, sensual pleasure of laughter . . ."

Meanwhile Madame Raphael was forlornly roaming the streets of that small town on the Mediterranean coast. Suddenly she raised her head as if a fragment of melody carried on the wings of a breeze were reaching her from afar, or as if a distant scent had struck her nostrils. She stopped and heard within her skull the shriek of a rebellious void wanting to be filled. It seemed to her that somewhere nearby a flame of great laughter was blazing, that perhaps somewhere nearby people were holding hands and dancing in a ring . . .

She stood this way for a while, looking around nervously, and then the mysterious music abruptly vanished (Michelle and Gabrielle had stopped laughing; suddenly they looked wearied by the prospect of a night devoid of love), and Madame Raphael, oddly anguished and unsatisfied, made her way home through the warm streets of the small coastal town.

6

I too once danced in a ring. It was in 1948. In my country, the Communists had taken power, the Socialist and democratic Christian ministers had taken refuge abroad, and I took other Communist students by the hands or shoulders and we took two steps in place, one step forward, raised the left leg to one side and then the right to the other, and we did this nearly every month, because we always had something to celebrate, an anniversary or some other event, old injustices were redressed, new injustices were perpetrated, factories were nationalized, thousands of people went to prison, medical care was

free, tobacconists saw their shops confiscated, aged workers vacationed for the first time in expropriated villas,
and on our faces we had the smile of happiness. Then one
day I said something I should not have said, was expelled
from the party, and had to leave the ring dance.

That is when I understood the magical meaning of
the circle. If you go away from a row, you can still come
back into it. A row is an open formation. But a circle
closes up, and if you go away from it, there is no way
back. It is not by chance that the planets move in circles
and that a rock coming loose from one of them goes
inexorably away, carried off by centrifugal force. Like a
meteorite broken off from a planet, I left the circle and
have not yet stopped falling. Some people are granted
their death as they are whirling around, and others are
smashed at the end of their fall. And these others (I am
one of them) always retain a kind of faint yearning for
that lost ring dance, because we are all inhabitants of a
universe where everything turns in circles.

It was God knows what anniversary and the streets of
Prague were once again filled with young people dancing in rings. I wandered among them, I came very close
to them, but I was forbidden to enter any of their rings.
It was June 1950, and Milada Horakova had been
hanged the day before. She had been a Socialist deputy
and the Communist tribunal had accused her of plotting
against the state. Zavis Kalandra, a Czech surrealist and
a friend of André Breton and Paul Éluard, was hanged
at the same time. And the dancing young Czechs, knowing that the day before, in the same city, a woman and

a surrealist had been swinging from the end of ropes, were dancing all the more frenetically, because their dance was a demonstration of their innocence, in shining contrast to the guilty darkness of the two who were hanged, those betrayers of the people and its hopes.

André Breton did not believe Kalandra had betrayed the people and its hopes, and in Paris he called on Éluard (in an open letter dated June 13, 1950) to protest the insane accusation and try to save their old friend. But Éluard was busy dancing in a gigantic ring between Paris, Moscow, Prague, Warsaw, Sofia, and Greece, between all the socialist countries and all the world's Communist parties, and everywhere he recited his beautiful poems about joy and brotherhood. After reading Breton's letter, he took two steps in place, then one step forward, he shook his head, refusing to defend a betrayer of the people (in the June 19, 1950 issue of the weekly *Action*), and started to recite in a metallic voice:

> "We shall fill innocence
> With the strength that so long
> We lacked
> We shall no longer be alone."

I wandered through the streets of Prague, rings of laughing, dancing Czechs swirled around me, and I knew that I did not belong to them but belonged to Kalandra, who had also come loose from the circular trajectory and had fallen, fallen, to end his fall in a condemned man's coffin, but even though I did not belong to them, I nonetheless watched the dancing with envy and yearning, unable to take my eyes off them. And that is when I saw him, right in front of me!

He had his arms around their shoulders and along with them was singing two or three simple notes and raising his left leg to one side and then his right leg to the other. Yes, it was he, Prague's darling Éluard! And suddenly the people he was dancing with fell silent, continuing to move in absolute silence while he chanted to the stamping of their feet:

> "We shall flee rest, we shall flee sleep,
> We shall outrun dawn and spring
> And we shall shape days and seasons
> To the measure of our dreams."

And then everyone abruptly began again to sing the three or four simple notes, speeding up the steps of their dance. They were fleeing rest and sleep, outrunning time, and filling their innocence. They were all smiling, and Éluard leaned over a girl he had his arm around:

"A man possessed by peace is always smiling."

And the girl started laughing and stamping her feet harder so that she rose a few centimeters above the pavement, pulling the others up after her, and a moment later not one of them was touching the ground, they were all taking two steps in place and one step forward without touching the ground, yes, they were soaring over Wenceslaus Square, their dancing ring resembled a great wreath flying off, and I ran on the ground below and looked up to see them, as they soared farther and farther away, raising the left leg to one side and then the right to the other, and there below them was Prague with its cafés full of poets and its prisons full of betrayers of the people, and from the crematorium where they were incinerating a Socialist deputy and a surrealist writer the smoke ascended to the heavens like a good omen, and I heard Éluard's metallic voice:

"Love is at work it is tireless."

And I ran after that voice through the streets so as not to lose sight of the splendid wreath of bodies gliding over the city, and I realized with anguish in my heart that they were flying like birds and I was falling like a stone, that they had wings and I would never have any.

7

Eighteen years after his execution, Kalandra was totally rehabilitated, but some months later Russian tanks burst into Bohemia and soon tens of thousands of people were in turn accused of betraying the people and its hopes, some of them thrown into prison and most of them driven from their jobs, and two years later (twenty years, that is, after Éluard soared away over Wenceslaus Square), one of these newly accused (I myself) was writing an astrology column in an illustrated Czech magazine for young people. A year after I wrote my last astrological article, on Sagittarius, I was visited by a young man I did not know. Without a word, he gave me an envelope. I tore it open and read the letter, but it took me a while to realize that it was from R. The handwriting was entirely different. She must have been very agitated when she wrote that letter. She had tried so hard to phrase it in terms only I could understand that even I understood only half of it. The only thing I really grasped was that, after a year, my identity as author had been discovered.

At that time I had a studio apartment on Bartolomejska Street in Prague. It's a short but famous street. All but two of the buildings (one of which I lived in) belong to the police. When I looked out of my large fifth-floor window, I saw, up above the rooftops, the towers of Hradcany Castle and, down below, the police courtyards. Up above paraded the glorious history of the Bohemian kings, down below unfolded the history of renowned prisoners. They had all passed through there, Kalandra and Horakova, Slansky and Clementis, and my friends Sabata and Hübl.

The young man (everything about him indicated he was R.'s fiancé) looked around with great caution. He clearly thought the police had hidden microphones in my apartment. With silent nods we agreed to go outside. We walked at first in continuing silence, and only when we entered the din of Narodni Avenue did he tell me that R. wished to see me and that a friend of his, whom I didn't know, had offered to lend his apartment in a suburb for this secret meeting.

So the next day, I took a long streetcar ride, my hands freezing in the December cold, to the outskirts of Prague, to the dormitory towns that were entirely empty at that midmorning hour. Finding the right building thanks to the young man's description, I took the elevator to the fourth floor, looked at the calling cards fastened to the doors, and rang the bell at one of them. The apartment was silent. I rang again, but no one came to the door. I went back down to the street and walked around in the freezing cold for half an hour, thinking R. had been delayed and we would meet on the deserted sidewalk on her way from the streetcar stop. But no one came. I took the elevator up again to the fourth floor. I rang once more. A few seconds later, I heard the sound of water flushing from inside the apartment. In that instant it was as though someone had dropped an ice cube of anguish into me. Inside my own body I felt the fear of the young woman unable to open the door because her anxiety was upsetting her bowels.

When she opened the door, she was pale but smiling, trying hard to be as pleasant as always. She joked awkwardly about our being alone at last in an empty apartment. We sat down, and she told me she had recently been summoned by the police. They had interrogated her for a whole day. The first two hours, they asked her about a lot of unimportant things, making her feel so in control of the situation that she joked with them and insolently asked if they expected her to miss lunch over such foolishness. Just then they asked her: So who is it, dear Miss R., that writes the astrology articles for your magazine? She blushed and tried to say something about a well-known physicist whose name she couldn't reveal. They asked her: Do you know Mr. Kundera? She said she knew me. Was there anything wrong with that? They replied:

There's nothing wrong with that, but do you know that Mr. Kundera is interested in astrology? I don't know anything about it, she said. You don't know anything about it? they asked, laughing. All Prague is talking about it, and you don't know anything? She spoke again for a few moments about the nuclear physicist, and then one of the cops started shouting at her: Just stop lying!

She told them the truth. The editorial board wanted to have an interesting astrology column but didn't know anybody who could write one, and R. knew me and so she asked me to help out. She was certain she hadn't violated any law. They said she was right. She hadn't violated any law. She had only infringed the internal administrative regulations that prohibited working with persons guilty of having abused the confidence of the party and the state. She pointed out that nothing very serious had occurred: Mr. Kundera's name had remained hidden under a pseudonym and thus couldn't have offended anyone. As for the fees Mr. Kundera was paid, they weren't even worth mentioning. Again they said she was right: nothing serious had happened, that was true, and they were merely going to draw up a statement about what actually had happened and she was going to sign it and would have nothing to worry about.

She signed the statement and two days later the editor in chief called her in and told her she was dismissed, effective immediately. The same day she went to the radio offices, where she had friends who had long been offering her a job. They greeted her happily, but when she came the next day to fill out the forms, the head of personnel, who liked her very much, met her with a look of distress: "What a stupid thing you've done, my dear! You've messed up your life. There's absolutely nothing I can do for you."

Initially she hesitated to talk to me, because she had to promise the police not to breathe a word about the interrogation to anyone. But when she was again summoned by the police (she was due there the next day), she decided it would be best to meet me in secret to agree on a story and avoid contradicting each other if I too was summoned.

Please understand that R. was not fearful but young and unworldly. She had just sustained her first unexpected, incomprehensible blow, and she would never forget it. I realized I had been chosen to be the mailman who delivers warnings and punishments to people, and I began to be afraid of myself.

"Do you think," she asked me with a lump in her throat, "they know about the thousand crowns you got for the horoscope?"

"Don't worry. Someone who spent three years in Moscow studying Marxism-Leninism wouldn't dare admit he had his horoscope cast."

She laughed, and though the laugh lasted barely half a second, it rang in my ears like a tentative promise of salvation. For it was just this laughter I wanted to hear when I wrote those silly little articles on Pisces, Virgo, and Aries, it was just this laughter I imagined as my reward, but it never reached me, not from anywhere, because in the meantime throughout the world the angels had occupied all positions of authority, all the general staffs, had taken over the left and the right, the Arabs and the Jews, the Russian generals and the Russian dissidents. They stared at us icily from all sides, that stare stripping us of the amiable costume we wear as playful hoaxers and unmasking us as pathetic impostors who work at a socialist youth magazine while believing neither in youth nor in socialism, who cast a horoscope for an editor in chief while making fun of both editor in chief and horoscopes, who busy ourselves with paltry things when all those around us (left and right, Arabs and Jews, generals and dissidents) are fighting for the future of the human race. We felt the weight of their stares turning us into insects to be crushed underfoot.

Overcoming my anguish, I tried to come up with the most sensible plan for R. to follow in her replies to the police the next day. Several times during our conversation she got up to go to the toilet. Each time, she came back to the sound of water flushing and with a look of embarrassed panic. That brave girl was ashamed of her fear. That woman of taste was ashamed of her bowels raging in front of a stranger.

8

Twenty or so young people of various nationalities sat at their desks looking inattentively at Michelle and

Gabrielle, who were standing tensely before the dais where Madame Raphael sat. Both were holding several sheets of paper, covered with the text of their talk, and an odd cardboard object fitted with a rubber band.

"We're going to talk about the Ionesco play *Rhinoceros*," said Michelle, and bent her head to place the cardboard cone, decorated with multicolored pieces of glued-on paper, over her nose and fasten it around the back of her head with the rubber band. Gabrielle did the same. Then they looked at each other and emitted high-pitched, short, spasmodic sounds.

The class swiftly enough understood that the two girls were showing, one, that a rhinoceros has a horn instead of a nose and, two, that Ionesco's play is comic. They had decided to express these two ideas not only in words but most of all with their own bodies' actions.

The long cones swayed on their faces, and the class fell into a kind of embarrassed compassion, as if someone had stood up in front of their desks to display his amputated arm.

Only Madame Raphael admired her young favorites' inspiration, responding to their shrill, spasmodic sounds with similar shrieks of her own.

Satisfied with that, the girls nodded their long noses and Michelle started to read her share of their talk.

One of the students was a Jewish girl named Sarah. A few days before, she had asked the two American girls to let her have a look at their notes (everybody knew they took down every one of Madame Raphael's words), but they had refused: "You cut class and went to the beach." Ever since, Sarah had heartily detested them, and now she was delighted to see them making fools of themselves.

Michelle and Gabrielle took turns reading their analysis of *Rhinoceros*, the long cardboard cones extending from their faces like futile supplications. Sarah realized that it would be a pity to let such an opportunity go by. During the pause when Michelle signaled Gabrielle to take over, Sarah got up from her seat and headed toward the two girls. Instead of continuing with her part, Gabrielle fixed the gaze of the astonished orifice of her false nose on Sarah and stood there gaping. When she reached the two students, Sarah went around them (as if the added noses were weighing down their heads, the American girls did not even turn to see what was happening) and, taking a running start, gave Michelle a kick in the buttocks, then, with another running start, booted Gabrielle's behind. Then she calmly, indeed with dignity, returned to her seat.

For a moment there was absolute silence.

Then Michelle's tears began to flow, and a moment later Gabrielle's.

Then the whole class exploded in tremendous laughter.

Then Sarah sat down again.

Then Madame Raphael, who had initially been caught off guard and was stupefied, realized that Sarah's intervention was an episode devised for a carefully prepared student prank whose aim was to shed light on the subject of their analysis (the inter-

pretation of a work of art cannot be limited to the traditional theoretical approach; a modern approach is
needed, reading by means of praxis, of action, of a
happening), and unable to see her favorites' tears
(facing the class, they had their backs to her), she
tilted her head backward and burst into acquiescent
laughter.

Hearing their beloved teacher laughing behind
them, Michelle and Gabrielle felt betrayed. Now the
tears flowed from their eyes as from a faucet. The
humiliation was so painful they began to writhe as if
with stomach cramps.

Madame Raphael thought her favorite students' convulsions were a dance, and all at once a force more powerful than her professorial gravity flung her out of her
chair. She laughed until she cried, and she spread her
arms and wiggled her body so hard that her head was
thrown back and forth on her neck like an upside-down
bell in the hand of the sexton vigorously ringing it.
Approaching the convulsively writhing girls, she took
Michelle by the hand. Now all three of them were in front
of the student desks, all three of them writhing and in
tears. Madame Raphael took two steps in place, raised
her left leg to one side, then the right leg to the other, and
the two girls in tears started timidly to imitate her. The
tears ran along their cardboard noses, and they writhed
and hopped in place. Then *Madame le professeur* seized
Gabrielle's hand; now they formed a circle in front of the
desks, all three, hand in hand, taking steps in place and
to each side and turning in a ring on the classroom floor.

They threw the right and then the left leg forward, and imperceptibly Gabrielle and Michelle's grimace of sobbing became the grimace of laughter.

The three women danced and laughed, the cardboard noses jiggled, and the class looked at them in mute horror. But by now the three dancing women were unaware of the others, they were concentrating entirely on themselves and on their sensual pleasure. Suddenly Madame Raphael stamped her foot harder and rose a few centimeters above the floor and then, with the next step, was no longer touching the ground. She pulled her two companions after her, and in a moment all three were revolving above the floor and rising slowly in a spiral. When their hair touched the ceiling, it started little by little to open. They rose higher and higher through that opening, their cardboard noses were no longer visible, and now there were only three pairs of shoes passing through the gaping hole, but these too finally vanished, while from on high, the dumbfounded students heard the fading, radiant laughter of three archangels.

9

My meeting with R. in the borrowed apartment was decisive for me. Only then did I understand definitively that I had become a bearer of ill tidings and could not go on living among the people I loved if I wished them no harm, and that the only thing remaining for me to do was to leave my country.

But I have yet another reason to recall that last meeting with R. I had always been very fond of the young woman, in the most innocent, least sexual way possible. It was as if her body were always perfectly concealed behind her radiant intelligence and, as well, behind the modesty of her behavior and the tastefulness of her clothes. She had never offered me the smallest gap through which I could have caught sight of a glimmer of her nakedness. And now, like a butcher knife, fear had suddenly cut her open. I had the impression of seeing her before me like the carcass of a heifer hanging from a hook in a shop. We were sitting side by side on the daybed in that borrowed apartment, hearing the slosh of water refilling the toilet tank, and suddenly I felt a wild desire to make love to her. More exactly: a wild desire to rape her. To throw myself on her and seize her in a single embrace along with all her unbearably exciting contradictions, with her perfect clothes and her rebellious intestines, with her reason and her fear, with her pride and her shame. And it seemed to me that lying hidden in these contradictions was her very essence, that treasure, that nugget of gold, that diamond concealed in her depths. I wanted to pounce on her and tear it out of her. I wanted to contain her entirely, with her shit and her ineffable soul.

But I saw two anguished eyes fixed on me (anguished

eyes in an intelligent face), and the more anguished those eyes, the greater my desire to rape her—and all the more absurd, idiotic, scandalous, incomprehensible, and unachievable.

When I left the borrowed apartment that day and was once more on the deserted suburban dormitory-town street (R. stayed in the apartment for a time, fearing to be seen with me), I could think of nothing for a long while but the immense desire I had felt to rape my lovely friend. That desire has remained with me, captive like a bird in a sack, a bird that from time to time awakens and flutters its wings.

It may be that the insane desire to rape R. was merely a desperate effort to grab at something in the midst of falling. Because ever since they expelled me from the ring dance, I have not stopped falling, I am still falling, and all they have done now is push me once again to make me fall still farther, still deeper, farther and farther from my country into the deserted space of a world where the fearsome laughter of the angels rings out, drowning all my words with its jangle.

I know that Sarah exists somewhere, Sarah the Jewish girl, Sarah my sister, but where will I find her?

(Quotations are from the following works: Annie Leclerc, *Parole de femme*, 1976; Paul Éluard, *Le visage de la paix*, 1951; Eugène Ionesco, *Rhinocéros*, 1959.)

PART FOUR

Lost Letters

1

I calculate that two or three new fictional characters are baptized here on earth every second. That is why I am always hesitant about joining that vast crowd of John the Baptists. But what can I do? After all, my characters need to have names. This time, to make clear that my heroine is mine and only mine (I am more attached to her than to any other), I am giving her a name no woman has ever before borne: Tamina. I imagine her as tall and beautiful, thirty-three years old, and originally from Prague.

I see her walking down a street in a provincial town in the west of Europe. Yes, you're right to have noticed: I refer to faraway Prague by name, while leaving anonymous the town where my story takes place. That breaks all the rules of perspective, but you'll just have to make the best of it.

Tamina works as a waitress in a small café belonging to a married couple. The café brings in so little, the husband had to take the first job he could find, and Tamina was hired to replace him. The difference between the pitiful amount the owner earns at his new job and the still more pitiful amount they pay Tamina accounts for their slender profit.

Tamina serves coffee and calvados to the customers (there aren't all that many, the room being always half empty) and then goes back behind the bar. Almost always there is someone sitting on a barstool, trying to talk to her. Everyone likes Tamina. Because she knows how to listen to people.

But is she really listening? Or is she merely looking at them so attentively, so silently? I don't know, and it's not very important. What matters is that she doesn't interrupt anyone. You know what happens when two people talk. One of them speaks and the other breaks in: "It's absolutely the same with me, I . . ." and starts talking about himself until the first one manages to slip back in with his own "It's absolutely the same with me, I . . ."

The phrase "It's absolutely the same with me, I . . ." seems to be an approving echo, a way of continuing the other's thought, but that is an illusion: in reality it is a brute revolt against a brutal violence, an effort to free our own ear from bondage and to occupy the enemy's ear by force. Because all of man's life among his kind is nothing other than a battle to seize the ear of others. The whole secret of Tamina's popularity is that she has no desire to talk about herself. She submits to the forces occupying her ear, never saying: "It's absolutely the same with me, I . . ."

2

Bibi is ten years younger than Tamina. For nearly a year she has been talking to Tamina about herself, day after day. Not long ago (that, in fact, was when it all began), she told her she was planning to go with her husband on vacation to Prague that summer.

With that, Tamina thought she was awakening from a sleep of several years. Bibi went on talking, and Tamina (contrary to her habit) broke in:

"Bibi, if you go to Prague, could you drop by at my father's and get something for me? It's nothing big, just a small parcel. It'll easily fit into your suitcase."

"I'd do anything for you!" said Bibi with great eagerness.

"I'll be eternally grateful," said Tamina.

"You can count on me," said Bibi. The two women talked a bit about Prague, and Tamina's cheeks were burning.

"I want to write a book," Bibi said next.

Thinking about her small parcel back in Bohemia, Tamina realized she had to make sure of Bibi's friendship. So she immediately offered Bibi her ear: "A book? About what?"

Bibi's year-old daughter was crawling around under her mother's barstool, making a lot of noise.

"Be quiet!" said Bibi down at the floor, and drew on

her cigarette with a pensive look. "About the world as I see it."

The little girl's cries grew more and more shrill, and Tamina asked: "Would you know how to write a book?"

"Why not?" she said, looking pensive again. "Of course, I have to get a bit of information on how you go about writing a book. Do you by any chance know Banaka?"

"Who is that?" asked Tamina.

"A writer," said Bibi. "He lives around here. I've got to meet him."

"What has he written?"

"I don't know," said Bibi, and added pensively: "Maybe I should read one of his things."

3

Instead of an exclamation of joyful surprise, what came through the receiver was an icy: "Well, well! You still remember me?"

"You know I'm not rolling in money. Phoning you is expensive," Tamina said in apology.

"You could write. As far as I know, stamps aren't so expensive there. I don't even recall when I got your last letter."

Realizing that the conversation with her mother-in-law was off to a bad start, Tamina set out to question her at length about her health and about what she was doing, before she could bring herself to say: "I have a favor to ask of you. When we were leaving the country, we left a parcel with you."

"A parcel?"

"Yes. Pavel and you put it away in his father's old desk, and he locked the drawer. You'll recall he always had a drawer of his own in that desk. And then he gave you the key."

"I don't have your key."

"But you've got to have it! I'm sure Pavel gave it to you. I was there."

"You didn't give me a thing."

"It's been quite a few years, and maybe you've forgotten. All I'm asking you is to look for that key. You'll certainly find it."

"And what do you want me to do with it?"

"Just look and see if the parcel is still there."

"And why wouldn't it be? Didn't you put it there?"

"Yes."

"Then why should I open the drawer? What do you think I've done with your notebooks?"

That stunned Tamina: How could her mother-in-law know there were notebooks in the drawer? They were wrapped and the parcel was carefully sealed with gummed tape. But she did not let her surprise show:

"I'm not suggesting anything like that. I just want you to look and see if everything's there. I'll tell you more next time."

"You can't tell me what this is about?"

"I can't keep talking, it's so expensive!"

Her mother-in-law started to sob: "Then don't phone me, if it's too expensive!"

"Don't cry, please," said Tamina. She knew her sobs by heart. Whenever her mother-in-law had wanted something from them, she would weep. Weeping was her way of blaming them, and there was nothing more aggressive than her tears.

The receiver shook with her sobs, and Tamina said: "Goodbye now, I'll phone again soon."

Tamina did not dare hang up before her mother-in-law stopped weeping and said goodbye. But the sobs went on, with every tear adding to the phone call's cost.

Tamina hung up.

"You've talked for a very long time," said the owner's wife, aggrieved, and pointed to the telephone meter. Then she calculated how much the call to Bohemia would cost, and Tamina was horrified by the amount. She would have to count every coin to make it to the next payday. But she paid up without batting an eye.

4

Tamina and her husband had left Bohemia illegally. They had signed up with the official travel agency for a group going to the Yugoslav coast. Once there, they abandoned the group and, after crossing the Austrian border, headed west.

Afraid of drawing attention during their time with the group, they took only one large suitcase each. At the last moment, they had not dared to take with them the bulky parcel containing their letters to each other and Tamina's notebooks. If a police officer of occupied Bohemia had made them open their baggage at customs, they immediately would have been under suspicion for bringing along on a two-week seaside vacation the entire archive of their private life. And knowing that their apartment would be confiscated by the state after their departure, they did not want to leave the parcel there, and so they deposited it at Tamina's mother-in-law's, in a drawer of the soon-to-be-unused desk left behind by her deceased father-in-law.

Abroad, Tamina's husband had fallen ill, and Tamina could only look on as death slowly took him. When he died, they asked her whether she wanted to have him buried or cremated. She told them to cremate him. Then they asked her if she wanted to keep him in an urn or preferred to have the ashes scattered. Having no home, she was afraid she would be carrying her husband around all the rest of her life like a piece of hand luggage. She had his ashes scattered.

I imagine the world rising higher and higher around Tamina like a circular wall, and that she is a bit of lawn down at the bottom. Growing on that bit of lawn, there is only a single rose, the memory of her husband.

Or I imagine Tamina's present (which consists of serving coffee and offering her ear) as a raft adrift on the water, with her on that raft looking back, looking only back.

After a while, she fell into despair because the past was becoming more and more faint. All she had left of her husband was his passport photo, the other photographs having remained in the confiscated Prague apartment. Looking at that pathetic stamped dog-eared full-face photo of her husband (like a criminal's mug shot), she saw that it was scarcely like him. Every day, she engaged in a kind of spiritual exercise before this picture, trying to visualize her husband in profile, then half profile, then three-quarter. Recapturing the lines of his nose and chin, she was horrified every day to notice the imaginary sketch showing newly questionable points introduced by the uncertain memory that was doing the drawing.

During these exercises, she tried to evoke his skin, its color and all its tiny blemishes—warts, growths, freckles, small veins. It was difficult, almost impossible. The colors her memory supplied were unreal, and with such colors there was no way to simulate human skin. So she had settled on a special recollection technique of her own. Whenever she sat facing a man, she would use his head as material for sculpture: gazing intently at him, she would imagine remaking the contours of the face, giving him a darker complexion and putting warts and freckles on it, reducing the ears' size, coloring the eyes blue.

But all these efforts only showed that her husband's image was irrevocably slipping away. At the beginning of their time together, he had asked her (ten years older than she, he had already gotten some idea of human memory's wretchedness) to keep a diary that would record their life. She had resisted, declaring it would make light of their love. She loved him too much to admit that what she considered unforgettable could ever be forgotten. Finally, of course, she obeyed him, but with no enthusiasm. The notebooks showed it: there were many empty pages, and the entries were fragmentary.

5

She had lived with her husband in Bohemia for eleven years, and the notebooks left at her mother-in-law's were also eleven in number. Not long after her husband's death, she bought a school notebook and divided it in eleven sections. She of course managed to recollect a good many half-forgotten events and situations, but she had no idea in what part of the school notebook to enter them. The chronological order was irremediably lost.

She tried initially to recover memories that could serve as reference points in time's flow and become the underlying framework of a reconstructed past. Their vacations, for example. There must have been eleven of them, but she could recall only nine. Two had been lost forever.

Then she tried to distribute the nine rediscovered vacations among the eleven sections of the school notebook. She could manage that with certainty only for years marked by something exceptional. In 1964, Tamina's mother had died, and a month later they had vacationed sadly in the Tatras. And she knew that the year after that they had gone to the Bulgarian seashore. She also recalled the vacations of 1968 and the following year, because they were the last they spent in Bohemia.

But if she succeeded after a fashion in reconstructing most of their vacations (though she was unable to date all of them), she completely failed to recollect their Christmases and New Years. Of eleven Christmases, she found only two in her mind's recesses, and of twelve New Years she could recall only five.

She also tried to remember all the names he had bestowed on her. Only during their first two weeks had he called her by her real name. His tenderness was a nonstop nickname machine. As the names quickly wore out, he incessantly gave her new ones. In their twelve years together, she had had some twenty or thirty, each one belonging to a specific period of their life.

But how to rediscover the lost link between a nickname and the rhythm of time? Only rarely does

Tamina manage to find it. She remembers, for example, the days after her mother's death. Her husband insistently whispered her name into her ear (that time's name, the name of the moment), as if trying to wake her from a dream. It is a nickname she remembers and can confidently enter in the section headed "1964." But all the other names are soaring outside time, free and mad like birds escaped from an aviary.

That is why she so desperately wants to have that parcel of notebooks and letters.

She knows, of course, that there are also quite a few unpleasant things in the notebooks, days of dissatisfaction, arguments, and even boredom, but that is not what matters. She does not want to give back to the past its poetry. She wants to give back to it its lost body. What is urging her on is not a desire for beauty. It is a desire for life.

For Tamina is adrift on a raft and looking back, looking only back. Her entire being contains only what she sees there, far behind her. Just as her past contracts, disintegrates, dissolves, so Tamina is shrinking and losing her contours.

She wants to have her notebooks so that the flimsy framework of events, as she has constructed them in her school notebook, will be provided with walls and become a house she can live in. Because if the tottering structure of her memories collapses like a clumsily pitched tent, all that Tamina will be left with is the present, that invisible point, that nothingness moving slowly toward death.

6

Why then hadn't she told her mother-in-law long ago to send her the parcel?

In her native country, correspondence with foreign countries passes through the hands of the secret police, and Tamina could not accept the idea of police officials poking their noses into her private life. And then, her husband's name (which was also hers) had surely remained on the blacklists, for the police took an unfailing interest in any document pertaining to the lives of their adversaries, even those who were dead. (Tamina was not mistaken on that score: our only immortality is in the police files.)

Because of this, Bibi was her only hope, and she was willing to do anything to further their friendship. If Bibi was to be introduced to Banaka, Tamina thought her friend should be familiar with the plot of at least one of his books. It was in fact absolutely essential for her to slip into their conversation remarks like "Yes, that's just what you say in your book" or "You're just like your characters, Mr. Banaka!" Tamina knew that there wasn't a single book at Bibi's and that reading bored her. So she wanted to learn a bit about Banaka's books to prepare her friend for her meeting with the writer.

As Tamina was serving a customer his coffee, she asked him: "Hugo, do you know Banaka?"

Hugo had bad breath, but apart from that, Tamina rather liked him: he was a quiet, shy young fellow, about five years younger than she. He would come to the café once a week, now looking through a pile of books, now at Tamina standing behind the bar.

"Yes," he said.

"I'd like to know the subject of one of his books."

"Don't forget, Tamina," replied Hugo, "that no one has ever read anything by Banaka. Anyone who reads a book of Banaka's is considered an idiot. Everyone knows that Banaka is a second-rate or third-rate or even tenth-rate writer. Believe it or not, Banaka himself is such a victim of his own reputation that he looks down on people who read his books."

She stopped trying to obtain Banaka's books, simply deciding to go ahead and arrange Bibi's meeting with the writer. From time to time Tamina lent the room she lived in, which was empty during the day, to a tiny Japanese married woman nicknamed Joujou, for her trysts with an equally married philosophy professor. The professor knew Banaka, and Tamina made the lovers promise to bring him along to her place one day when Bibi would be there, visiting.

When Bibi heard the news, she said to her: "Maybe Banaka's good-looking and your sex life's finally going to change."

7

It's true that Tamina had not made love since the death of her husband. Not on principle. Her posthumous fidelity, on the contrary, seemed almost ridiculous to her, and she never boasted about it. But whenever she imagined undressing before a man (and she imagined it often), she saw her husband's image before her. She knew she would see him if she actually did so. She knew she would see his face and see his eyes watching her.

It was obviously incongruous, it was even absurd, and she was aware of that. She didn't believe in the life after death of her husband's soul, nor did she think she would offend his memory by taking a lover. But there was nothing she could do about it.

She even had a peculiar thought: It would have been much easier than it was now to be unfaithful to her husband when he was still alive. Her husband had been cheerful, brilliant, strong, and she, feeling much weaker, had the impression that, try as she might, she would have been unable to wound him.

But now everything was different. Now she would be harming someone unable to defend himself, who was at her mercy like a child. Because now that he was dead, her husband had no one but her, no one but her in the entire world!

That is why, the moment she even considered the possibility of physical love with another man, her husband's image suddenly appeared, and with it an agonizing yearning, and with that yearning an immense desire to weep.

8

Banaka was ugly and found it difficult to awaken a woman's dormant sensuality. Tamina poured him a cup of tea, and he thanked her very respectfully. Everyone felt at home at Tamina's, and Banaka, turning to Bibi with a smile, quickly broke into the rambling conversation:

"I gather you want to write a book. A book about what?"

"Very simple," Bibi answered. "A novel. About the world as I see it."

"A novel?" asked Banaka disapprovingly.

Bibi corrected herself evasively: "It won't necessarily be a novel."

"Just think about what a novel is," said Banaka. "About the multitude of different characters. Are you trying to make us believe that you know all about them? That you know what they look like, what they think, how they're dressed, the kind of family they come from? Admit it, you're not interested in any of that!"

"That's right," Bibi acknowledged. "I'm not."

"You know," said Banaka, "the novel is the fruit of

a human illusion. The illusion of the power to understand others. But what do we know of one another?"

"Nothing," said Bibi.

"That's true," said Joujou.

The philosophy professor nodded his head in approval.

"All anyone can do," said Banaka, "is give a report on oneself. Anything else is an abuse of power. Anything else is a lie."

Bibi agreed enthusiastically: "That's true! That's absolutely true! I don't really want to write a novel! I didn't make myself clear. I want to do just what you said, write about myself. Give a report on my life. But I don't want to hide that my life is absolutely ordinary, normal, and that I've never experienced anything special."

Banaka smiled: "That's not important! Looked at from the outside, I've never experienced anything special either."

"Yes," cried Bibi, "that's right! Looked at from the *outside*, I haven't experienced anything. Looked at from the outside! But I have a feeling that my experience *inside* is worth writing about and could be interesting to everybody."

Tamina refilled the teacups, delighted that the two men, who had descended into her apartment from the Olympus of the mind, were being nice to her friend.

The philosophy professor drew on his pipe, hiding behind the smoke as though he were ashamed.

"Since James Joyce," he said, "we have known that the greatest adventure of our lives is the absence of adventure. Ulysses, who fought at Troy, returned home by crisscrossing the seas, he himself steering his ship, and had a mistress on every island—no, that is not the way we lead our lives. Homer's odyssey has been taken inside. It has been interiorized. The islands, the seas, the sirens seducing us, Ithaca summoning us—nowadays they are only the voices of our interior being."

"Yes! That's just how I feel!" Bibi exclaimed, and then she again turned to Banaka. "And that's why I wanted to ask you how to go about doing it. I often have the impression my whole body is filled with the desire to express itself. To speak. To make itself heard. Sometimes I think I'm going crazy, because I'm so bursting with it I have an urge to scream, you certainly must know about that, Mr. Banaka. I want to express my life and my feelings, which I know are absolutely original, but when I sit down in front of a piece of paper, I suddenly don't know anymore what to write. Then I think it must be about technique. Obviously there's something you know that I don't know. You've written such beautiful books. . . ."

9

I'll spare you the lecture on the art of writing the two Socrateses gave the young woman. I want to talk about something else. Some time ago, I went across Paris in a taxi with a garrulous driver. He couldn't sleep nights. He had chronic insomnia. Had it ever since the war. He was a sailor. His ship sank. He swam three days and three nights. Then he was rescued. He spent several months between life and death. He recovered, but he had lost the ability to sleep.

"I've had a third more of life than you," he said, smiling.

"And what do you do with that extra third?" I asked him.

"I write."

I asked him what he was writing.

He was writing his life story. The story of a man who swam in the sea for three days and three nights, who had struggled against death, who had lost the ability to sleep but kept the strength to live.

"Are you writing it for your children? As a family chronicle?"

He chuckled bitterly: "For my children? They're not interested in that. I'm writing a book. I think it could help a lot of people."

That conversation with the taxi driver suddenly made clear to me the essence of the writer's occupation. We write books because our children aren't interested in us. We address ourselves to an anonymous world because our wives plug their ears when we speak to them.

You might say that the taxi driver is not a writer but a graphomaniac. So we need to be precise about our concepts. A woman who writes her lover four letters a day is not a graphomaniac. She is a lover. But my friend who makes photocopies of his love letters to publish them someday is a graphomaniac. Graphomania is not a desire to write letters, personal diaries, or family chronicles (to write for oneself or one's close relations) but a desire to write books (to have a public of unknown readers). In that sense, the taxi driver and Goethe share the same passion. What distinguishes Goethe from the taxi driver is not a difference in passions but one passion's different results.

Graphomania (a mania for writing books) inevitably takes on epidemic proportions when a society develops to the point of creating three basic conditions:

(1) an elevated level of general well-being, which allows people to devote themselves to useless activities;

(2) a high degree of social atomization and, as a consequence, a general isolation of individuals;

(3) the absence of dramatic social changes in the nation's internal life. (From this point of view, it seems to me symptomatic that in France, where practically nothing happens, the percentage of writers is twenty-one times higher than in Israel. Bibi is, moreover, right to say that *looked at from the outside,* she hasn't experienced anything. The mainspring that drives her to write is just that absence of vital content, that void.)

But by a backlash, the effect affects the cause. General isolation breeds graphomania, and generalized graphomania in turn intensifies and worsens iso-

lation. The invention of printing formerly enabled
people to understand one another. In the era of universal graphomania, the writing of books has an opposite meaning: everyone surrounded by his own words
as by a wall of mirrors, which allows no voice to filter
through from outside.

10

"Tamina," said Hugo one day as they were chatting in
the empty café, "I know I don't stand a chance with
you. So I'm not going to try anything. But just the
same, may I invite you to lunch on Sunday?"

The parcel is with her mother-in-law in a provincial
town, and Tamina wants to have it sent to her father
in Prague, where Bibi could go pick it up. At first
sight, nothing could be simpler, but it will take a good
deal of time and money to persuade these two capri-
cious old people to do their parts. Telephoning is
expensive, and Tamina earns barely enough for food
and rent.

"Yes," said Tamina, remembering that Hugo had a
telephone.

He came for her in his car, and they went to a
restaurant in the country.

Tamina's precarious situation should have made it

easy for Hugo to play the role of conquering sovereign, but behind the person of the underpaid waitress he saw the mysterious experience of the foreigner and widow. He felt intimidated. Tamina's kindness was like a bulletproof vest. He wanted to attract her attention, captivate her, gain entry into her mind!

He did his best to come up with something interesting. On the way, he stopped the car to visit a zoo set up on the grounds of a beautiful country château. They walked among monkeys and parrots in a setting of Gothic towers. They were all alone except for a rustic gardener sweeping fallen leaves from the broad paths. Passing a wolf, a beaver, and a tiger, they came to a wire fence surrounding a large field where the ostriches were.

There were six of them. When they caught sight of Tamina and Hugo, they ran toward them. Now bunched up and pressing against the fence, they stretched out their long necks, stared, and opened their straight, broad bills. They opened and closed them feverishly, with unbelievable speed, as if they were trying to outtalk one another. But these bills were hopelessly mute, making not the slightest sound.

The ostriches were like messengers who had learned an important message by heart but whose vocal cords had been cut by the enemy on the way; so that when they reached their destination, they could do no more than move their voiceless mouths.

Tamina gazed bewitched, as the ostriches kept on talking more and more insistently. Then, as she and

Hugo were moving away, they ran after them along the fence, clacking their bills to warn them about something, but what that could be Tamina did not know.

11

"That was a scene from a horror story," said Tamina, cutting her pâté. "It was as if they were trying to tell me something very important. But what? What were they trying to tell me?"

Hugo pointed out that they were young ostriches and always behaved this way. The last time he had been in that zoo, all six of them had run up to the fence, just as they did today, and opened their mute bills.

Tamina was still disturbed: "You know, I left something behind in Bohemia. A parcel with some papers in it. If I were to have it mailed to me, chances are the police would confiscate it. Bibi is going to Prague this summer. She's promised to bring it back to me. And now I'm afraid. I wonder whether the ostriches were warning me something's happened to that parcel."

Hugo knew Tamina's husband had had to emigrate for political reasons.

"Are they political documents?" he asked.

Tamina had long been convinced that to make people here understand anything about her life, it had to be simplified. It would have been extremely difficult to explain why that private correspondence and those personal diaries chanced being seized by the police and why she cared about them so much. She said: "Yes, they're political documents."

Next she was afraid Hugo would ask for details about these documents, but her fears were groundless. Had anyone here ever asked her any questions? People would sometimes tell her what they thought about her country, but they were not at all interested in her experiences.

Hugo asked: "Does Bibi know they're political documents?"

"No," said Tamina.

"That's best," said Hugo. "Don't tell her it's something political. She'll get scared at the last moment and won't go and get your parcel. You can't imagine the things people are afraid of, Tamina. Bibi should be made to think it's something completely insignificant and ordinary. Your love letters, for example. That's it—tell her there are love letters in your parcel!"

Hugo chuckled over his idea: "Love letters! Yes! That's her kind of thing! Bibi'll understand that!"

Tamina reflects on Hugo's thinking that love letters are insignificant and ordinary. It never occurs to anyone that she might have loved someone and that it was important.

Hugo added: "If she ends up not going on that trip, you can count on me. I'll go over there and get your parcel."

"Thank you," Tamina said warmly.

"I'll go and get it even if it gets me arrested."

"Come on!" Tamina protested. "Nothing would happen to you!" And she tried to explain that foreign tourists ran no risks in her country. Life there was dangerous only for the Czechs, and they no longer noticed it. Suddenly she was talking excitedly and at length, and as she knew the country inside out, I can confirm that what she said was entirely right.

An hour later, she was pressing Hugo's telephone receiver to her ear. This conversation with her mother-in-law ended no better than the first. "You never gave me the key! You've always hidden everything from me! Why are you forcing me to remember how you've always treated me?"

12

If Tamina cares so much about her memories, why doesn't she simply go back to Bohemia? The emigrants who left the country illegally after 1968 have since been amnestied and invited to return. What is Tamina afraid of? She is too insignificant in her country to be in danger!

Yes, she could go back without fear. And yet she cannot.

In that country everyone had betrayed her husband.

By going back to live among them, she thought she too would be betraying him.

When they were transferring him to more and more inferior posts and had finally driven him from his occupation, no one defended him. Not even his friends. Of course, Tamina knew that deep down, people were with her husband. It was fear alone that kept them silent. But just because they were really with him, they were all the more ashamed of their fear, and when they met him in the street they pretended not to see him. The couple started avoiding people in order not to elicit that shame. Soon they felt like lepers. When they left Bohemia, her husband's former colleagues signed a public statement slandering and condemning him. Surely they did that only so as not to lose their jobs as Tamina's husband had lost his job not long before. But they did it. They thus dug a chasm between themselves and the two exiles, which Tamina would never agree to leap over by going back there.

On the first morning after their flight, when they awoke in a small hotel in an Alpine village and realized that they were alone, cut off from the world where all of their lives had been spent, she experienced a feeling of liberation and relief. They were in the mountains, marvelously alone. Around them unbelievable silence reigned. Tamina welcomed that silence as an unexpected gift, leading her to reflect that her husband had left his homeland to escape persecution and she to find silence; silence for her husband and for herself; silence for love.

When her husband died, she was gripped by a sudden longing for her native country, where the eleven years of their life together had everywhere left their imprint. In a surge of feeling, she sent death announcements to about ten friends. She did not receive a single response.

A month later, with what was left of her savings, she went to the seashore. She put on her bathing suit and swallowed a tubeful of tranquilizers. Then she swam far toward the open sea. She thought the tablets would make her very tired and she would drown. But the cold water and her athletic stroke (she had always been an excellent swimmer) prevented her from falling asleep, and the tablets most likely were weaker than she had supposed.

She came back to shore, went to her room, and slept for twenty hours. When she awoke, she was calm and at peace. She resolved to live in silence and for silence.

13

The silver-blue light of Bibi's television set shone on the people in the room: Tamina, Joujou, Bibi, and her husband, Dédé, a traveling salesman who had returned the day before from a four-day trip. A faint odor of urine hung in the air, and on the screen a big,

round, bald old head was being addressed provoca-
tively by an invisible interviewer:

"There are some shocking erotic confessions in your
memoirs."

It was a weekly program where a popular journalist
conversed with authors of books published the week
before.

The big bald head smiled smugly: "Oh no! There's
nothing shocking! It's only arithmetic, very exact
arithmetic! Let's figure it out together. My sex life
started at fifteen." The round old head turned to look
proudly at his fellow writers: "Yes, at fifteen. I am now
sixty-five. So I have had a sex life of fifty years. I
assume—and it's a very modest estimate—that I made
love an average of twice a week. That makes a hundred times a year or five thousand in my life. Let's go
on with the calculation. If an orgasm lasts five seconds,
I have had twenty-five thousand seconds of orgasm.
That makes a total of six hours and fifty-six minutes
of orgasm. Not bad, eh?"

Everyone in the room nodded seriously except
Tamina, who was imagining the bald old man racked
by an unremitting orgasm: in contortions, he clutches
at his heart, within fifteen minutes his denture falls
out, and five minutes after that he falls down dead.
She burst out laughing.

Bibi called her to order: "What's so funny? Six
hours and fifty-six minutes of orgasm is a pretty good
total!"

Joujou said: "For years I didn't have any idea what

an orgasm was. But in the past few years I've been having orgasms very regularly."

While everyone started talking about Joujou's orgasms, a new face, expressing indignation, appeared on the screen.

"Why is he so angry?" asked Dédé.

On the screen the writer said:

"It's very important. Very important. I explain it in my book."

"What's so very important?" asked Bibi.

"That he spent his childhood in the village of Rourou," Tamina pointed out.

The character who spent his childhood in the village of Rourou had a long nose so weighing him down that his head bent lower and lower, at times appearing about to fall off the screen into the room. The face weighed down by its long nose was extremely agitated as he said:

"I explain that in my book. All of my writing is bound up with the little village of Rourou, and anyone who fails to understand that will be unable to understand anything about my work. After all, that's where I wrote my first poems. Yes. In my opinion, it's very important."

"There are men," said Joujou, "I've never had an orgasm with."

"Don't forget," said the writer, his face more and more agitated, "it was in Rourou that I first rode a bike. Yes, I tell about it in detail in my book. And you all know what the bicycle signifies in my work. It's a symbol. For me, the bicycle is the first step taken by humanity out of the patriarchal world and into the world of civilization. The first flirtation with civilization. The flirtation of a virgin before her first kiss. Still virginity and already sin."

"That's true," said Joujou. "Tanaka, a girl I worked with, had her first orgasm riding a bicycle when she was still a virgin."

Everyone started discussing Tanaka's orgasm, and Tamina asked Bibi: "May I make a telephone call?"

14

The urine smell was stronger in the next room. It was Bibi's daughter's room.

"I know the two of you aren't on speaking terms," whispered Tamina. "But unless you do it I'll never get my parcel back. The only way is for you to go there and take it from her. If she doesn't find the key, make her force open the drawer. They're things of mine. Letters and such. I have a right to them."

"Tamina, don't make me talk to her!"

"Papa, just take it upon yourself and do it for me. She's afraid of you and won't dare refuse you."

"Listen, if your friends come to Prague, I'll give them a fur coat for you. That's more important than some old letters."

"But I don't want a fur coat. I want my parcel!"

"Speak louder! I can't hear you!" said her father, but his daughter was purposely speaking in an undertone because she did not want Bibi to hear the Czech words, which would reveal that the call was international and each of its seconds expensive.

"I said I want my parcel, not a fur!" Tamina repeated.

"You're always interested in foolishness!"

"Papa, this telephone call is horribly expensive. Really, would you please go see her?"

The conversation was difficult. Her father kept making her repeat things and obstinately refusing to go see her mother-in-law. He ended by saying:

"Phone your brother and ask him to go see her! He's got nothing better to do! And then he can bring me your parcel!"

"But he doesn't even know her!"

"That's the point," said her father, and laughed. "If he did, he'd never go near her."

Tamina thought swiftly. It wasn't such a bad idea to send her energetic and brusque brother to her mother-in-law. But Tamina did not want to telephone him. They had not exchanged a single letter since she had gone abroad. Her brother had a well-paying job he was able to keep by cutting all ties with her émigré sister.

"Papa, I can't phone him. Maybe you could explain it to him yourself. Please, Papa!"

15

Papa was short and puny, and long ago, when he walked down the street holding Tamina by the hand, he would be puffed up as if he were showing the whole world a monument to the heroic night when he created her. He had never liked his son-in-law and waged an endless war against him. When he offered to send Tamina a fur coat (most likely gotten from a deceased relative), he had in mind that old rivalry, not his daughter's health. He wanted her to choose her father (the fur coat) over her husband (the parcel of letters).

Tamina was horrified by the idea that the fate of her letters was in the hostile hands of her father and her mother-in-law. For some time now she had been imagining more and more often that her notebooks were being read by outsiders, and she thought that the gaze of those outsiders was like rain obliterating inscriptions on walls. Or like light falling too soon on photographic paper immersed in the fixing bath and ruining the picture.

She realized that what gave her written memories their meaning and worth was that they were intended for *her alone*. As soon as they lost that quality, the intimate tie binding her to them would be cut, and she would be able to read them no longer with her own eyes but only with the eyes of readers perusing a document about some other person. Then even she who had written them would become for her some other person, an outsider. The striking similarity that would nonetheless remain between her and the author of the notes would have the effect of parody, of mockery. No, she would never be able to read her notes if they had been read by outsiders.

That is why she was bursting with impatience and wanted to recover those notebooks and letters as swiftly as possible, while the picture of the past fixed in them was not yet ruined.

16

Bibi appeared suddenly in the café and sat down at the bar: "Hello, Tamina! Give me a whisky!"

Bibi usually had coffee or, in exceptional circumstances, some port. By ordering whisky, she was showing she was in an unusual frame of mind.

"How's your book going?" asked Tamina, pouring the drink into a glass.

"I need to be in a better mood," said Bibi. She emptied her glass in one gulp and ordered another.

Some more customers came into the café. Tamina asked them what they wanted, returned behind the bar to get her friend another whisky, and then went off to serve the other customers. When she came back, Bibi told her:

"I can't stand Dédé anymore. When he comes home from one of his selling trips, he stays in bed two whole days. Two days in pajamas! Would you put up with that? And the worst is when he wants to fuck. He can't understand that I don't enjoy fucking, absolutely not a bit. I should leave him. He spends all his time planning his stupid vacation. In bed in his pajamas and holding an atlas. First he wanted to go to Prague. Now he never mentions it. He found a book about Ireland, and he wants to go there no matter what."

"So you're going to Ireland on vacation?" asked Tamina with a lump in her throat.

"Are *we? We're* not going anywhere. Me, I'm going to stay right here and I'm going to write. He's not going to make me go anywhere. I don't need Dédé. He's not a bit interested in me. I'm writing, and would you believe he's still not even asked me what I'm writing about? I realize now that we have nothing more to say to each other."

Tamina wanted to ask: "So you're not going to Prague anymore?" But she had that lump in her throat and could not speak.

Just then Joujou, the little Japanese woman, came into the café and hopped onto the barstool next to Bibi's. She said: "Would you be able to make love in public?"

"What do you mean?" asked Bibi.

"Here, for instance, on the floor of the café, in front

of everybody. Or at the movies during the intermission."

"Be quiet!" Bibi shrieked down to the foot of her barstool, where her daughter was making a racket. Then she said: "Why not? It's natural. Why should I be ashamed of something natural?"

Again Tamina prepared herself to ask Bibi if she was going to Prague. But she realized the question was superfluous. It was all too obvious. Bibi was not going to Prague.

The owner's wife came out of the kitchen and, smiling at Bibi, said: "How are you?"

"We need a revolution," said Bibi. "Something's got to happen! Something's finally got to happen!"

That night Tamina dreamed about the ostriches. They were standing against the fence, all talking to her at once. She was terrified. Unable to move, she watched their mute bills as if she were hypnotized. She kept her lips convulsively shut. Because she had a golden ring in her mouth, and she feared for that ring.

17

Why do I imagine her with a golden ring in her mouth?

I can't help it, that's how I imagine her. And suddenly a phrase comes back to me: "a faint, clear, metallic tone—like a golden ring falling into a silver basin."

When he was very young, Thomas Mann wrote a naïvely entrancing story about death: in that story death is beautiful, as it is beautiful to all those who dream of it when they are very young, when death is still unreal and enchanting, like the bluish voice of distances.

A mortally ill young man gets on a train and, descending at an unknown station, enters a town whose name he does not know and rents rooms in an ordinary house from an old woman with a mossy growth on her brow. No, I'm not going to relate what happens then in that rented lodging, I only wish to recall a single trivial occurrence: passing through the front room, the ill young man "believed he heard, in between the thud of his footsteps, a sound coming from next door, a faint, clear, metallic tone—but perhaps it was only an illusion. Like a golden ring falling into a silver basin, he thought. . . ."

In the story, that small acoustical detail remains inconsequential and unexplained. From the action's standpoint alone, it could have been omitted without loss. The sound simply happens; all by itself; just like that.

I think Thomas Mann sounded that "faint, clear, metallic tone" to create silence. He needed that silence to make beauty audible (because the death he was speaking of was *death-beauty*), and for beauty to be perceptible, it needs a minimal degree of silence (of which the precise measure is the sound made by a golden ring falling into a silver basin).

(Yes, I realize you don't know what I'm talking about, because beauty vanished long ago. It vanished under the surface of the noise—the noise of words, the noise of cars, the noise of music—we live in constantly. It has been drowned like Atlantis. All that remains of it is the word, whose meaning becomes less intelligible with every passing year.)

The first time Tamina heard that silence (as precious as the fragment of a marble statue from sunken Atlantis) was when she woke up in a mountain hotel surrounded by forests on the morning after she had fled her country. She heard it a second time when she was swimming in the sea with a stomach full of tablets that brought her not death but unexpected peace. She wanted to shelter that silence with her body and within her body. That is why I see her in her dream standing against the wire fence; in her convulsively shut mouth she has a golden ring.

Facing her are six long necks topped by tiny heads with straight bills opening and closing soundlessly. She does not understand them. She does not know whether the ostriches are threatening her, warning her, exhorting her, or imploring her. And because she does not know, she feels immense anguish. She fears for the golden ring (that tuning fork of silence) and keeps it convulsively in her mouth.

Tamina will never know what those great birds

came to tell her. But I know. They did not come to warn her, scold her, or threaten her. They are not at all interested in her. Each one of them came to tell her about itself. Each one to tell her how it had eaten, how it had slept, how it had run up to the fence and seen her behind it. That it had spent its important childhood in the important village of Rourou. That its important orgasm had lasted six hours. That it had seen a woman strolling behind the fence and she was wearing a shawl. That it had gone swimming, that it had fallen ill and then recovered. That when it was young it rode a bike and that today it had gobbled up a sack of grass. They are standing in front of Tamina and talking to her all at once, vehemently, insistently, aggressively, because there is nothing more important than what they want to tell her.

18

A few days later, Banaka turned up in the café. Staggering drunk, he fell off a barstool twice before managing to stay on it, order a calvados, and put his head down on the counter. Tamina noticed he was crying.

"What's the matter, Mr. Banaka?" she asked him.

Banaka looked up at her tearfully and pointed to his

chest: "I'm nothing, do you understand? I'm nothing! I don't exist!"

Then he went to the toilet and from the toilet straight out into the street, without paying.

When Tamina told Hugo what had happened, he showed her, by way of explanation, a newspaper page with book reviews, among them a sarcastic four-line note on Banaka's entire output.

The episode of Banaka's pointing to his chest and crying because he did not exist reminds me of a line from Goethe's *West-East Divan*: "Is one alive when other men are living?" Hidden within Goethe's question is the mystery of the writer's condition: By writing books, a man turns into a universe (don't we speak of the universe of Balzac, the universe of Chekhov, the universe of Kafka?), and it is precisely the nature of a universe to be unique. The existence of another universe threatens it in its very essence.

Provided their shops are not on the same street, two cobblers can live in perfect harmony. But if they start writing books on the cobbler's lot, they are soon going to get in each other's way and ask: "Is a cobbler alive when other cobblers are living?"

Tamina has the impression that a single outsider's glance can destroy the entire worth of her intimate notebooks, and Goethe is convinced that a single glance of a single human being which fails to fall on lines written by Goethe calls into question Goethe's very existence. The difference between Tamina and Goethe is the difference between human being and writer.

Someone who writes books is either everything (a unique universe in himself and to all others) or nothing. And because it will never be given to anyone to be *everything,* all of us who write books are *nothing.* We are unrecognized, jealous, embittered, and we wish the others dead. In that we are all equals: Banaka, Bibi, I, and Goethe.

The irresistible proliferation of graphomania among politicians, taxi drivers, childbearers, lovers, murderers, thieves, prostitutes, officials, doctors, and patients shows me that everyone without exception bears a potential writer within him, so that the entire human species has good reason to go down into the streets and shout: "We are all writers!"

For everyone is pained by the thought of disappearing, unheard and unseen, into an indifferent universe, and because of that everyone wants, while there is still time, to turn himself into a universe of words.

One morning (and it will be soon), when everyone wakes up as a writer, the age of universal deafness and incomprehension will have arrived.

19

Now Hugo was her only hope. He invited her to dinner, and this time she accepted immediately.

Facing her across the restaurant table, he has only one thought: Tamina continues to elude him. He lacks confidence with her and does not dare to make a frontal attack. And the more he suffers from being unable to hit so modest and determinate a target, the greater his wish to conquer the world, that immensity of the indeterminate. He takes a magazine out of his pocket, opens it, and hands it to Tamina. On the opened spread is the beginning of a long article signed with his name.

He launches into a long speech. He talks about the review he has just given her: yes, at the moment its circulation is mainly local, but it's a solid theoretical review, the people who put it out are courageous and will go far. Hugo talks and talks, and his words attempt to be a metaphor for his erotic aggressiveness, a parade of his strength. There is in these words the beautiful maneuverability of the abstract rushing in to replace the intractability of the concrete.

Tamina is looking at Hugo and rectifying his face. This spiritual exercise has become a habit. She no longer knows how else to look at a man. It takes an effort, mobilizing all the power of her imagination, but Hugo's brown eyes then really do change color, suddenly turning blue. Tamina fixes her eyes on him, because to prevent the blue from vanishing, she must keep it in Hugo's eyes with all the strength of her stare.

That stare disturbs Hugo, and so he talks and talks still more, his eyes a beautiful blue and his brow gently widening on both sides until the only hair remaining in front is a narrow triangle pointing down.

"I've always directed my criticisms exclusively against our Western world. But the injustice that prevails here has led us to a mistaken indulgence toward other countries. Thanks to you, you know, thanks to you, Tamina, I've realized that the problem of power is the same everywhere, in your country and in ours, in the East as well as in the West. We should not try to replace one type of power with another, we should repudiate the very *principle* of power and repudiate it everywhere."

As Hugo leans over the table toward Tamina, the sour smell of his breath so disrupts her spiritual exercises that Hugo's thick hair once again grows low over his brow. Hugo starts to repeat that he realizes all this thanks to her.

"How can that be?" Tamina breaks in. "We've never talked about it!"

There is now only one blue eye left on Hugo's face, and then it too slowly turns brown.

"I didn't need you to talk to me about it, Tamina. It was enough for me to think a lot about you."

The waiter leans over to serve their appetizers.

"I'll read this at home," says Tamina, putting the review in her bag. Then she says: "Bibi isn't going to Prague."

"Just as I thought," says Hugo, and then he adds: "Don't worry, Tamina. I've promised. I'll go there for you."

20

"I've got good news for you. I talked to your brother. He's going to see your mother-in-law on Saturday."

"Really? And did you explain everything to him? Did you tell him that if she doesn't find the key he should force open the drawer?"

When Tamina hung up, she had the impression she was drunk.

"Good news?" asked Hugo.

"Yes."

With her father's cheerful, energetic voice still in her ear, she reflected that she had been unjust to him.

Hugo got up and went over to his liquor cabinet. He took out two glasses and poured whisky into them.

"Tamina," he said, "you can phone from here whenever you want and as often as you want. I'm going to say it again. I feel good with you, even though I know you'll never sleep with me."

He forced himself to utter "I know you'll never sleep with me" just to prove to himself he could say certain words to this inaccessible woman's face (though in a cautiously negative form), and he felt almost daring.

Tamina got up and went over to Hugo for her glass. She was thinking about her brother: they no longer spoke to each other, yet they really loved and were ready to help each other.

"May all your wishes come true!" said Hugo, and emptied his glass.

Tamina too downed her whisky in one gulp, and put her glass on the coffee table. She was about to sit down again, when Hugo suddenly embraced her.

She did not defend herself, merely averted her head. Her mouth was twisted and her brow furrowed.

He had taken her in his arms without knowing how it happened. He was frightened initially by his own gesture, and if Tamina had pushed him away, he would have retreated timidly and virtually apologized. But Tamina did not push him away, and her grimace and averted head aroused him enormously. None of the few women he had known up to now had ever responded so eloquently to his caresses. If they decided to make love with him, they would undress very placidly, with a kind of indifference, and then wait to see what he was going to do with their bodies. Tamina's grimacing gave their embrace a depth he had never dreamed of. He gripped her with frenzy and tried to tear off her clothes.

But why did Tamina not defend herself?

For three years now she had fearfully been imagining such a moment. For three years now she had been living under the hypnotic stare of such a moment. And now it had arrived, just as she had imagined it. That is why she did not defend herself. She accepted it as one accepts the inescapable.

All she could do was avert her head. But that was no use. Her husband's image was before her, and as she swiveled her face about the room his image followed accordingly. It was a large portrait of a grotesquely large husband, larger than life, yes, just what she had imagined for three years.

And then she was entirely naked, and Hugo, aroused by what he took to be her arousal, was amazed to discover that Tamina was dry.

21

She had once undergone minor surgery without anesthesia, forcing herself during the operation to review English irregular verbs. Now she tried to do the same by concentrating entirely on her notebooks. She thought about how they would soon be safe with her father, and this nice Hugo would go and get them for her.

Nice Hugo had already been moving fiercely on her for some time when she became aware that he was oddly raised on his forearms and thrashing his hips around in all directions. She realized he was dissatisfied with her responses, finding her insufficiently aroused, and therefore trying to penetrate her from various angles and find somewhere in her depths the mysterious sensitivity that was hiding itself from him.

Not wanting to see his labored efforts, she moved her head away. She tried to control her thoughts and bring them back to her notebooks. She forced herself to review the sequence of vacations, as she had managed, if only incompletely, to reconstruct it: the first vacations on the shore of a small lake in Bohemia, then Yugoslavia, then the small lake in Bohemia again, and a spa, also in Bohemia; but the sequence of these vacations was uncertain. In 1964 they had gone to the Tatras and the next year to Bulgaria, but after that the trail vanished. In 1968 they had spent their entire vacation in Prague, the following year they had gone to a spa, and then they emigrated and had their last vacations in Italy.

Hugo withdrew from her and tried to turn her body over. She realized he wanted her on all fours. At that instant she recalled that Hugo was younger than she, and she was ashamed. But she made an effort to stifle all her feelings and obey him with total indifference. Then she felt the hard blows of his body on her rump. She realized he was trying to dazzle her with his strength and endurance, he was joined in a decisive battle, he was taking a test to prove he could conquer and be worthy of her.

She did not know that Hugo could not see her. The fleeting sight of Tamina's rump (of the open eye of that mature and beautiful rump, of the eye that stared at him pitilessly) had so aroused him that he closed his eyes, slowed his tempo, and breathed deeply. Now he too tried hard to think of something else (it was the only thing they had in common), so as to be able to go on making love to her.

And during all this, Tamina saw her husband's gigantic face in front of her on the white surface of Hugo's wardrobe. She swiftly closed her eyes and again reviewed the sequence of their vacations, as if they were irregular verbs: first the vacations at the lake; then Yugoslavia, the lake, and the spa—or rather the spa, Yugoslavia, the lake; then the Tatras and Bulgaria, and then the trail vanished; later on, Prague, the spa, and finally Italy.

Hugo's heavy breathing tore her away from her memories. She opened her eyes and saw her husband's face on the white wardrobe.

Suddenly Hugo too opened his eyes. He caught sight of the eye of Tamina's rump, and pleasure ran through him like lightning.

22

When Tamina's brother went to get the notebooks, he did not have to force open the drawer. It was not locked, and the eleven notebooks were all there. They were not wrapped but thrown in every which way. The letters were also jumbled; they were a shapeless pile of papers. Along with the notebooks, Tamina's brother stuffed them into a briefcase that he brought to his father.

Over the telephone, Tamina asked her father to wrap everything carefully, to seal the parcel with gummed tape, and, above all, stressed that neither he nor her brother was to read any of it.

Nearly offended, he assured her it had never occurred to them to imitate Tamina's mother-in-law by reading something that was no concern of theirs. But I know (and Tamina knows it too) that there are sights whose temptation no one can resist: auto accidents, for instance, or other people's love letters.

So the intimate writings were finally with her father. But did Tamina still value them? Hadn't she said a hundred times over that the gaze of outsiders was like rain obliterating inscriptions?

No, she had been wrong. She wanted them more than ever, they were more than ever dear to her. Those notebooks had been ravaged and violated as she had been ravaged and violated, so that she and her memories had a kindred fate. She loved them all the more.

But she felt sullied.

A very long time ago, when she was seven years old, her uncle had come upon her when she was naked in her bedroom. She had been terribly ashamed, and her shame had turned into rebellion. She made a solemn, childish vow never to look at him again in her whole life. They could scold her, yell at her, make fun of her, but she never looked at her uncle, who came often to visit.

Now she was in a similar situation. Although she was grateful to them, she no longer wanted to see her father or her brother. More clearly than ever before, she realized she would never go back to them.

23

Hugo's unexpected sexual success brought him an equally unexpected disappointment. He could now make love to her whenever he wanted (she could hardly deny him what she had once granted), but he felt he had succeeded neither in captivating nor in dazzling her. How, oh how, could a naked body under his own body be so indifferent, so out of reach, so distant and foreign? Had he not wanted her to be part of his inner world, that imposing universe shaped by his blood and thoughts?

Sitting across from her in a restaurant, he says: "I want to write a book, Tamina, a book about love, you know, about you and me, about the two of us, our most intimate diary, the diary of our two bodies, you know, I want to sweep away all the taboos and tell everything, tell everything about me, about what I am and what I think, and it'll be a political book too, a political book about love and a book of love about politics . . ."

Tamina stares at Hugo, and suddenly he can no longer endure that stare and loses the thread of what he is saying. He wants to imprison her in the universe of his blood and thoughts, but she is utterly enclosed in her own world. Remaining unshared with her, the words he is saying become heavier and heavier in his mouth, and his delivery becomes slower and slower:

". . . a book of love about politics, you know, because the world has to be re-created on a human scale, our scale, the scale of our bodies, of your body, Tamina, of my body, you know, so that someday there will be a new way of kissing and a new way of loving . . ."

The words are heavier and heavier, like big mouthfuls of meat too tough to chew. Hugo falls silent. Tamina is beautiful, and he hates her. He thinks she is exploiting her fate. She is perched on her émigré and widow past as on a skyscraper of false pride from which she is looking down on everyone. Filled with envy, Hugo is pondering the tower of his own that he has been trying to put up facing her skyscraper and she has been refusing to see: a tower made out of one published article and a projected book about their love.

Then Tamina asks him: "When are you going to Prague?"

And Hugo realizes she has never loved him. She is with him only because she needs him to go to Prague. He is seized by an irresistible desire to take revenge on her:

"Tamina," he says, "I thought you would have figured it out by yourself. You've read my article, after all!"

"Yes," she says.

He does not believe her. And if she read it, she took no interest in it. She had never referred to it. And Hugo is aware that the only deep feeling he is capable of is fidelity to the unrecognized, abandoned tower (the tower of the published article and the projected book about his love for Tamina), that he is capable of going to war for the tower and forcing Tamina to open her eyes to it and marvel at its height.

"After all, you know that in my article I talk about the problem of power. I analyze how power works. And I criticize what's going on in your country. I talk about it without pulling any punches."

"Look! Do you really think they know your article in Prague?"

Hugo is wounded by her irony: "You've been away from your country a long time, you've forgotten what your police can do. That article has caused a great stir. I've gotten lots of letters. Your police know who I am. I know they do."

Tamina is silent and more and more beautiful. My God, he would agree to go to and from Prague a hundred times if only she would open her eyes a bit to the universe he wanted to take her to, the universe of his blood and thoughts! And he abruptly alters his tone:

"Tamina," he says sadly, "I know you're annoyed with me because I can't go to Prague. At first I thought I could hold off publishing the article, but then I realized I didn't have the right to keep silent for such a long time. Do you understand?"

"No," says Tamina.

Hugo knows he is saying ridiculous things that are taking him where he does not at all want to let himself be dragged, but he can no longer retreat, and this makes him despair. Red blotches mottle his face and his voice quavers: "You don't understand? I don't want things to end up with us here the way they did with you there! If we all keep silent, we'll end up slaves."

Just then a terrible disgust took hold of Tamina, and she got up from her chair and ran to the toilet; stomach rising to her throat, she knelt in front of the toilet bowl to vomit, her body doubled up as if she were sobbing, and before her eyes was the image of that boy's balls, cock, and pubic hair, and she smelled his sour breath, felt the contact of his thighs with her buttocks, and it crossed her mind that she could no longer visualize her husband's genitals and pubic thatch, that the memory of revulsion is therefore stronger than the memory of tenderness (oh yes, my God, the memory of revulsion is stronger than the memory of tenderness!), and that nothing is going to remain in her poor head but this boy with bad breath, and she vomited, doubled up and vomited.

She left the toilet, and her mouth (still filled with that acid smell) was firmly shut.

He was embarrassed. He wanted to escort her home, but she did not say a word, keeping her mouth firmly shut (as in the dream where she had a golden ring in her mouth).

When he spoke, her only response was to quicken her pace. Soon he had nothing more to say, and he walked a few more meters alongside her in silence, then stopped and stood motionless. She went on walking straight ahead, without even a backward glance.

She continued to serve coffee and never again telephoned Prague.

PART FIVE

Litost

Who Is Kristyna?

Kristyna is a woman of about thirty, who has a child, a butcher husband she gets along with quite well, and a very intermittent affair with a local mechanic, who now and then makes love to her after hours amid the discomforts of the auto-repair shop. The small town hardly lends itself to extramarital love, or rather it requires a wealth of ingenuity and audacity, qualities Kristyna is not abundantly endowed with.

Meeting the student turned her head powerfully. He had come to the town to spend his summer vacation with his mother, had twice stared at the butcher's wife as she stood behind the shop counter, and the third time, when he spoke to her at the local swimming place, he was so charmingly timid that the young woman, accustomed to the butcher and the mechanic, could not resist. Ever since her marriage (a good ten years now), she had not dared touch another man except in the safety of the locked repair shop, among dismantled cars and old tires, and suddenly she had found the audacity for amorous meetings out in the open, exposed to prying eyes. Though the spots they chose for their walks were the most isolated and the likelihood of anyone intruding on them negligible,

Kristyna's heart would pound and she would be filled with stimulating fear. But the more bravely she faced the danger, the more reserved she was with the student. They did not go very far. He got only some brief hugs and tender kisses, she would often slip out of his arms entirely, and when he was fondling her body she kept her legs tightly together.

It was not that she did not want the student. It was that she had fallen in love with his tender timidity and wanted to preserve it for herself. Hearing a man expound ideas about life and mention the names of poets and philosophers was something that never before had happened to Kristyna. The student, poor boy, could talk about nothing else; the range of his seducer's eloquence was very limited, and he could not adapt it to women of varying social levels. Anyway, he felt no need to blame himself in this regard, because the quotations from the philosophers produced much more of an effect on that simple butcher's wife than on any fellow student. One thing nonetheless escaped him: an effective quotation from a philosopher might charm the butcher's wife's soul, but it stood as an obstacle between the butcher's wife's body and his own. For Kristyna vaguely imagined that by giving her body to the student she would lower their affair to the butcher's or the mechanic's level and she would never again hear a word about Schopenhauer.

With the student she suffered from an embarrassment she had never known before. With the butcher and the mechanic she always arrived quickly and cheerfully at an understanding about things. For instance, both men agreed to be very careful, because the doctor had told her after her child was born that she could risk her health if not her life by having another. This story happened a very long time ago, when abortion was strictly forbidden and women themselves had no means of limiting their fertility. The butcher and the mechanic well understood Kristyna's apprehensions, and before she allowed them to enter her, she would make sure with good-humored naturalness that they had taken the required precautions. But the thought that she would have to behave like that with her angel, who had come down to her from the cloud where he conversed with Schopenhauer, made her feel she would be unable to find the words she needed. I therefore conclude that her erotic reserve had two motives: to keep the student as long as possible in the enchanted territory of tender timidity and to avoid as long as possible the disgust sure to be inspired in him, as she saw it, by the crude instructions and precautions without which physical love could not take place.

But the student, despite all his refinement, was persistent. Though Kristyna kept her thighs tightly closed, he bravely got hold of her rump, meaning that someone who likes to quote Schopenhauer is not for all that ready to give up a body that pleases him.

Anyway, vacation ended and the two lovers realized it would be hard for them to go a whole year without seeing each other. Kristyna had only to find an excuse to go see him. They both understood what that visit would mean. In Prague, the student lived in a small attic room, and Kristyna would have to end up spending the night there.

What Is Litost?

Litost is an untranslatable Czech word. Its first syllable, which is long and stressed, sounds like the wail of an abandoned dog. As for the meaning of this word, I have looked in vain in other languages for an equivalent, though I find it difficult to imagine how anyone can understand the human soul without it.

Let me give an example: The student went swimming in the river one day with his girlfriend, a fellow student. She was athletic, but he was a very poor swimmer. He could not time his breathing properly and swam slowly, his head held tensely high above the surface. She was madly in love with him and tactfully swam as slowly as he did. But when their swim was coming to an end, she wanted to give her athletic instincts a few moments' free rein and headed for the opposite bank at a rapid crawl. The student made an effort to swim faster too and swallowed water. Feeling humbled, his physical inferiority laid bare, he felt *litost*. He recalled his sickly childhood, lacking in physical exercise and friends and spent under the constant gaze of his mother's overfond eye, and fell into despair about himself and his life. They walked back to the city together in silence on a country lane. Wounded and humiliated, he felt an irresistible desire to hit her. "What's the matter with you?" she asked him, and he started to reproach her: she knew about the current near the other bank, and that he had forbidden her to swim there because of the risk of drowning—and then he slapped her face. The girl began to cry, and when he saw the tears on her cheeks, he took pity on her and put his arms around her, and his *litost* melted away.

Or take an instance from the student's childhood: His parents made him take violin lessons. He was not very gifted and his teacher would interrupt him to criticize his mistakes in a cold, unbearable voice. He felt humiliated, and he wanted to cry. But instead of trying to play in tune and not make mistakes, he would deliberately play wrong notes, the teacher's voice would become still more unbearable and harsh, and he himself would sink deeper and deeper into his *litost*.

What then is *litost*?

Litost is a state of torment created by the sudden sight of one's own misery.

One of the customary remedies for misery is love. Because someone loved absolutely cannot be miserable. All his faults are redeemed by love's magical gaze, under which even inept swimming, with the head held high above the surface, can become charming.

Love's absolute is actually a desire for absolute

identity: the woman we love ought to swim as slowly as we do, she ought to have no past of her own to look back on happily. But when the illusion of absolute identity vanishes (the girl looks back happily on her past or swims faster), love becomes a permanent source of the great torment we call *litost*.

Anyone with wide experience of the common imperfection of mankind is relatively sheltered from the shocks of *litost*. For him, the sight of his own misery is ordinary and uninteresting. *Litost*, therefore, is characteristic of the age of inexperience. It is one of the ornaments of youth.

Litost works like a two-stroke engine. Torment is followed by the desire for revenge. The goal of revenge is to make one's partner look as miserable as oneself. The man cannot swim, but the slapped woman cries. It makes them feel equal and keeps their love going.

Since revenge can never reveal its true motive (the student cannot confess to the girl that he slapped her because she swam faster than he did), it must put forward false reasons. *Litost*, therefore, is always accompanied by a pathetic hypocrisy: the young man proclaims he is terrified his girlfriend will drown, and the child incessantly playing off key feigns an irremediable lack of talent.

Initially this chapter was entitled "Who Is the Student?" But to deal with *litost* was to describe the student, who is *litost* incarnate. No wonder the fellow student he loves finally left him. It's not very pleasant to be slapped for knowing how to swim.

The butcher's wife, whom he had met in his hometown, had come to him like a huge adhesive bandage, prepared to cover all his wounds. She adored him, she worshiped him, and when he talked about Schopenhauer, she did not try to display her own independent personality by raising objections (as did the girlfriend of grievous memory) but looked at him with eyes in which, moved by Kristyna's emotion, he thought he was seeing tears. And too, let us not forget to add that he had not made love to a woman since breaking up with his girlfriend.

Who Is Voltaire?

Voltaire is a lecturer in the university faculty of arts and letters, he is witty and aggressive, and he eyes his adversaries with a malicious look. Reason enough to call him Voltaire.

He liked the student, and that is no slight distinction, because Voltaire was particular about the company he kept. After the seminar one day, he went up to him to ask whether he was free the following evening. The following evening, alas, was when Kristyna was coming. It took courage for the student to tell Voltaire he was busy. But Voltaire waved the objection away: "Well, just reschedule. You won't regret it." And then he told him that the country's best poets were getting together tomorrow at the Writers Club and that he,

Voltaire, wanted to introduce the student to them.

Yes, the great poet about whom Voltaire was writing a monograph and whose house he frequented would also be there. He was ill and walked with crutches. That is why he rarely went out, and an opportunity to meet him was all the more to be valued.

The student knew the books of all the poets who would be there next day, but of the great poet's verse he knew whole pages by heart. He had never wanted anything more ardently than to spend an evening in their company. Then he remembered he had not made love to a woman in months, and he said again that it would be impossible for him to come.

Voltaire did not understand what could be more important than meeting great men. A woman? Can't that be put off? Suddenly his glasses were flashing ironically. But the student was seeing before him the image of the butcher's wife who had shyly evaded him during a long vacation month, and though it took great effort, he shook his head. Just then, Kristyna was worth all his country's poetry.

The Compromise

She arrived in the morning. During the day, she ran the errand that would serve as her alibi. The student had arranged to meet her in the evening at a restaurant he had chosen himself. When he entered, he became nearly frightened: the room was full of drunks, and the small-town sylph of his vacation was sitting in the corner near the toilets, at a table meant not for customers but for dirty dishes. She had dressed with the awkward formality of a provincial lady visiting the capital after a long absence and wanting to sample all its delights. She was wearing a hat, garish beads around her neck, and black high-heeled pumps.

The student felt his cheeks burning—not with excitement but with disappointment. The impression Kristyna created against the backdrop of a small town, with its butchers, mechanics, and pensioners, was entirely different in Prague, the city of pretty students and hairdressers. With her ridiculous beads and her discreet gold tooth (in an upper corner of her mouth), she seemed to personify the negation of that youthful feminine beauty in jeans who had been cruelly rejecting him for months. He made his way uncertainly to her, bringing his *litost* along with him.

The student was disappointed, and Kristyna no less so. The restaurant he had invited her to had a nice name—King Wenceslaus—and Kristyna, who did not know Prague well, had imagined a deluxe establishment, where the student would dine with her before she was shown the fireworks display of Prague's pleasures. When she noticed that the King Wenceslaus was just the kind of place where the mechanic drank his beer and that she was waiting for the student in the corner near the toilets, she did not experience the feeling I have referred to as *litost* but rather felt quite ordinary anger. By which I mean that she felt neither miserable nor humiliated but thought her student did not know how to behave. She did not, moreover, hesitate to tell him so. She looked furious and talked to him as she did to the butcher.

They stood face-to-face, she volubly and loudly reproaching him and he feebly defending himself. His distaste for her intensified. He wanted to take her to his room quickly, hide her from everyone's sight, and wait for the privacy of their refuge to revive the vanished charm. But she refused. She had not been to the capital for a long time, and she wanted to go out, see things, have a good time. Her black pumps and big garish beads were noisily demanding their rights.

"But this is a great little place. All the best people come here," the student pointed out, implying that the butcher's wife understood nothing about what was interesting in the capital and what was not. "Unfortunately, there's no room now, so I'll have to take you somewhere else." But as if deliberately, all the other places were just as crowded, it was a distance from one to the other, and Kristyna seemed unbearably comic to him with her little hat, beads, and shining gold tooth. The streets were filled with young women, and the student realized he would never forgive himself for giving up, for Kristyna's sake, the opportunity to spend an evening with his country's giants. But neither did he want to incur her hostility, because, as I have said, he had not been to bed with a woman in a long time. Only a masterfully constructed compromise could bring the dilemma to an end.

They finally found a table in an out-of-the-way café. The student ordered two aperitifs and looked sadly into Kristyna's eyes: Here in Prague, he announced, life is full of surprises. Just yesterday the country's most famous poet had phoned him.

When he said his name, Kristyna gave a start. She had learned his poems by heart in school. The great men whose names we learn in school have something unreal and immaterial about them, having been admitted, while still alive, to the majestic gallery of the dead. Kristyna could not really believe that the student knew him personally.

Of course he knew him, the student declared. He was even writing his master's thesis on him, a monograph that was likely to be published as a book someday. The reason he had never spoken of it before was that she would have thought he was bragging, but he had to talk about him now because the great poet had suddenly gotten in their way. A private meeting of the country's poets was taking place this evening at the Writers Club, and only a few critics and insiders had been invited. It's an extremely important meeting. There will be a debate, and sparks will fly. But obviously the student is not going. He is thrilled to be here with Kristyna!

In my sweet, singular country, the charm of poets still agitates women's hearts. Kristyna felt admiration for the student and a kind of maternal desire to advise him and defend his interests. With striking and unexpected altruism, she declared it would be a pity if the student were to miss an event attended by the great poet.

The student said he had tried everything to enable Kristyna to come with him, because he knew how happy she would be to see the great poet and his friends. Unfortunately, that was not possible. Even the great poet would not be bringing his wife. The discussion was intended exclusively for specialists. Initially he had actually even considered not going, but now he realized that Kristyna was probably right. Yes, it was a good idea. He could run over there for an hour or so. Kristyna would wait for him at his place, and then they would be together, just the two of them.

The temptations of the theaters and the variety shows were forgotten, and Kristyna went with the student and entered his attic room. At first she experienced the same disappointment she had felt upon entering the King Wenceslaus. It was not an apartment, merely a tiny room with no anteroom and no furniture but a daybed and a desk. But she was no longer sure of her judgments. She had entered into a world with a mysterious scale of values she did not understand. So she rapidly reconciled herself to this uncomfortable and filthy room and called on all her feminine talent to make herself feel at home in it. The student invited her to remove her hat, gave her a kiss, made her sit down on the daybed, and showed her his small library, where she would find something to distract her while he was gone.

Then Kristyna had an idea: "Do you have a copy of his book?" She was thinking of the great poet.

Yes, the student had his book.

She went on very shyly: "Would you like to give it to me as a present? And ask him to inscribe it to me?"

The student was exultant. The great poet's inscription would replace, for Kristyna, the theaters and variety shows. She had given him a bad conscience, and he was ready to do anything for her. As he expected, the intimacy of his attic room had revived Kristyna's charm. The young women coming and going on the streets had vanished, and the enchantment of her modesty silently invaded the room. The disappointment slowly wore off, and the student left for the Writers Club calmed and delighted by the thought of the splendid double program the evening promised him.

The Poets

He waited for Voltaire in front of the Writers Club and then went up with him to the second floor. They passed through the cloakroom and into the vestibule, where a jovial din reached them. When Voltaire opened the door to the function room, the student saw, sitting around a large table, all of his country's poetry.

I am watching them from the great distance of two thousand kilometers. It is the autumn of 1977, my country has been sweetly dozing for nine years now in the strong embrace of the Russian empire, Voltaire has been expelled from the university, and my books, having been gathered up from all the public libraries, are locked away in some state cellar. I waited for a few years, and then I got into a car and drove as far west as possible, to the Breton town of Rennes, where on the first day I found an apartment on the top floor of the tallest high-rise tower. When the sun woke me the next morning, I realized its large windows faced east, toward Prague.

And so I am watching them from the height of my lookout, but the distance is too great. Fortunately, there is a tear in my eye, which, like a telescope lens, brings me nearer to their faces. Now I can clearly make out the great poet, seated solidly among the others. He is surely more than seventy, but his face is still handsome, his eyes are still lively and wise. His crutches lean against the table next to him.

I see them all against the backdrop of the luminous Prague of fifteen years ago, when their books had not yet been locked away in a state cellar and when they chatted loudly and cheerfully around the large table laden with bottles. Because I am very fond of them all, I hesitate to give them ordinary names taken at random from the telephone book. If we must hide their faces behind the masks of assumed names, I want to give them as gifts, as adornments and in homage.

Since his students nicknamed the lecturer Voltaire,

what prevents me from calling the beloved great poet Goethe?

Facing him is Lermontov.

And the one over there, with the dark dreamy eyes, I want to call Petrarch.

And then there are Verlaine, Yesenin, and several others not worth mentioning, as well as someone who surely is there by mistake. From far away (from that distance of two thousand kilometers), it is obvious that Poetry has not kissed his brow and that he does not like verse. He is called Boccaccio.

Voltaire took two chairs from against the wall, pushed them over to the table laden with bottles, and introduced the student to the poets. The poets nodded to him courteously, all but Petrarch, who was too absorbed in an argument he was having with Boccaccio to notice him. He ended the debate with these words: "Something in women always gives them the upper hand. I could talk about that for weeks."

And to egg him on, Goethe said: "Weeks is a bit much. But give us at least ten minutes of it."

Petrarch's Story

"Last week, an unbelievable thing happened to me. My wife had just taken her evening bath, she was in her red bathrobe with her golden hair undone, and she was beautiful. At ten past nine the doorbell rang. When I opened the apartment door I saw a girl pressed against the wall. I recognized her immediately. Once a week I go to a girls' school. They've organized a poetry club and secretly worship me.

"I said: 'May I ask what you're doing here?'

"'I need to talk to you!'

"'What do you have to tell me?'

"'I have to tell you something terribly important!'

"'Listen,' I said, 'it's late, you can't come in now, get yourself downstairs and wait for me at the cellar door.'

"I went back into the bedroom and told my wife someone had the wrong door. And then, picking up two empty buckets, I casually announced I had to go down to the cellar for some coal. That was damned stupid. My gallbladder had been bothering me all day, and I'd been lying down. Such unexpected zeal made my wife suspicious."

"You have gallbladder trouble?" asked Goethe with interest.

"I've had it for years now," said Petrarch.

"Why don't you have an operation?"

"Not a chance!"

Goethe nodded sympathetically.

"Where was I?" Petrarch asked.

"Your gallbladder hurts and you're holding two coal buckets," prompted Verlaine.

"I found the girl at the cellar door," Petrarch went on, "and I told her to come down there with me. I picked up a shovel and, while I was filling the buckets, tried to find out what she wanted. She kept repeating she *had* to see me. I couldn't get anything more out of her.

"Then I heard footsteps on the staircase above. I grabbed the full bucket and ran up out of the cellar. My wife was on the way down. I passed her the bucket: 'Please take this up right away, I'm going to fill the other one.' My wife went back up with the bucket, and I went back down to the cellar and told the girl we couldn't stay there and she should wait for me on the street. I quickly filled the other bucket and ran upstairs. Then I gave my wife a kiss and told her to go to bed, that I wanted to take a bath before going to sleep. She went off to bed, and I went into the bathroom and turned on the faucets. The water gushed noisily into the tub. I took off my slippers and in my socks went to the apartment door, where I'd put the shoes I wore that day. I left them there to show that I hadn't gone far. I took another pair of shoes from the wardrobe, put them on, and slipped out of the apartment."

Here Boccaccio interrupted: "Petrarch, we all know you're a great poet. But now I see you're also very methodical, a wily strategist who not even for a moment allows himself to be blinded by passion! What you did with the slippers and the two pairs of shoes is a masterpiece!"

All the poets agreed with Boccaccio and showered Petrarch with praise, which visibly flattered him.

"She was waiting for me on the street. I tried to calm

her. I told her I had to go back inside and suggested she return next day in the afternoon, when my wife would be away at work. There's a streetcar stop right in front of the building. I insisted she go over to it. But when the streetcar arrived, she started laughing and tried to rush to the building door."

"You should have pushed her under the streetcar," said Boccaccio.

"My friends," Petrarch announced almost solemnly, "there are times when, against your will, it's necessary to be nasty to a woman. So I said to her: 'If you won't go home of your own accord, I'll lock the building door. Don't forget, this is my home and I can't turn it into a barnyard!' And keep in mind, my friends, that while I was arguing with her in front of the building, upstairs the bathtub faucets were running and the tub was about to overflow!

"I turned around and dashed through the building door. She started to run after me. And to top things off, some people were entering the building just then and she edged her way in with them. I went up those stairs like a sprinter! I could hear her footsteps behind me. We live on the fourth floor! It was quite a feat! But I was faster, and I practically slammed the door in her face. And I had just enough time to tear the doorbell wire off the wall so no one could hear her ringing, because I knew she was going to push the button and not let go of it. After that I ran on tiptoe into the bathroom."

"Had the tub overflowed?" asked Goethe solicitously.

"I shut the faucets at the last instant. Then I went to

take a quick look at the apartment door. I opened the peephole and saw she was still there, standing motionless, with her eyes riveted on the door. My friends, that frightened me. I wondered whether she was going to stay there all night."

Boccaccio Behaves Badly

"Petrarch, you're an incorrigible worshiper," Boccaccio interrupted. "I can imagine how these girls who started a poetry club invoke you as their Apollo. Nothing would make me want to meet any of them. A woman poet is doubly a woman. That's too much for a misogynist like me."

"Listen, Boccaccio," said Goethe, "why are you always bragging that you're a misogynist?"

"Because misogynists are the best of men."

All the poets reacted to these words with hooting. Boccaccio was forced to raise his voice:

"Please understand me. Misogynists don't despise women. Misogynists don't like femininity. Men have always been divided into two categories. Worshipers of women, otherwise known as poets, and misogynists, or, more accurately, gynophobes. Worshipers or poets revere traditional feminine values such as feelings, the home, motherhood, fertility, sacred flashes of hysteria, and the divine voice of nature within us, while in misogynists or gynophobes these values inspire a touch of terror. Worshipers revere women's femininity, while misogynists always prefer women to femininity. Don't forget: a woman can be happy only with a misogynist. No woman has ever been happy with any of you!"

These words provoked another round of hostile clamor.

"Worshipers or poets can bring drama, passion, tears, and worries to women, but never any pleasure. I knew one once. He worshiped his wife. Then he took up worshiping someone else. He didn't like humiliating the one by deceiving her and the other by making her a clandestine mistress. So he confessed everything to his wife, asked her to help him, his wife fell ill, he spent all his time crying, so his mistress finally couldn't stand it anymore and announced she was leaving him. He lay down on the tracks in front of a streetcar. Unfortunately, the motorman saw him in time, and that worshiper had to pay fifty crowns for impeding traffic."

"Boccaccio is a liar!" shouted Verlaine.

"The story Petrarch just told us," Boccaccio went on, "is the same old stuff. Does your wife with the golden hair deserve your taking that hysterical girl seriously?"

"What do you know about my wife?" Petrarch shouted. "My wife is my faithful friend! We have no secrets from each other!"

"Then why did you change shoes?" asked Lermontov.

But Petrarch was not flustered. "My friends, at that

crucial moment, when the girl was out there and I really didn't know what to do, I went to my wife in the bedroom and told her everything."

"Just like my worshiper!" said Boccaccio, and laughed. "To tell everything! It's the reflex of every worshiper! Surely you asked her to help you!"

Petrarch's voice was filled with tenderness: "Yes, I asked her to help me. She'd never refused me her help. Not this time either. She went to the door by herself. I stayed in the bedroom, because I was afraid."

"I'd be afraid too," said Goethe, filled with understanding.

"When she came back she was quite calm. After looking through the peephole she'd opened the door, and no one was there. One might have said I'd invented the whole thing. But suddenly we heard loud banging behind us, and then the sound of shattering glass; as you know, we live in one of those old buildings where the apartment windows and entrance doors give onto a gallery facing the courtyard. When no one answered the ringing doorbell, the girl got a metal bar somewhere and went along the gallery breaking all our windows, one after the other. We watched from inside the apartment, unable to do anything, nearly terrified. Then, coming from the dark other side of the gallery, we saw three white shadows. They were the old ladies from the apartment opposite. The shattering glass had awakened them. They were rushing around eagerly and impatiently in their nightgowns, happy with this unexpected scene. Just imagine! A beautiful teenager with a metal bar in her hand, surrounded by the malevolent shadows of three witches!

"Then the girl broke the last window and came through it into the bedroom.

"I tried to go talk to her, but my wife took me by the arms and begged me, 'Don't go, she'll kill you!' And the girl stood there in the middle of the room with the metal bar in her hand, beautiful and majestic like Joan of Arc with her lance! I tore myself away from my wife's arms and headed for the girl. The nearer I got to her, the more she lost her threatening look, it softened, radiated a celestial peacefulness. I grabbed the metal bar, threw it on the floor, and took the girl by the hand."

Insults

"I don't believe a word of your story," Lermontov announced.

"Of course, it didn't happen quite the way Petrarch told it," Boccaccio again interrupted, "but I believe it really happened. The girl is a hysteric, and any normal man in that kind of situation would long since have slapped her a couple of times. Worshipers or poets have always been perfect prey for hysterics, who know they'll never be slapped by them. Worshipers are disarmed when faced by a woman, because they're still in their mothers' shadows. In every woman they see a messenger from their mother and submit to her. Their mothers' skirts spread over them like the sky." That last image pleased him so much he repeated it several times: "Poets, what you're seeing overhead is not the sky but your mothers' enormous skirts! You're all living under your mothers' skirts!"

"What did you say?" Yesenin yelled out with incredible loudness, springing up from his chair. He was tottering. From the start, he had been drinking more than anyone else. "What did you say about my mother? What did you say?"

"I wasn't talking about your mother," said Boccaccio gently. He knew that Yesenin lived with a famous dancer thirty years older than he, and he felt genuinely sorry for him. But the spit was already on Yesenin's lips, and he leaned forward and let fly. But he was too drunk, and the gob landed on Goethe's collar. Boccaccio took out his handkerchief and wiped it off the great poet.

Spitting had made Yesenin feel deathly tired, and he fell back into his chair.

Petrarch went on: "Listen, all of you, my friends, to what she said to me, it was unforgettable. She said to me, and it was like a prayer, like a litany, 'I'm a simple girl, I'm quite an ordinary girl, I have nothing to offer you, but I came here because I was sent by love, I came'—and now she squeezed my hand very hard— 'so that you'll know what real love is, so that you'll experience it once in your life.' "

"And what did your wife say to that messenger of love?" asked Lermontov with heavy irony.

Goethe laughed: "What wouldn't Lermontov give to have a woman come and break his windows! He'd even pay her to do it!"

Lermontov cast a look of hatred at Goethe, and Petrarch went on: "My wife? You're mistaken, Lermontov, if you think this is just a funny Boccaccio story. The girl turned to my wife with a celestial look and said to her, and again it was like a prayer, like a litany, 'You shouldn't hold it against me, because you're good and I love you too, I love you both,' and with her free hand, she took my wife by the hand."

"If it were a scene from a funny Boccaccio story, I'd have nothing against it," Lermontov said. "But what you've just told us is something worse. It's bad poetry."

"You're just jealous!" Petrarch shouted at him. "It's never happened to you in your whole life, being alone in a room with two beautiful women who love you! Do you know how beautiful my wife is in a red bathrobe, with her golden hair undone?"

Lermontov laughed mockingly, and this time Goethe decided to punish him for his caustic comments: "You're a great poet, Lermontov, we all know that, but why do you have such complexes?"

For a few moments Lermontov was stunned, then he said to Goethe, barely controlling himself: "Johann, you shouldn't have said that to me. It's the worst thing you could have said to me. It's boorish."

Goethe, a lover of harmony, would not have gone on

teasing Lermontov, but Voltaire laughingly interrupted:
"It's as plain as the nose on your face, Lermontov, that
you're loaded with complexes," and he started to analyze all his poetry, which lacked both Goethe's happy
natural charm and Petrarch's impassioned inspiration.
He even started to dissect each of his metaphors to
show brilliantly that Lermontov's inferiority complex
was the direct source of his imagination and that it had
taken root in a childhood marked by poverty and the
oppressive influence of an authoritarian father.

Just then Goethe leaned over to Petrarch and said in a
whisper that resounded throughout the room, to be heard
by everyone, including Lermontov: "Come off it! What a
bunch of nonsense. Lermontov's trouble is hypercelibacy!"

The Student Takes Lermontov's Side

The student kept quiet, pouring himself wine (a discreet waiter noiselessly removed empty bottles and
brought full ones) and listening attentively to the conversation with its flying sparks. He couldn't swivel his
head fast enough to follow their giddy whirl.

He tried to decide which of the poets he liked most.
He venerated Goethe just as much as Kristyna venerated him, just as much, for that matter, as the entire
country. Petrarch cast a spell on him with his burning

eyes. But strangely enough it was the much-insulted Lermontov for whom he felt the greatest affinity, especially after Goethe's last remark, which led him to think that even a great poet (and Lermontov really was a great poet) could experience the same difficulties as an ordinary student, such as himself. He looked at his watch and noted it was time he returned home if he wanted to avoid ending up just like Lermontov.

Nonetheless, he could not tear himself away from the great men, and instead of going back to Kristyna, he went to the toilet. Filled with grandiose thoughts as he stood in front of the white tiles, he heard Lermontov's voice next to him: "You heard them. They're not *subtle*. Do you understand? They're not *subtle*."

Lermontov said the word "subtle" as if it were in italics. Yes, there are words unlike all the others, those words whose particular meaning is known only to initiates. The student did not know why Lermontov said the word "subtle" as if it were in italics, but I, who am among the initiates, know that Lermontov once read Pascal's *pensée* about subtle minds and geometrical minds, and ever since had divided the human race into two categories: those who are subtle, and all the others.

"You think they're *subtle*, don't you?" he said aggressively to the silent student.

Buttoning his fly, the student noticed that Lermontov, just as Countess Rostopchin had noted in her diary one hundred fifty years before, had very short legs. He felt grateful to him as the first great poet to ask him a serious question and await an equally serious answer.

The student said the word "subtle" in roman type: "They're not subtle at all."

Lermontov stood still on his short legs: "No, not *subtle* at all." And raising his voice, he added: "But I'm *proud*! Do you understand, I'm *proud*!"

The word "proud" was another that came from his mouth in italics, to indicate that only a fool could think Lermontov's pride was like a girl's in her beauty or a shopkeeper's in his goods, for it was a singular kind of pride, a pride justified and noble.

"I'm *proud*," shouted Lermontov, and he returned with the student to the function room, where Voltaire was delivering a panegyric to Goethe. Lermontov then went into a frenzy. Planting himself at the edge of the table, which at once made him a head taller than the seated others, he said: "And now I'm going to show you what I'm *proud* of! Now I'm going to tell you something, because I'm *proud*! There are only two poets in this country: Goethe and me."

This time it was Voltaire who raised his voice: "You may be a great poet, but you're a small man! I can say you're a great poet, but you don't have the right to say it."

Lermontov was taken aback for a moment. Then he stammered: "Why don't I have the right to say it? I'm *proud*!"

Lermontov repeated several more times that he was proud, Voltaire roared with laughter, and then the others roared with him.

The student realized that the moment he was waiting for had arrived. He stood up like Lermontov and looked around at the assembled poets: "You don't understand Lermontov. A poet's pride is not ordinary pride. Only the poet himself can know the value of what he writes. Others don't understand it until much later, or they may never understand it. So it's the poet's duty to be proud. If he weren't, he would betray his own work."

A moment before, they had been roaring with laughter, but now at a single stroke they all agreed with the student, because they were just as proud as Lermontov and were only ashamed to say so, not realizing that when the word "proud" is properly enunciated it stops being laughable and becomes witty and noble. So they were grateful to the student for giving them such good advice, and one of them, probably Verlaine, even applauded.

Goethe Turns Kristyna into a Queen

The student sat down and Goethe turned to him with a kindly smile: "My boy, you certainly know what poetry is."

The others were again immersed in their drunken discussions, leaving the student alone with the great poet. He wanted to make the most of the precious opportunity, but suddenly he did not know what to say. Because he was looking hard for a suitable remark—

Goethe was merely smiling at him in silence—he was unable to come up with anything, and so he just smiled back. And then the thought of Kristyna came to his aid.

"Right now, I'm going out with a girl, I mean a woman. She's married to a butcher."

That greatly pleased Goethe, who responded with a friendly laugh.

"She venerates you. She gave me one of your books for you to inscribe."

"Hand it over," said Goethe, and took the book of his verse from the student. Opening to the title page, he went on: "Tell me about her. What is she like? Is she beautiful?"

The student could not lie to Goethe's face. He admitted that the butcher's wife was no beauty. On top of that, today she was dressed in a ridiculous outfit. She had gone around Prague all day wearing big beads around her neck and old-fashioned black pumps.

Goethe listened with sincere interest and said, with a bit of yearning: "That's wonderful."

Becoming bolder, the student went so far as to admit that the butcher's wife had a gold tooth shining in her mouth like a gilded fly.

Excited, Goethe laughed and suggested: "Like a ring."

"Like a lighthouse!" replied the student.

"Like a star!" said Goethe with a smile.

The student told him the butcher's wife was really the most ordinary kind of small-town woman, and that was exactly what had attracted him to her.

"I know what you mean," said Goethe. "It's just those

details—poorly chosen clothes, slightly flawed teeth, delightful mediocrity of soul—that make a woman lively and real. The women on posters or in fashion magazines, the ones almost all women nowadays try to imitate, lack charm because they're unreal, because they're merely the sum total of a set of abstract instructions. They're not born of human bodies but of computers! I assure you, my friend, your small-town woman is just what a poet needs, and I congratulate you!"

Then he bent over the title page, took out his pen, and started to write. Enthusiastically, nearly in a trance, his face radiant with love and understanding, he filled the whole page.

The student took back the book and blushed proudly. What Goethe had written to a woman unknown to him was beautiful and sad, yearning and sensual, lively and wise, and the student was certain that such beautiful words had never before been addressed to any woman. He thought of Kristyna and desired her infinitely. Poetry had cast a cloak woven of the most sublime words over her ridiculous clothes. She had been turned into a queen.

Carrying a Poet

The waiter entered the room, this time with no new bottles. He asked the poets to get ready to leave. It was time to close up the building. The caretaker was threatening to lock them in for the night.

He had to repeat this announcement several times, loudly and softly, to all of them collectively and to each one individually, before the poets finally realized that the part about the caretaker was no joke. Petrarch suddenly remembered his wife in her red bathrobe and got up from the table as if he had been kicked in the pants.

Goethe then said, with infinite sadness: "Leave me here, boys. I want to stay here." His crutches were still leaning against the table next to him, and to the poets trying to persuade him to leave with them, he merely responded by shaking his head.

They all knew his wife, a harsh, spiteful lady. They were all afraid of her. They knew that if Goethe did not come home on time his wife would make a terrible scene in front of all of them. They implored him: "Be reasonable, Johann, you've got to go home!" and they took him shyly by the armpits and tried to lift him from his chair. But the Olympian god was heavy, and their arms were hesitant. He was at least thirty years their elder and their true patriarch; all of a sudden, when they were lifting him and passing him his crutches, they all felt small and embarrassed. And he kept repeating that he wanted to stay there!

No one agreed with him except Lermontov, who seized the opportunity to be more cunning than the others: "Leave him here, boys, and I'll keep him company till morning. Don't you understand? When he was young, he'd stay away from home whole weeks at a time. He's trying to regain his youth! Don't you understand that, you morons? Right, Johann? The two of us are going to lie down on the rug and stay here with this bottle of red wine till morning, and all the rest of them have to get out! Petrarch can go run to his wife, with her red bathrobe and her hair undone!"

But Voltaire knew it was not nostalgia for his youth that was keeping Goethe there. Goethe was ill and forbidden to drink. When he drank, his legs refused to carry him. Voltaire seized the crutches and ordered the others to give up their unnecessary hesitancy. And so the tipsy poets' feeble arms took hold of Goethe's armpits and lifted him from his chair. They carried him through the function room to the vestibule, or rather dragged him (sometimes Goethe's feet touched the floor, sometimes they were above it like the feet of a child being swung by its parents). But Goethe was heavy and the poets were drunk: they dropped him in the vestibule, and Goethe moaned and cried out: "Let me die right here, boys!"

Voltaire got angry and shouted to the poets to pick Goethe up again immediately. This shamed the poets. Some took Goethe by the arms, others by the legs, and they lifted him and carried him through the club door to the staircase. Everyone was carrying him. Voltaire was carrying him, Petrarch was carrying him, Verlaine was carrying him, Boccaccio was carrying him, and even the staggering Yesenin was holding on to Goethe's leg, for fear of falling.

The student too tried to carry the great poet, knowing it was a once-in-a-lifetime opportunity. But in vain, because Lermontov had become so fond of him. He took him by the arm and could not stop finding things to say to him.

"Not only are they not *subtle*, they're also clumsy. They're all spoiled children. Look how they're carrying him! They're going to drop him! They've never worked with their hands. Do you know I worked in a factory?"

(We should not forget that all the heroes of that time and country did factory work, either voluntarily, out of revolutionary enthusiasm, or under duress, as punishment. In either case they were equally proud of it, because it seemed to them that in the factory, Hard Life herself, that noble goddess, had kissed their brows.)

Holding their patriarch by the arms and legs, the poets carried him downstairs. The stairwell was square, with several right-angle turns that put their strength and agility to a hard test.

Lermontov went on: "Do you know, my friend, what it is to carry a crossbeam? You've never carried one. You're a student. But these characters have never carried one either. Look how stupidly they're carrying him! They're letting him fall!" He shouted at them: "Hold on to him, you idiots, you're letting him fall! You've never worked with your hands!" And clinging to the student's arm, he came slowly down behind the staggering poets carrying the increasingly heavy Goethe with growing anguish. They finally arrived on the sidewalk with their burden and leaned him against a lamppost. Petrarch and Boccaccio kept him propped up while Voltaire went out into the street to try to flag down one of the passing cars.

Lermontov said to the student: "Do you realize what you're seeing? You're a student, you don't know anything about life. But this is a great scene! They're carrying a poet. Do you know what a poem it would make?"

Goethe, however, had slumped to the ground; Petrarch and Boccaccio tried to prop him up again.

"Look," said Lermontov to the student, "they can't even lift him up. They have no strength in their arms. They don't have any idea what life is. Carrying a poet. What a magnificent title. Do you understand? Right now I'm putting together two collections of verse. Two entirely different collections. One is in strictly classical form, rhymed and in a definite meter. And the other is in free verse. It's going to be called *Accounts Rendered*. The last poem in this collection will be 'Carrying a Poet.' It'll be a harsh poem. But honest. *Honest.*"

That was the third word Lermontov said in italics. The word expressed opposition to everything merely ornamental or witty. It expressed opposition to Petrarch's reveries and Boccaccio's pranks. It expressed the pathos of the worker's labor and a passionate faith in the aforementioned goddess, Hard Life.

Intoxicated by the night air, Verlaine was standing on the sidewalk, looking up at the stars and singing. Yesenin had sat down against the building wall and fallen asleep. Voltaire, still waving his arm in the street, finally succeeded in getting a taxi. Then, with Boccaccio's help, he settled Goethe in the back seat. He shouted to Petrarch to sit down next to the driver, because Petrarch was the only one with any chance of mollifying Mrs. Goethe. But Petrarch frantically defended himself:

"Why me? Why me? She scares me!"

"You see," said Lermontov to the student. "When a friend needs help, he takes off. Not a single one of them is capable of talking to Goethe's old lady." Then, leaning inside the car, where Goethe, Boccaccio, and Voltaire were now crammed together in the back seat, he said: "Boys, I'm coming with you. I'll take care of Mrs. Goethe." And he got into the empty seat next to the driver.

Petrarch Condemns Boccaccio's Laughter

The taxi loaded with poets vanished and the student remembered it was time to go back to Kristyna.

"I have to go home," he said to Petrarch.

Petrarch nodded, took him by the arm, and went off with him in the opposite direction.

"You know," he said, "you're a sensitive boy. You're the only one there who was capable of listening to what the others were saying."

The student took it from there: "That girl standing in the middle of the room like Joan of Arc with her lance—I can repeat everything you said, in your own words exactly."

"Besides, those drunks didn't even hear the end of the story! Are they interested in anything other than themselves?"

"Or when you said your wife was afraid the girl wanted to kill you, and then you approached her and her look radiated a celestial peacefulness, it was like a small miracle."

"Ah, my friend, you are the one who is a poet! You and not they!"

Petrarch was holding the student by the arm and leading him to his own distant suburb.

"And how does the story end?" asked the student.

"My wife took pity on her and let her stay in the apartment for the night. But imagine this! My mother-in-law sleeps in a kind of storage room behind the kitchen and gets up very early. When she saw the windows were all broken, she quickly went to get the glaziers who by chance were working in the building next door, and all the windows were replaced by the time we woke up. There wasn't a trace of the evening's events. I felt I had dreamed them."

"And the girl?" asked the student.

"Gone too. She must have left quietly very early in the morning."

Just then, Petrarch stopped in the middle of the street and looked at the student with an almost stern expression: "You know, my friend, it would pain me greatly if you were to take my story for one of those Boccaccio anecdotes that end up in a bed. You should know this: Boccaccio is a jackass. Boccaccio never understands anyone, because to understand is to merge and to identify with. That is the secret of poetry. We consume ourselves in the beloved woman, we consume ourselves in the idea we believe, we burn in the landscape we are moved by."

The student listened to Petrarch ardently and saw before him the image of his Kristyna, about whose charms he had had his doubts some hours earlier. He was ashamed of those doubts now, because they belonged to the less good (Boccaccian) half of his being; they sprang from his weakness, not his strength: they proved that he did not dare enter into love completely, with all his being, proved that he was afraid of being consumed in the beloved woman.

"Love is poetry, poetry is love," said Petrarch, and the student resolved to love Kristyna with a love ardent and grand. A short time earlier, Goethe had arrayed her in a royal cloak, and now Petrarch was adding to the fire in the student's heart. The night awaiting him would be blessed by two poets.

"Laughter, on the other hand," Petrarch went on, "is an explosion that tears us away from the world and throws us back into our own cold solitude. Joking is a barrier between man and the world. Joking is the enemy of love and poetry. That's why I tell you yet again, and want you to keep in mind: Boccaccio doesn't understand love. Love can never be laughable. Love has nothing in common with laughter."

"Yes," agreed the student enthusiastically. The world seemed to him to be divided in two, the side of love and the side of joking, and he knew that he belonged and would go on belonging to Petrarch's army.

Angels Hover Above the Student's Bed

She was not pacing tensely in the attic room, she was not angry, she was not sulking, she was not languishing at the open window. She was curled up in her nightgown under his blanket. He woke her with a kiss on the lips, and to forestall any reproaches told her with forced loquacity about the unbelievable evening, about the dramatic confrontation between Boccaccio and Petrarch, about Lermontov insulting all the other poets. She was not interested in his explanation and interrupted him suspiciously:

"I bet you forgot about the book."

When he handed her the book with Goethe's long inscription, she could not believe her eyes. Again and again she reread those unlikely phrases that seemed to embody all of her equally unlikely adventure with the student, all of last summer with its secret walks on unknown woodland paths, all the delicacy and all the tenderness apparently so alien to her life.

Meanwhile the student undressed and lay down beside her. She took him firmly in her arms. It was an embrace such as he had never before experienced. A sincere, vigorous, ardent, maternal, sisterly, amicable, and passionate embrace. Several times that evening, Lermontov had used the word "honest," and the student thought Kristyna's embrace well deserved that term, which synthesized an entire cohort of adjectives.

The student felt that his body was outstandingly well disposed toward love. With a disposition so certain, hard, and durable, he could take his time and do nothing but savor the long, sweet minutes of that motionless embrace.

She thrust her tongue sensually into his mouth and a moment later showered most sisterly kisses all over his face. With the end of his tongue he felt her gold tooth on the upper left side, remembering what Goethe had said to him: Kristyna was born not of a computer but of a human body! She was just what a poet needed! He wanted to shout for joy. And Petrarch's words rang out in his mind, telling him that love is poetry and poetry is love and that to understand is to merge with the other and burn within her. (Yes, all three poets were here with him, hovering above the bed like angels, singing, rejoicing, and blessing him!) Overflowing with immense enthusiasm, the student decided it was time to transform the Lermontovian honesty of the motionless embrace into a real work of love. He turned over onto Kristyna's body and tried to open her legs with his knee.

But what's this? Kristyna is resisting! She is keeping her legs tightly together with the same obstinacy as on their woodland walks!

He wanted to ask her why she was resisting him, but he could not speak. Kristyna was so shy, so delicate, that love's functions lost their names in her presence. He dared use only the language of breathing and touching. Weren't they beyond the heaviness of words? Wasn't he burning within her? They were both burning with the same flame! And so, in stubborn silence, he kept attempting with his knee to force open Kristyna's tightly closed thighs.

She too was silent. She too was afraid to speak and tried to express everything with kisses and caresses. But finally, on his twenty-fifth attempt to open her thighs, she said: "No, please, no. It would kill me."

"What?"

"It would kill me. It's true. It would kill me," Kristyna repeated, and again she thrust her tongue deep into his mouth, yet keeping her thighs very tightly together.

The student felt despair tinged with bliss. He wildly desired to make love to her and at the same time wanted to weep for joy. Kristyna loved him as no one had before. She loved him so much it would kill her, she loved him to the point of being afraid to make love with him because if she were to make love with him, she would never be able to live without him and she would die of grief and desire. He was happy, he was madly happy, because he had suddenly, unexpectedly, and without having done anything to deserve it attained what he had always desired, the infinite love compared to which all the earth with all its continents and all its seas is as nothing.

"I understand you! I'll die with you!" he murmured, caressing and kissing her and almost weeping for love of her. All the same, these grand, tender feelings did nothing to stifle his physical desire, which had become nearly intolerably painful. He again made some attempts to lever his knee between Kristyna's thighs and thus open the way into her body, which was suddenly more mysterious to him than the Holy Grail.

"No, not you, nothing would happen to you. *I'm* the one it would kill!" said Kristyna.

He imagined infinite pleasure, such pleasure that it would kill him, and he said: "We'll die together! We'll die together!" And he went on pushing his knee between her thighs, still in vain.

They didn't know what more to say. They were still pressed against each other. Kristyna shook her head as he launched a few more assaults on the fortress of her thighs before finally giving up. Resigned, he turned over and lay on his back beside her. She took hold of the scepter of her love standing up in her honor, and grasped it with all her splendid honesty: sincerely, vigorously, ardently, maternally, sisterly, amicably, and passionately.

At the student's, the bliss of an infinitely beloved man mingled with the despair of a rejected body. And the butcher's wife was still holding his weapon of love, not thinking about substituting, with some simple movements, for the carnal act he desired, but holding it in her hand like something rare, something precious, something she did not want to damage and wanted for a long, long time to keep just as it was, erect and hard.

But enough of that night, which went on without much change until nearly morning.

The Drab Light of Morning

Since they fell asleep very late, they did not wake up until just before noon, both with headaches. Soon Kristyna would be taking her train. Neither of them said much. Kristyna had put her nightgown and Goethe's book into her overnight bag and was again perched on her ridiculous black pumps and wearing her ill-chosen necklace.

As if the drab light of morning had broken the seal of silence, as if a day of prose had followed a night of poetry, Kristyna told the student quite simply: "You know, you shouldn't want it from me, it really could kill me. The doctor told me after I had my baby I should never get pregnant again."

The student gave her a despairing look: "Did you think I was going to make you pregnant? What do you take me for?"

"That's what they all say. They're always sure of themselves. I know what's happened to my friends. Young ones like you are terribly dangerous. And when it happens, that's it, you're stuck."

Despairingly, he told her he was not some inexperienced novice and would never have made her pregnant. "Are you really comparing me with your friends' boyfriends?"

"I know," she said almost apologetically. The student no longer needed to find ways to convince her. She believed him. He was no peasant and probably knew

204

more about matters of love than any mechanic. She probably had been wrong to resist him last night. But she did not regret it. A night of love with its brief coupling (in Kristyna's mind physical love could only be brief and hurried) always left her with the impression of something nice but also dangerous and deceitful. What she had experienced with the student was infinitely better.

He went with her to the railroad station, she already thrilled by the thought of sitting down in her compartment and recalling it all. She kept telling herself, with a simple woman's avaricious pragmatism, that she had experienced something "no one could take away" from her: she had spent the night with a young man who had always seemed unreal, elusive, and distant, and for a whole night had held him by his erect member. Yes, for a whole night! That's something which never happened to her before! She might never see him again, but she had never believed she could go on seeing him. She was happy with the thought of keeping something of his that was permanent: the Goethe book with its unbelievable inscription, which she could use at any time to prove to herself that her adventure had not been a dream.

The student, for his part, was in despair. Last night, one sensible sentence would have been enough! It would have been enough to call things by their right names, and he could have had her! She was afraid he would make her pregnant, and he thought she was frightened by the immensity of her love! Casting his eyes into the unfathomable depths of his stupidity, he wanted to burst into laughter, into whimpering, hysterical laughter.

He returned from the railroad station to his wasteland of loveless nights, and *litost* came with him.

Further Notes Toward a Theory of Litost

With two examples taken from the student's life, I explained the two basic reactions of someone faced with his own *litost*. If our counterpart is the weaker, we find an excuse to hurt him, like the student hurting the girl who swam too fast.

If our counterpart is the stronger, all we can do is choose circuitous revenge—the indirect blow, a murder by means of suicide. The child plays a wrong note on his violin over and over until the teacher goes mad and throws him out the window. As he falls, the child is delighted by the thought that the nasty teacher will be charged with murder.

These are the two classic methods, and if the first is commonly found among lovers and spouses, what we conventionally call the history of mankind offers innumerable examples of the other kind of behavior. Everything our teachers called heroism may only be the form of *litost* I have illustrated with the example of the child and the violin teacher. The Persians conquered the Peloponnesus when the Spartans made one military mistake after another. Just like the child refusing to play in tune, they were blinded by tears of rage and refused to take any reasonable action, being capable neither of fighting better nor of surrendering or fleeing, and it is through *litost* that they allowed themselves to be killed to the last man.

The idea occurs to me in this connection that it is no accident the notion of *litost* originated in Bohemia. The story of the Czechs—an endless story of rebellions against the stronger, a succession of glorious defeats that launched their history and led to ruin the very people who had done the launching—is a story of *litost*. When in August 1968 thousands of Russian tanks occupied that amazing small country, I saw a slogan written on the walls of a town: "We don't want compromise, we want victory!" You must understand, by then there was no more than a choice among several varieties of defeat, but this town rejected compromise and wanted victory! That was *litost* talking! A man possessed by it takes revenge through his own annihilation. The child lies shattered on the sidewalk, but its immortal soul is going to be eternally thrilled because the violin teacher has hanged himself from the window catch.

But how could the student hurt Kristyna? Before he had a chance to think about it, she was on the train. Theoreticians are familiar with this kind of situation and call it "*litost* block."

It is the worst that can happen. The student's *litost* was like a tumor growing by the minute, and he did not know what to do about it. Since he had no one on whom to take revenge, he hoped at least for consolation. That is why he thought about Lermontov. He thought about how Goethe had insulted and Voltaire had humiliated Lermontov, and that he had stood up to them all by shouting about his pride as if all the poets around the table were violin teachers he was trying to provoke into flinging him out the window.

Wanting Lermontov the way one wants a brother, the student thrust his hand into his pocket. His fingers felt a folded sheet of paper. It was a large sheet torn from a notebook, and on it was written: "I await you. I love you. Kristyna. Midnight."

He understood. The jacket he was wearing had been hanging in his attic room yesterday evening. The message belatedly found only confirmed what he already knew. He had failed to have Kristyna's body because of his own stupidity. The *litost* that filled him to the brim could find no channel of escape.

In the Depths of Despair

It was late afternoon, and he thought the poets must at last be up and around after the drinking bout of the night before. Maybe they were back at the Writers Club. Taking four steps at a time, he rushed up to the second floor, passed through the cloakroom, and turned right into the restaurant. Not being an habitué, he paused at the entrance to look inside. Petrarch and

Lermontov were sitting at the far end of the room with two men unknown to him. There was a vacant table very near them; he went and sat down there. No one seemed to notice him. He even had the impression that Petrarch and Lermontov had glanced at him without recognizing him. He ordered a cognac from the waiter; the infinitely sad and infinitely beautiful text of Kristyna's message resounded painfully through his head: "I await you. I love you. Kristyna. Midnight."

He stayed there for about twenty minutes, taking tiny sips of cognac. Far from comforting him, the sight of Petrarch and Lermontov only brought him still more sadness. He had been abandoned by everyone, abandoned by Kristyna and by the poets. He was alone here, with nothing for company but a large sheet of paper with "I await you. I love you. Kristyna. Midnight" written on it. He had a craving to get up and wave the sheet of paper over his head, so everyone could see it, so everyone could know that he, the student, had been loved, infinitely loved.

He called the waiter over to pay him. Then he lit a cigarette. He no longer had any desire to stay at the Writers Club, but he was repelled by the thought of returning to his attic room, where no woman awaited him. Just as he was finally stubbing the cigarette out in the ashtray, he noticed Petrarch motioning to him with his hand. But it was too late, *litost* was driving him out of the club and toward his sad solitude. He got up and, at the last moment, once more took out of his pocket the sheet of paper with Kristyna's love message on it. That sheet of paper would no longer give him any pleasure. But if he left it lying on the table here, someone might notice it and would know that the student had been infinitely loved.

He headed for the exit.

Unexpected Glory

"My friend!" The student heard a voice behind him and turned around. It was Petrarch, who had motioned to him and was now approaching him: "Are you leaving already?" He apologized for not having recognized him immediately. "When I've been drinking, I'm completely dazed the next day."

The student explained that he had not wished to disturb Petrarch because he did not know the gentlemen with him.

"They're idiots," said Petrarch, walking back with the student to sit down with him at the table he had just left. The student looked with anguish at the large sheet of paper lying casually on the table. If only it had been a discreet little piece of paper—but that large sheet loudly cried out the clumsily obvious intention with which it had been forgotten there.

Rolling his dark eyes with curiosity, Petrarch immediately noticed the sheet of paper and examined it: "What's this? Ah, my friend, it's yours, isn't it?"

Clumsily trying to feign the embarrassment of a man who has left a confidential communication lying around, the student tried to snatch the sheet of paper out of Petrarch's hands.

But he was already reading it aloud: "'I await you. I love you. Kristyna. Midnight.'"

He looked the student in the eyes and asked: "What midnight was that? It wasn't yesterday, I hope!"

The student lowered his eyes: "Yes, it was," he said. He had stopped trying to snatch the sheet of paper out of Petrarch's hands.

Meanwhile Lermontov was approaching their table on his squat little legs. He shook hands with the student: "I'm glad to see you. Those two," he said, indicating the table he had just come from, "are horrible cretins." And he sat down.

Petrarch immediately read Lermontov the text of Kristyna's message, read it several times in a row in a sonorous, melodic voice as if it were verse.

Which makes me think that when someone can neither slap a girl who swims too fast nor get himself killed by the Persians, when he has no means of escaping from *litost*, then poetry's charm flies to his assistance.

What remains of this beautiful and thoroughly bungled story? Only the poetry. Inscribed in Goethe's book, the words that Kristyna is taking away with her, and on a lined sheet of paper, the words that have adorned the student with unexpected glory.

"My friend," said Petrarch, seizing the student by

the arm, "admit it, admit that you write verse, admit that you're a poet!"

The student lowered his eyes and admitted that Petrarch was right.

And Lermontov Remains Alone

Lermontov is the one the student came to the Writers Club to see, but from that moment on he is lost to Lermontov and Lermontov is lost to him. Lermontov detests happy lovers. He frowns and speaks with disdain of the poetry of mawkish feelings and lofty words. He says that a poem must be as honest as an object fashioned by a worker's hands. He scowls and he is unpleasant with Petrarch and the student. We know full well what it is about. Goethe knows too. It is about hypercelibacy. About the terrible *litost* that comes from hypercelibacy.

Who could understand this better than the student? But that incorrigible idiot can only see Lermontov's gloomy face, only hear his spiteful words and be insulted by them.

I watch them from afar, from the top of my high-rise in France. Petrarch and the student stand up. They coldly take leave of Lermontov. And Lermontov remains alone.

My dear Lermontov, the genius of that sorrow my sad Bohemia calls *litost*.

PART SIX

The Angels

1

In February 1948, the Communist leader Klement
Gottwald stepped out on the balcony of a Baroque
palace in Prague to harangue hundreds of thousands
of citizens massed in Old Town Square. That was a
great turning point in the history of Bohemia. It was
snowing and cold, and Gottwald was bareheaded.
Bursting with solicitude, Clementis took off his fur hat
and set it on Gottwald's head.

Neither Gottwald nor Clementis knew that every
day for eight years Franz Kafka had climbed the same
stairs they had just climbed to the historic balcony,
because under Austria-Hungary the palace had
housed a German school. Nor did they know that on
the ground floor of the same building Hermann Kafka,
Franz's father, had a shop whose sign showed a jackdaw painted next to his name, *kafka* meaning jackdaw
in Czech.

Gottwald, Clementis, and all the others were
unaware even that Kafka had existed, but Kafka had
been aware of their ignorance. In his novel, Prague is
a city without memory. The city has even forgotten its
name. No one there remembers or recalls anything,
and Josef K. even seems not to know anything about

his own life previously. No song can be heard there to evoke for us the moment of its birth and link the present to the past.

The time of Kafka's novel is the time of a humanity that has lost its continuity with humanity, of a humanity that no longer knows anything and no longer remembers anything and lives in cities without names where the streets are without names or with names different from those they had yesterday, because a name is continuity with the past and people without a past are people without a name.

Prague, as Max Brod said, is the city of evil. When the Jesuits, after the defeat of the Czech Reformation in 1621, tried to reeducate the people in the true Catholic faith, they swamped Prague with the splendor of Baroque cathedrals. The thousands of petrified saints gazing at you from all sides and threatening you, spying on you, hypnotizing you, are the frenzied occupation army that invaded Bohemia three hundred fifty years ago to tear the people's faith and language out of its soul.

The street Tamina was born on was called Schwerinova Street. That was during the war, when Prague was occupied by the Germans. Her father was born on Cernokostelecka Avenue. That was under Austria-Hungary. When her mother married her father and moved in there, it was Marshal Foch Avenue. That was after the 1914–1918 war. Tamina spent her childhood on Stalin Avenue, and it was on Vinohrady Avenue that her husband picked her up to take her to her new home. And yet it was always the same street, they just kept changing its name, brainwashing it into a half-wit.

Wandering the streets that do not know their names are the ghosts of monuments torn down. Torn down by the Czech Reformation, torn down by the Austrian Counter-Reformation, torn down by the Czechoslovak Republic, torn down by the Communists; even the statues of Stalin have been torn down. In place of those destroyed monuments, statues of Lenin are nowadays springing up in Bohemia by the thousands, springing up like weeds among ruins, like melancholy flowers of forgetting.

2

If Franz Kafka is the prophet of a world without memory, Gustav Husak is its builder. After T. G. Masaryk, who was called the Liberator President (every last one of his monuments has been destroyed), after Benes, Gottwald, Zapotocky, Novotny, and Svoboda, he is the seventh president of my country, and he is called the President of Forgetting.

The Russians put him in power in 1969. Not since 1621 has the Czech people experienced such a devastation of culture and intellectuals. Everyone every-

The Book of Laughter and Forgetting

where thinks that Husak was merely persecuting his political enemies. But the struggle against the political opposition was instead the perfect opportunity for the Russians to undertake, with their lieutenant as intermediary, something much more basic.

I consider it very significant from this standpoint that Husak drove one hundred forty-five Czech historians from the universities and research institutes. (It's said that for each historian, as mysteriously as in a fairy tale, a new Lenin monument sprang up somewhere in Bohemia.) One day in 1971, one of those historians, Milan Hübl, wearing his extraordinarily thick-lensed eyeglasses, came to visit me in my studio apartment on Bartolomejska Street. We looked out the window at the towers of Hradcany Castle and were sad.

"You begin to liquidate a people," Hübl said, "by taking away its memory. You destroy its books, its culture, its history. And then others write other books for it, give another culture to it, invent another history for it. Then the people slowly begins to forget what it is and what it was. The world at large forgets it still faster."

"And the language?"

"Why bother taking it away? It will become a mere folklore and sooner or later die a natural death."

Was that just hyperbole dictated by excessive gloom?

Or is it true that the people will be unable to survive crossing the desert of organized forgetting?

None of us knows what is going to happen. One thing, however, is certain. In moments of clear-sightedness, the Czech people can see the image of its own death near at hand. Neither as a fact nor as an inescapable future, but nonetheless as a quite concrete possibility. Its death is right there with it.

3

Six months later, Hübl was arrested and sentenced to many years in prison. My father was dying at the time.

During the last ten years of his life, he gradually lost the power of speech. At first there were some words he either could not recall or replaced with similar-sounding ones that immediately made him laugh at himself. But in the end he could utter only a very small number of words, and every attempt to define his thoughts resulted in the same sentence, one of the last sentences remaining to him: "That's strange."

He said "That's strange," and his eyes showed the immense astonishment of knowing everything and being able to say nothing. Things had lost their names and were merged into single, undifferentiated being. I was the only one who by talking to him could momentarily retrieve from that wordless infinitude the world of entities with names.

The huge blue eyes in his handsome face still expressed wisdom as before. I often took him for walks. We always walked once around the block, because it was all Papa had the strength for. He walked poorly, taking tiny steps, and when he became at all tired, his body would bend forward and he would lose his balance. We often had to stop so he could rest, his brow leaning against a wall.

During these walks we talked about music. When Papa could speak normally, I had asked him very few questions. Now I wanted to make up for lost time. So we talked about music, but it was a strange conversation, between someone who knew nothing but a great many words and one who knew everything but not a single word.

Throughout the ten years of his illness, Papa worked on a big book about Beethoven's sonatas. He probably wrote a little better than he spoke, but even while writing he had more and more trouble finding words, and finally his text had become incomprehensible, consisting of nonexistent words.

He called me into his room one day. Open on the piano was the variations movement of the Opus 111 sonata. "Look," he said, pointing to the music (he could no longer play the piano), and again, "Look," and then, after a prolonged effort, he succeeded in saying: "Now I know!" and kept trying to explain something important to me, but his entire message consisted of unintelligible words, and seeing that I did not understand him, he looked at me in surprise and said: "That's strange."

I know of course what he wanted to talk about,

because it was a question he had been asking himself for a long time. Variation form was Beethoven's favorite toward the end of his life. At first glance, it seems the most superficial of forms, a simple showcase of musical technique, work better suited to a lacemaker than to a Beethoven. But Beethoven made it a sovereign form (for the first time in the history of music), inscribing in it his most beautiful meditations.

Yes, all that is well known. But Papa wanted to know how it should be understood. Why exactly choose variations? What meaning is hidden behind it?

That is why he called me into his room, pointed to the music, and said: "Now I know!"

4

The silence of my father, from whom all words slipped away, the silence of the hundred forty-five historians, who have been forbidden to remember, that multiple silence resounding through Bohemia, forms the background of the picture I am painting of Tamina.

She continued to serve coffee in a café in a small town in the west of Europe. But she had lost the sparkle of solicitous concern, which used to attract the customers. The desire to offer them her ear had gone away.

One day, when Bibi was sitting on a barstool while

her child crawled around on the floor, howling, Tamina, after giving Bibi some time to restore order, finally lost patience and said: "Can't you make your brat shut up?"

In a huff, Bibi retorted: "Why do you hate children so?"

There is no reason to think that Tamina hated children. Yet it didn't escape her that Bibi's voice betrayed an entirely unexpected hostility. Without Tamina's knowing why, they had ceased to be friends.

Then one day Tamina did not come to work. That had never happened before. The owner's wife went over to her place to see what was wrong. She rang at her door, but no one opened it. She went back the next day and again rang in vain. She called the police. They forced the door open, but found only a carefully tidied apartment with nothing missing, nothing suspicious.

Tamina did not come back the following days. The police continued to take an interest in the case but discovered nothing new. Tamina's disappearance was filed with the unsolved cases.

5

On the fateful day, a young fellow in jeans sat down at the bar. Tamina was alone in the café. The young man ordered a Coke and sipped it slowly. He looked at Tamina, and Tamina looked out into space.

After a while, he said: "Tamina."

If he was trying to impress her, he failed. It was not very hard to learn her name; all the customers in the neighborhood knew it.

"I know you're sad," the young man went on.

Tamina was not particularly won over by that remark. She knew that there were many ways to conquer a woman and that one of the surest roads to her flesh led through her sadness. Even so, she looked at the young man with greater interest than before.

They got into a conversation. What intrigued Tamina were his questions. Not their content, but the simple fact that he was asking them. My God, it had been so long since anyone had asked her about anything! It seemed like an eternity! Only her husband had kept asking her questions, because love is a continual interrogation. I don't know of a better definition of love.

(In that case, my friend Hübl would have pointed out to me, no one loves us more than the police. That's true. Just as every *height* has its symmetrical *depth,* so love's interest has as its negative the police's curiosity. We sometimes confuse depth with height, and I can easily imagine lonely people hoping to be taken to the police station from time to time for an interrogation that will enable them to talk about themselves.)

6

The young man looks into her eyes, he listens to her and then tells her that what she calls remembering is really something entirely different: Under a spell, she watches her forgetting.

Tamina nods in agreement.

The young man goes on: Her looking back sadly is no longer the expression of her faithfulness to a dead man. The dead man has disappeared from her field of vision, and she is only looking behind her into space.

Into space? But then what is it that renders her look so heavy?

It is not heavy with memories, the young man explains, but heavy with remorse. Tamina will never forgive herself for forgetting.

"So what should I do?" asks Tamina.

"Forget your forgetting," says the young man.

Tamina smiles bitterly: "Tell me how you manage that."

"Haven't you ever felt like going away?"

"Yes," admits Tamina. "I want terribly to go away. But where?"

"Some place where things are as light as the breeze. Where things have lost their weight. Where there's no remorse."

"Yes," says Tamina dreamily. "Where things weigh nothing at all."

And as in a tale, as in a dream (of course it's a tale! of course it's a dream!), Tamina comes out from behind the bar where she has spent several years of her life and leaves the café with the young man. A red sports car is parked at the curb. The young man sits down at the wheel and invites Tamina to get in beside him.

7

I understand Tamina's self-reproaches. When Papa died, I did the same. I could not forgive myself for asking him about so little, for knowing so little about him, for allowing myself to lack him. And it is just that very remorse which suddenly made me realize what he most likely wanted to tell me when he was pointing to the Opus 111 sonata.

I am going to try to explain it with a comparison. A symphony is a musical epic. We might say that it is like a voyage leading from one thing to another, farther and farther away through the infinitude of the exterior world. Variations are also like a voyage. But that voyage does not lead through the infinitude of the exterior world. In one of his *pensées,* Pascal says that man lives between the abyss of the infinitely large and the abyss of the infinitely small. The voyage of variations leads

into that *other* infinitude, into the infinite diversity of
the interior world lying hidden in all things.

Beethoven thus discovered in variations another
area to be explored. His variations are a new "invita-
tion to the voyage."

Variation form is the form in which concentration is
brought to its maximum; it enables the composer to
speak only of essentials, to go straight to the core of
the matter. A theme for variations often consists of no
more than sixteen measures. Beethoven goes inside
those sixteen measures as if down a shaft leading into
the interior of the earth.

The voyage into that other infinitude is no less
adventurous than the voyage of the epic. It is how the
physicist penetrates into the wondrous depths of the
atom. With every variation Beethoven moves farther
and farther away from the initial theme, which resem-
bles the last variation as little as a flower its image
under a microscope.

Man knows he cannot embrace the universe with its
suns and stars. Much more unbearable is for him to be
condemned to lack the other infinitude, that infinitude
near at hand, within reach. Tamina lacked the infinitude of her love, I lacked Papa, and all of us are lacking in our work because in pursuit of perfection we go
toward the core of the matter but never quite get to it.

That the infinitude of the exterior world escapes us
we accept as natural. But we reproach ourselves until
the end of our lives for lacking that other infinitude.
We ponder the infinitude of the stars but are uncon-

cerned about the infinitude our papa has within him.

It is not surprising that in his later years variations became the favorite form for Beethoven, who knew all too well (as Tamina and I know) that there is nothing more unbearable than lacking the being we loved, those sixteen measures and the interior world of their infinitude of possibilities.

8

This book is a novel in the form of variations. The various parts follow each other like the various stages of a voyage leading into the interior of a theme, the interior of a thought, the interior of a single, unique situation, the understanding of which recedes from my sight into the distance.

It is a novel about Tamina, and whenever Tamina goes offstage, it is a novel for Tamina. She is its principal character and its principal audience, and all the other stories are variations on her own story and meet with her life as in a mirror.

It is a novel about laughter and about forgetting, about forgetting and about Prague, about Prague and about the angels. So it is not at all by chance that the young man sitting at the wheel is named Raphael.

The landscape became more and more of a waste-

land, with less and less green and more and more
ocher, fewer and fewer plants and trees and more and
more sand and clay. Then the car left the road and
turned onto a narrow lane that came abruptly to an
end at a steep slope. The young man stopped the car.
They got out. They stood at the edge of the slope; some
ten meters below them was a thin strip of clayey shore,
and beyond it, a body of murky brownish water
extended as far as the eye could see.

"Where are we?" asked Tamina, with a lump in her
throat. She wanted to tell Raphael that she wished to
go back, but she did not dare: she was afraid he would
refuse, and she knew that his refusal would heighten
her anguish.

They were at the edge of the slope, the water in front
of them and nothing but clay, clay sodden and plantless all around them as though the clay had been
extracted right here. And in fact there was an abandoned dredge not far off.

This landscape took Tamina back to the area of Bohemia, about one hundred kilometers from Prague,
where her husband, after being driven from his occupation, had found his last job, as a bulldozer operator.
During the week, he lived in a trailer at the site, coming
to Prague to see Tamina only on Sundays. She once went
out there to visit him, and they took a walk through a
landscape very much like this one: wet, treeless, and
plantless ground, squeezed between ocher and yellow
underfoot and heavy gray clouds up above. They walked
side by side in rubber boots that slipped and sank in the

mud. They were alone in the world, filled with anguish, love, and despairing concern for each other.

The same despair now penetrated her, and she was thrilled suddenly, surprisingly, to find in it a lost fragment of her past. The memory had been completely lost, it was coming back to her for the first time. She should write it down in her school notebook! She even knew the exact year!

She wanted to tell the young man that she wished to go back. No, he was wrong when he said that her sadness was only form without content! No, no, her husband was still alive in that sadness, he was merely lost and she must go search for him! Search the whole world for him! Yes, yes! At last she knew! Whoever wishes to remember must not stay in one place, waiting for the memories to come of their own accord! Memories are scattered all over the immense world, and it takes voyaging to find them and make them leave their refuge!

She wanted to say all that to the young man and ask him to drive her back. But just then, down at the edge of the water, someone whistled.

9

Raphael seized Tamina by the arm. It was a strong grip from which there could be no thought of escape.

A narrow, slippery path zigzagged down the slope. He led Tamina down it.

On the shore, where moments before there had been not the slightest sign of life, a boy of about twelve stood waiting. In his hand was the line of a rowboat that rocked gently at the edge of the water, and he was smiling at Tamina.

She turned to Raphael. He too was smiling. She looked from one to the other, then Raphael burst out laughing and so did the boy. It was strange laughter, because nothing funny had happened, but also pleasant and infectious: it invited her to forget her anguish and promised her something vague—perhaps it was joy, perhaps it was peace—so that Tamina, who wanted to get away from her anguish, obediently started laughing with them.

"You see?" said Raphael. "There's nothing to be afraid of."

When Tamina stepped into the boat, it began to roll under her weight. She sat down on the seat in the stern. The seat was wet. She was wearing a light summer dress and felt the wetness on her buttocks. That slimy contact with her skin revived her anguish.

The boy pushed off and started rowing, and Tamina turned her head around: on shore, Raphael was watching them go, and he was smiling. Tamina saw something odd about that smile. Yes! He was smiling and slightly shaking his head! Smiling and shaking his head very, very slightly.

10

Why didn't Tamina ask where she was going?

If you don't care about the destination, you don't ask where you're going!

She watched the boy sitting across from her and rowing. He looked weak, and she thought the oars were too heavy for him.

"Wouldn't you like me to take over?" she asked him. The boy readily agreed and gave up the oars.

They changed places. He sat down in the stern, glanced at Tamina rowing, and then picked up a small tape recorder from under his seat. Soon the air was filled with rock music, with electric guitars and song lyrics, and the boy began to writhe in time to it. Tamina looked at him with revulsion: the child was swiveling his hips with flirtatious adult movements she found obscene.

She lowered her eyes to avoid seeing him. The boy turned up the volume and began to sing along softly. After a while, when Tamina again raised her eyes, he asked her: "Why aren't you singing?"

"I don't know that song."

"What do you mean, you don't know it? Everybody knows it."

He went on writhing on his seat, and Tamina was feeling tired: "Would you take over now for a while?"

"Keep rowing!" the boy replied, and he laughed.

But Tamina was really tired. She shipped the oars to rest a bit: "Are we nearly there?"

The boy pointed straight ahead. Tamina turned around. They were close to shore. The landscape was different from the one they had left behind: it was green with plants, covered with trees.

In a few moments, the boat touched bottom. On shore, ten children were playing with a ball and looking at them curiously. Tamina and the boy stepped out of the boat. The boy tied it to a stake. A lane lined with plane trees extended from the sandy shore. They took it and, barely ten minutes later, reached a large, low, white building. In front of it were some large colored objects, whose function Tamina did not know, and several volleyball nets. Tamina was struck by something odd about them. Yes, they were hanging very close to the ground.

The boy put two fingers into his mouth and whistled.

11

A little girl no more than nine came forward. She had a charming little face and the coquettishly rounded belly of the virgins in Gothic paintings. She looked at Tamina with no particular interest, with the look of a woman who is conscious of her beauty and tries to emphasize it with a conspicuous indifference to everything that is not she.

The little girl opened the door to the white building. They went directly (there was neither a corridor nor an entrance hall) into a large room filled with beds. She looked all around the room as if she were counting the beds, then pointed to one: "That's where you'll sleep."

Tamina protested: "What? I'm going to sleep in a dormitory?"

"A child doesn't need its own room."

"What do you mean, a child? I'm not a child!"

"We're all children here!"

"But there have to be some grown-ups!"

"No, there aren't any here."

"Then what am I doing here?" Tamina shouted.

The little girl did not notice her agitation. She headed out, then stopped at the door: "I've put you with the squirrels," she said.

Tamina did not understand.

"I've put you with the Squirrels," the child repeated, sounding like a displeased teacher. "Everybody is assigned to teams named for animals."

Tamina refused to talk about the Squirrels. She wanted to go back. She asked about the boy who had brought her here.

The little girl pretended she had not heard what Tamina said, and went on with her explanation.

"I'm not interested in that!" shouted Tamina. "I want to go back! Where is that boy?"

"Don't shout!" No adult could have been as haughty as that beautiful child. "I don't understand you," she went on, shaking her head to express her surprise: "Why did you come here if you want to go back?"

"I didn't ask to come here!"

"Tamina, don't lie. People don't go on a long journey without knowing where they're going. You should break the habit of lying."

Tamina turned her back to the little girl and rushed out to the plane-tree lane. When she reached the shore, she looked for the boat the boy had tied to a stake barely an hour before. But there was neither boat nor stake.

She started running to inspect the shore. The sand beach soon gave way to a swamp that had to be skirted, and it took her a while to get back to the water. The shore always veered in the same direction, and (having found no trace of the boat or any kind of mooring) she was back after an hour at the spot where the plane-tree lane met the beach. She realized she was on an island.

She went slowly up the lane to the dormitory. Some ten children, girls and boys between the ages of six and twelve, were there in a circle, holding hands. When they saw her, they started to shout: "Tamina, come and join us!"

They opened the circle to make room for her.

Just then she remembered Raphael smiling and shaking his head.

She felt a pang of fear. Coldly passing the children by, she entered the dormitory and cowered on her bed.

12

Her husband died in a hospital. She had been with him there as much as she could, but he died at night, alone. When she arrived at the hospital the next day and found the bed empty, the old gentleman he had shared the room with said to her: "You should file a complaint! The way they treat the dead is criminal!" The fear in his eyes showed he knew it would soon be his turn. "They grabbed him by the feet and dragged him along the floor. They thought I was asleep. I saw his head hit the doorsill."

Death has a double aspect: It is nonbeing. But it is also being, the terrifyingly material being of a corpse.

When Tamina was very young, death would appear to her only in its first form, under the aspect of nothingness, and fear of death (vague as it then was) was fear of no longer being. Over the years, that fear diminished and nearly vanished (the thought that one day she would no longer see the sky or the trees did not frighten her), but on the other hand, she reflected more and more on death's other aspect, the material: she was terrified by the thought of becoming a corpse.

It was an unbearable insult to become a corpse. One moment you are a human being protected by modesty, by the sacrosanctity of nakedness and intimacy, and then the instant of death is enough to put your body suddenly at anyone's disposal—to undress it, to rip it open, to scrutinize its entrails, to hold one's nose against its stench, to shove it into the freezer or into the fire. When she wanted her husband cremated and his ashes scattered, it was also to avoid being tormented the rest of her life by the thought of what had become of that beloved body.

And when some months later she contemplated suicide, she decided to drown herself in the open sea so that the vileness of her dead body would be known only to fish, mute fish.

I spoke earlier of a Thomas Mann story: a young man suffering from a mortal illness gets on a train and descends in an unknown town. There is a wardrobe in his room, and every night a painfully beautiful naked woman steps out of it and tells him a long, sweetly sad tale, and that woman and that tale are death.

It is death sweetly bluish, like nonbeing. Because nonbeing is an infinite emptiness and empty space is blue and there is nothing more beautiful and more soothing than blue. Not at all by chance did Novalis, the poet of death, love blue and search for nothing else on his journeys. Death's sweetness is blue in color.

But if the nonbeing of Thomas Mann's young man is so beautiful, what happens to his body? Do they drag it by the feet across the doorsill? Do they rip it open? Do they throw it into a hole or into the fire?

Mann was twenty-four when he wrote the story, and Novalis never reached thirty. I am unfortunately older, and unlike them, I cannot avoid thinking about the body. For death is not blue, and Tamina knows it just as well as I know it. Death is terrible drudgery. My father lay dying for days with a fever, and I had the impression that he was working hard. He was bathed in sweat and concentrating entirely on his death pangs, as if death were beyond his strength. He no longer even knew I was sitting beside his bed, he was no longer aware of my presence, death's work totally exhausted him, he was concentrating like a rider on his horse trying to reach a far-off destination, but with no more than a final remnant of strength.

Yes, he was riding a horse.

Where was he going?

Somewhere far away, to hide his body.

No, not by chance do all poems about death depict it as a journey. Thomas Mann's young man gets on a train, Tamina gets into a red sports car. A person feels an immense desire to go away and hide his body. But the journey is in vain. He gallops off on a horse but ends up back on a bed and then with his head hitting the doorsill.

13

Why is Tamina on the children's island? Why do I imagine her just there?

I don't know.

Might it be because on the day my father was dying the air was filled with joyful songs sung by children's voices?

Everywhere east of the Elbe, children belong to what are called Pioneer organizations. They wear red kerchiefs around their necks, go to meetings like adults, and at times sing the "Internationale." They have the nice custom of sometimes knotting a red kerchief around the neck of an eminent adult and giving him the title Honorary Pioneer. The adults love that, and the older they are, the more they enjoy getting red kerchiefs from children for their coffins.

They all got one—Lenin got one, and so did Stalin, Masturbov, and Sholokhov, Ulbricht and Brezhnev, and Husak too got his that day at a grand celebration in the Prague Castle.

Papa's fever had gone down a bit. It was May, and we opened the window overlooking the garden. From the house opposite, the television broadcast of the ceremony was reaching us through the branches of the flowering apple trees. We heard the children singing in their high-pitched voices.

The doctor was in the room. He bent over Papa,

who could no longer say a single word. Then he turned to me and said aloud: "He's no longer conscious. His brain is deteriorating." I saw Papa's huge blue eyes open still wider.

When the doctor left, I was horribly uneasy and wanted to say something quickly to drive those words away. I pointed to the window: "Do you hear that? What a joke! They're making Husak an Honorary Pioneer!"

And Papa started to laugh. He laughed to show me that his brain was alive and I could go on talking and joking with him.

Husak's voice reached us through the apple trees: "Children! You are the future!"

And then: "Children, never look back!"

"I'm going to close the window so we don't have to hear any more!" I winked at Papa, and looking at me with his infinitely beautiful smile, he nodded.

A few hours later, his fever suddenly rose once more. He mounted his horse and rode it for several days. He never saw me again.

14

But what can she do now that she is lost among children, the boatman and his boat have disappeared, and she is surrounded by an immensity of water?

She is going to fight.

How sad it is: in the small town in the west of Europe, she never made an effort to achieve anything, and here, among children (in the world of things without weight), was she really going to fight?

And how does she intend to fight?

On the day she arrived, when she refused to play and took refuge on her bed as in a fortified castle, she felt the children's nascent hostility in the air and was afraid of it. Now she is trying to forestall it. She has decided to gain their friendship. To do that, she must identify with them, adopt their language. So she voluntarily takes part in all their games and contributes her ideas and physical strength to their activities, and the children are soon won over by her charm.

To identify with them she has to give up her privacy. She goes to the bathroom with them, though on that first day she had refused to accompany them there because it repelled her to wash herself with them looking on.

The large, tiled bathroom is at the center of the children's lives and secret thoughts. On one side are ten toilet bowls, on the other ten washbasins. While one team sits with hitched-up nightshirts on the toilet bowls, another stands naked at the washbasins. The seated ones look at the naked ones standing at the washbasins and the ones at the washbasins look over their shoulders at the ones on the toilet bowls, and the whole room is filled with a secret sensuality that awak-

ens in Tamina a vague memory of something long forgotten.

Tamina is sitting on the toilet bowl in her nightshirt,
and the naked Tigers standing at the washbasins have
eyes only for her. Then there is the gurgle of water
flushing, the Squirrels get off the toilets and remove
their long nightshirts, and the Tigers leave the washbasins for the dormitory, where the Cats are now coming from; they sit down on the vacated toilets and look
at big Tamina with her dark groin and big breasts
washing herself at a washbasin along with the other
Squirrels.

She is not ashamed. She feels that her adult sexuality makes her a queen who rules over those with hair-
less groins.

15

So it seems that the voyage to the island was not a con-
spiracy against her, as she had thought when she first
saw the dormitory and her bed. On the contrary, she
was finally where she had wished to be: she had fallen
far back to a time when her husband did not exist,
when he was neither in memory nor in desire, and thus
when there was neither weight nor remorse.

Her modesty had always been well developed (modesty was love's faithful shadow), and here she was displaying herself naked to tens of strangers. At first she found it startling and unpleasant, but she soon got used to it, because her nakedness was not immodest but had simply lost its significance and become inexpressive, mute, lifeless. A body whose every part was marked by Tamina's and her husband's love story had sunk into insignificance, and in that insignificance there was relief and repose.

But if her adult sensuality was vanishing, another world of arousals began slowly to emerge from the distant past. Long-gone memories came back to her. This one, for example (it's no wonder she had long ago forgotten it, because the adult Tamina would have found it unbearably ridiculous and unseemly): in the first grade of elementary school she worshiped her young, pretty teacher and dreamed for months of being in the bathroom with her.

Now she is sitting on the toilet bowl, smiling and with her eyes half closed. She imagines she is that teacher and the little girl with freckles sitting on the toilet next to hers and curiously looking sidelong at her is the child Tamina of long ago. So utterly does she identify with the sensual eyes above the little girl's freckled cheeks that somewhere in the distant reaches of her memory she feels, half awakened, the quiver of an old arousal.

16

Thanks to Tamina, the Squirrels won nearly all the games, and they decided to reward her formally. The children dispensed all punishments and rewards in the bathroom, and Tamina's reward was to have everyone at her service that evening: that evening she would have no right to touch herself—her totally devoted servants, the Squirrels, would diligently do everything for her.

And so they served her: they began by carefully wiping her as she sat on the toilet bowl, then they lifted her off it and flushed, took off her nightshirt, and led her to the washbasin, where they all tried to wash her breasts and belly and were eager to see what she looked like between her legs and what it felt like to touch. Now and then she tried to push them away, but that was very difficult: she was unable to be nasty to the children, because they were playing the game with admirable earnestness, pretending to be serving her as a way of rewarding her.

Finally they went to put her to bed for the night, and there they again found a thousand charming pretexts to press up against her and caress her entire body. There were so many of them she was unable to tell whose hand or mouth belonged to whom. She felt them pressing against her entire body, but especially where she was built unlike them. She closed her eyes and thought she felt her body rocking, slowly rocking as in a cradle: she experienced a singularly peaceful sensual pleasure.

She felt that pleasure making the corners of her lips quiver. She reopened her eyes and caught sight of a child's face closely watching her mouth and saying to another child's face: "Look! Look!" Now there were two children's faces leaning over her, eagerly observing the quivering corners of her lips as if they were looking at a watch taken to pieces or a fly with torn-off wings.

But she had the impression her eyes were seeing something entirely different from what her body felt, as if there had been no link between the children leaning over her and the silent, rocking pleasure sweeping through her. And so she closed her eyes again to enjoy her body, because for the first time in her life her body was taking pleasure in the absence of the soul, which, imagining nothing, remembering nothing, had quietly left the room.

17

This is what Papa told me when I was five years old: in music every key is a small royal court. The king (the first step of the scale) exercises power with the help of two princes (the fifth and fourth steps). Under their orders are four other dignitaries, each with his own special relation to the king and princes. The court also takes in five other tones, which are called chromatic. They of course occupy first-rank positions in other keys, but here they are only guests.

Because each of the twelve tones has its own position, title, and function, any piece of music we hear is more than just a mass of sound: it is an action developing before us. Sometimes the events are terribly tangled (as in Mahler or still more in Bartók or Stravinsky), with princes from several courts intervening and soon you no longer know which tone is serving which court or if it isn't serving several kings at once. But even then, the most naïve listener can still make a rough guess about what is going on. Even the most complex music is still speaking the *same language*.

That is what Papa told me, and what follows is all my own: one day, a great man saw that after a thousand years the language of music had worn itself out and could only keep on repeating the same old messages. By revolutionary decree he abolished the hierarchy of tones and made them all equal. He imposed a strict discipline to prevent any of them from appearing in a piece more often than any other and thus from reclaiming old feudal privileges. Royal courts were abolished once and for all and replaced by a single empire based on equality and called the twelve-tone system.

Maybe the sonority of music had become more interesting than before, but listeners, accustomed for a millennium to following the keys in their royal-court intrigues, heard a sound without understanding it. Anyway, the twelve-tone empire soon disappeared. After Schoenberg came Varèse, and he abolished not only keys but tones themselves (the tones of human voices and musical instruments), replacing them with a subtle, no doubt magnificent structure of noises, but also inaugurating the history of something different based on different principles and a different language.

When Milan Hübl in my Prague studio apartment developed his reflections on the possible disappearance of the Czech people into the Russian empire, we both knew that this perhaps justified idea was beyond us, that we were talking about the *unthinkable*. Even though man himself is mortal, he can imagine neither the end of space nor of time nor of history nor of a people, for he always lives in an illusory infinitude.

Those who are fascinated by the idea of progress do not suspect that everything moving forward is at the same time bringing the end nearer and that joyous watchwords like "forward" and "farther" are the lascivious voice of death urging us to hasten to it.

(If fascination with the word "forward" has become universal, isn't it mainly because death is already speaking to us from nearby?)

When Arnold Schoenberg founded the twelve-tone empire, music was richer than ever and intoxicated with its freedom. The idea that the end could be so

near crossed no one's mind. No fatigue! No twilight!
Schoenberg was animated by the most youthful spirit
of audacity. To have chosen the only possible way forward filled him with legitimate pride. The history of
music had ended in a flowering of audacity and desire.

18

If it is true that the history of music has ended, what
is left of music? Silence?

Not at all! There is more and more music, dozens,
hundreds of times more than in its most glorious eras.
It comes out of outdoor loudspeakers, out of the
appalling sound machines in apartments and restau-
rants, out of the little transistor radios people carry in
the streets.

Schoenberg is dead, Ellington is dead, but the gui-
tar is eternal. Stereotyped harmonies, banal melodies,
and rhythms all the more insistent the more monotonous they are—that is what remains of music, that is
music's eternity. Everyone can fraternize by means of
these simple combinations of tones, for it is being itself
that through them is shouting out its jubilant "I'm
here!" There is no more boisterous, no more unani-
mous agreement than the agreement with being. About
that, Arabs join with Jews and Czechs with Russians.

Bodies toss in rhythm, drunk with their awareness that they exist. That is why no work of Beethoven's has ever been experienced with such great collective passion as this unvaryingly repetitive thrumming of guitars.

About a year before Papa's death, while we were taking our habitual walk around the block, we heard singing coming at us from all sides. The sadder people were, the more the loudspeakers played. They were inviting the occupied country to forget the bitterness of history and indulge itself in enjoying life. Papa stopped and looked up at the device the noise was coming from, and I felt he wanted to confide something very important to me. He made a great effort to concentrate, to express what he was thinking, and then, slowly and with difficulty, he said: "The stupidity of music."

What did he mean by that? Was he really trying to insult music, the passion of his life? No, I think he wanted to tell me that there exists a *primeval state of music*, a state prior to its history, a state before the first questionings, before the first reflections, before the first games with motif and theme. That primeval state of music (music without thought) mirrors the human being's inherent stupidity. It required an immense effort of heart and mind for music to rise above that essential stupidity, and it is that splendid arc over centuries of European history which has been extinguished like a skyrocket at the peak of its trajectory.

The history of music is perishable, but the idiocy of guitars is eternal. Music nowadays has returned to its primeval state. It is the state after the last questioning, after the last reflection, the state after its history.

In 1972, when Karel Klos, a Czech pop singer, left the country, Husak became fearful. He immediately wrote a personal letter to him in Frankfurt, from which, inventing not a word, I quote the following: "Dear Karel: We want nothing from you. Please come back, we will do for you whatever you wish. We will help you, you will help us. . . ."

Think about it: without batting an eye, Husak allowed the emigration of doctors, scholars, astronomers, athletes, stage directors, filmmakers, workers, engineers, architects, historians, journalists, writers, painters, but he could not bear the thought of Karel Klos leaving the country. Because Karel Klos represented music without memory, the music under which the bones of Beethoven and Ellington, the ashes of Palestrina and Schoenberg, are forever buried.

The President of Forgetting and the Idiot of Music were two of a kind. They were doing the same work. "We will help you, you will help us." Neither could manage without the other.

19

But in the tower where the wisdom of music prevails, we sometimes yearn for the monotonous rhythm of the soulless cry coming to us from outside. It is dangerous to spend all one's time with Beethoven, just as all privileged positions are dangerous.

Tamina had always been a bit ashamed of admitting she was happy with her husband. She was afraid of giving people a reason to hate her.

Now she is torn between two feelings: Love is a privilege, and all privileges are undeserved and must be paid for. It is thus for punishment that she is here on the children's island.

But that feeling soon gives way to another: The privilege of love was not only a paradise, it was also a hell. Life in love was constant tension, fear, agitation. She is here among children to gain, at last, the rewards of calm and serenity.

Until now, her sexuality had been occupied by love (I say "occupied" because sex is not love but merely a territory love takes over), and it had therefore participated in something dramatic, responsible, serious. Here among children, in the kingdom of triviality, sexual activity has reverted to become what it had originally been: a small toy for the production of physical pleasure.

Or to put it another way: sexuality freed from its *diabolic* ties to love had become a joy of *angelic* simplicity.

20

If the children's first rape of Tamina was charged with that astonishing meaning, on repetition it swiftly lost its character as a message and became a more and more empty and dirty routine.

Soon the children were quarreling among themselves. Those who were fascinated by the sexual games started to hate those who were indifferent to them. And among Tamina's lovers there was a growing hostility between those who felt they were her favorites and those who felt rejected. And all these resentments began to turn against Tamina and weigh on her.

One day when the children were bent over her naked body (they were kneeling on the bed or standing beside it, sitting astride her body or squatting at her head and between her legs), she suddenly felt a sharp pain. A child had pinched her nipple. She let out a shriek and could no longer control herself: flailing her arms, she drove them all away from her bed.

She realized the pain had been caused neither by chance nor by sensuality: one of the brats hated her and wanted to hurt her. She put an end to the intimate encounters with the children.

21

And all of a sudden there is no longer peace in the kingdom where things are light as a breeze.

They are playing hopscotch, hopping from square to square, first on the right foot, then on the left, and then on both feet at once. Tamina too is hopping. (I see her tall body among the small figures of the children, hopping, with her hair flying around her face, and heavyhearted with immense boredom.) Just now, the Canaries are shouting that she stepped on the line.

The Squirrels, of course, protest: she did not step on the line. The two teams are bent over the line, looking for Tamina's footprint. But the line drawn in the sand is blurred, and so is the mark of Tamina's sole. The matter is arguable, and the children have been screaming at one another about it for fifteen minutes, with greater and greater urgency.

Tamina now makes a fatal gesture; she raises her arms and says: "All right, I stepped on it."

The Squirrels begin to shout at Tamina that it's not true, that she's crazy, that she's lying, that she didn't step on it. But they have lost their case. Their refutations of Tamina carry no weight, and the Canaries shriek cries of victory.

The Squirrels are furious, shouting at Tamina that she is a traitor, and a boy shoves her so violently she nearly falls. She tries to hit back, and this is a signal for them to pounce on her. Tamina defends herself, she is an adult, she is strong (and filled with hatred, oh yes, she hits out at the children as if she were hitting everything she has always hated), and soon children's noses are bloody, but then a flying stone strikes her brow and Tamina staggers and clutches her bleeding head as the children move aside. There is a sudden silence, and Tamina slowly returns to the dormitory. She stretches out on her bed, determined never to take part in the games again.

22

I see Tamina standing in the middle of the dormitory filled with children in their beds. She is the center of attention. A voice from a corner shouts "Tits, tits!," then all the others join in and Tamina hears the shout become a chant: "Tits, tits, tits . . ."

What until recently had been her pride and weapon—the black hair of her groin, her beautiful breasts—were now the target of abuse. In the children's eyes, her adulthood had turned into a monstrosity: her breasts were as absurd as tumors, her hairy groin was bestial.

She was now at bay. They were pursuing her all over the island, throwing stones and pieces of wood at her. She ran away, she tried to hide, but wherever she went she heard them calling her name: "Tits, Tits, Tits, Tits . . ."

Nothing is more degrading than the strong running away from the weak. But there were too many of them. She ran and was ashamed of running.

One day, she laid an ambush. She caught three of them; one went down under her blows, and the other two started to take off. But she is too swift for them and grabs them by the hair.

And then a net lands on her, and another and another. Yes, all those volleyball nets that had been hanging very close to the ground in front of the dormitory. They had been waiting for her. The three children she had just been pummeling were decoys. And now she is trapped, twisting and turning in a tangle of string as the howling children drag her along behind them.

23

Why are these children so bad?

Come on, they're not at all bad! On the contrary, they're kindhearted and always showing friendship for one another. None of them wants Tamina for himself alone. "Look, look!" they are always shouting. Tamina is trapped in a tangle of nets, the strings ripping into her skin, and the children are pointing to her blood, tears, and grimaces of pain. They are generously offering her to one another. She has become the cement of their brotherhood.

Her misfortune is not that the children are bad but that she is beyond their world's border. Humans do not revolt against the killing of calves in slaughterhouses. Calves are outside human law, just as Tamina is outside the children's law.

It is Tamina who is filled with bitter hatred, not the children. Their desire to hurt is positive and cheerful, a desire that can rightly be called joy. They want to hurt anyone beyond their world's border only in order to exalt their own world and its law.

24

Time does its work, and all joys and diversions wear out with repetition; even hunting down Tamina. Besides, the children are not really bad. The small boy who urinated on her when she lay beneath him tangled in the volleyball nets gave her a beautiful, innocent smile a day or so later.

Tamina takes part in the games again, but now in silence. Again she hops from one square to the other, first on one foot, then on the other, and then on both feet at once. She never again will enter their world, but she is careful not to find herself outside it either. She tries to stay right on the border.

But the lull, the normality, the *modus vivendi* based on compromise, brought with them all the horror of permanence. If a while ago her life as a hunted animal made Tamina forget the existence of time and its immensity, now that the violence of the attacks had fallen away, the wasteland of time had emerged from the shadows, excruciating and crushing, much like eternity.

Yet again, please engrave this image in your memory: Tamina must hop from square to square on one foot, then on the other, and then on both feet at once, and she must consider it important whether or not she steps on a line. She must go on hopping like this day after day, bearing on her shoulders as she hops the weight of time like a cross growing heavier from day to day.

Is she still looking back? Does she think about her husband and Prague?

No. Not anymore.

25

The ghosts of monuments torn down were wandering around the platform, and the President of Forgetting was at the rostrum with a red kerchief around his neck. The children were applauding and shouting his name.

Eight years have gone by since then, but I still hear his words coming to me through the flowering apple trees.

He said "Children! You are the future!" and now I realize these words have a meaning that was not initially apparent. Children are the future not because they will one day be adults but because humanity is becoming more and more a child, because childhood is the image of the future.

He shouted "Children, never look back!" and this meant that we must never allow the future to be weighed down by memory. For children have no past, and that is the whole secret of the magical innocence of their smiles.

History is a series of ephemeral changes, while eternal values are immutable, perpetuated outside history, and have no need of memory. Husak is president of the eternal, not of the ephemeral. He is on the side of children, and children are life, and living is "seeing, hearing, touching, drinking, eating, urinating, defecating, diving into the water and gazing at the sky, laughing and crying."

What appears to have happened after Husak finished his speech to the children (I had closed the window by then, and Papa was preparing to remount his horse) was that Karel Klos came out onto the platform and started to sing. This brought tears of emotion streaming down Husak's cheeks, and the sunny smiles shining everywhere were refracted in his tears. And just then a great miracle of a rainbow drew its curve over Prague.

Looking up at the rainbow, the children began to laugh and applaud.

The Idiot of Music finished his song, and the President of Forgetting spread his arms and shouted: "Children, 'living is being happy!'"

26

The island resounds with the shouting of a song and the din of electric guitars. A tape recorder has been set down on the play area in front of the dormitory. Standing over it is a boy who looks to Tamina like the boatman with whom she long ago came to the island. She is on the alert. If he is indeed the boatman, the boat must be here. She knows that she must not let this opportunity go by. Her heart is pounding, and all she can think of from now on is how to escape.

The boy is staring down at the tape recorder and wiggling his hips. Children come running to the play area to join him: flinging now one arm, now the other, forward, they throw their heads back and wave their hands, pointing their index fingers as if threatening someone, and shout along with the song coming from the tape recorder.

Tamina is hiding behind the thick trunk of a plane tree, unwilling to let them see her but unable to take her eyes off them. They are behaving with the provocative flirtatiousness of adults, thrusting their hips back and forth as if imitating coition. The obscenity of the motions superimposed on the children's bodies does away with the opposition between obscenity and innocence, purity and vileness. Sensuality becomes absurd, innocence becomes absurd, vocabulary decomposes, and Tamina feels nausea: as if her stomach were hollow.

The idiocy of the guitars keeps resounding, and the

children keep dancing, flirtatiously throwing their bellies forward, and she feels the nausea that emanates from weightless things. That hollowness in her stomach is exactly that unbearable absence of weight. And just as an extreme can at any moment turn into its opposite, so lightness brought to its maximum becomes the terrifying *weight of lightness,* and Tamina knows she cannot bear it for another moment. She turns around and starts to run.

She takes the plane-tree lane down to the water.

Now she is at its edge. She looks around. There is no boat.

As she did on the first day, she runs along the entire shore of the island, looking for the boat. She does not see it. Finally she comes back to the spot where the lane meets the beach. The children are excitedly running down it.

She stops.

The children notice her and rush toward her, shouting.

27

She dived into the water.

It was not because she was afraid. She had been thinking about it for a long time. After all, the crossing to the island by boat had not taken very long. Although the opposite shore was not visible, she would not need superhuman strength to swim to it!

Shouting, the children rushed to the spot where she had dived in, and some stones hit the water around her. But she swam fast and was soon beyond the range of their feeble arms.

Swimming, she felt well for the first time in a very long time. She could feel her body, feel her old strength. She had always been an excellent swimmer and was enjoying her every stroke. The water was cold, but she delighted in its chilliness, which seemed to be washing her skin of all the children's filth, of their saliva and their stares.

She swam for a long time, and the sun began to sink slowly into the water.

Then the darkness deepened, and soon it was pitch black, with no moon or stars, and Tamina did her best to keep heading in the same direction.

28

Just where was she trying to go back to? Prague?

She had even forgotten it existed.

To the small town in the west of Europe?

No. She simply wanted to go away.

Does that mean she wished to die?

No, no, not at all. On the contrary, she had a terrific desire to live.

Then she must have had some idea about the world she wanted to live in!

She had none. All she had left was a tremendous craving for life, and her body. Nothing but these two things, nothing more. She wanted to tear them away from the island and save them. Her body and that craving for life.

29

Day was breaking. She squinted to catch sight of the shore ahead.

But there was nothing in front of her, nothing but water. She turned and looked back. Not very far, barely one hundred meters away, was the shore of the green island.

What? Had she been swimming in place all night? Distress overcame her, and from the moment she lost hope her limbs were weak and the water was unbearably icy. She closed her eyes and tried to continue swimming. She no longer counted on reaching the other side, all she could think of now was her death, and she wanted to die somewhere midwater, far from all contact, alone with nothing but the fish. Her eyes closed, and she dozed off for an instant, getting water in her lungs, and in the midst of coughing and choking she suddenly heard children's voices.

Treading water, she coughed and looked around. Just a few strokes away was a boat loaded with children. They were shouting. When they noticed she had seen them, they fell silent. They came nearer, their eyes fixed on her. She saw how agitated they were.

She was afraid they would try to save her and make her play with them again. She felt exhaustion and a numbness in her limbs.

The boat was very near, and five children's faces were eagerly inclined over her.

Tamina shook her head desperately, as if to say, Let me die, don't save me.

But she had no reason to be afraid. The children were making no move, no one was offering an oar or a hand, no one was trying to save her. They were just staring at her, wide-eyed and eager, watching her. One of the boys used his oar as a rudder to keep the boat close by.

Water again got into her lungs, and she coughed and thrashed her arms, feeling she could no longer stay afloat. Her legs were getting heavier and heavier. They were dragging her down like weights.

Her head went under. With violent motions, she managed to raise it several times; each time, she saw the boat and the children's eyes watching her.

Then she vanished beneath the surface.

(Quotations on page 257 are from Annie Leclerc, *Parole de femme*, 1976.)

PART SEVEN

The Border

1

What he always found most interesting about a woman while making love was her face. The movements of the two bodies seemed to be unwinding a large reel of film, projecting on the woman's face, as on a television screen, a captivating movie filled with turmoil, expectations, explosions, pain, cries, emotion, and evil. But Edwige's face remained a blank screen, and Jan would stare at it, tormented by questions he could find no answers to: Was she bored with him? Was she tired? Was she making love reluctantly? Was she used to better lovers? Or was she, behind that immobile face, hiding sensations he had no inkling of?

Of course he could have asked her. But something uncommon had happened to them. Although they had always been talkative and open with each other, they would both lose the power of speech once their naked bodies embraced each other.

He had never quite known how to understand that silence. Maybe it was because, lovemaking aside, Edwige was always more enterprising than he. Even though she was younger, she had already uttered at least three times as many words and dispensed ten times as much instruction and advice. She was like a wise and tender mother taking him by the hand and guiding him through life.

He often imagined breathing obscene words into her ear while making love. But even in these reveries the venture ended in failure. He was certain that a tranquil smile of reproach and indulgent fondness would dawn on her face, the smile of a mother seeing her little boy filch a forbidden cookie from the cupboard.

Or he imagined whispering the greatest banality of all: "Do you like that?" With other women, this simple query always sounded depraved. By giving an act of love the respectable name "that," he would immediately awaken the desire for other words, words that would reflect physical love as in a hall of mirrors. But he seemed to know Edwige's response in advance: Of course I like that, she would tell him patiently. Do you think I would willingly do something I don't like? Be a bit logical, Jan!

And so he neither said obscene words nor asked her whether she liked that. He remained silent while their bodies moved long and vigorously, unwinding a reel with no film.

He often reflected that he was the one to blame for their nights in silence. He had contrived a caricature of Edwige as lover that now stood as a barrier between them, preventing him from reaching the real Edwige, her senses and her shrouded obsceneness. Anyway, after each of their nights in silence, he resolved not to make love to her the next time. He loved her as an intelligent, faithful, irreplaceable friend, not as a mistress. But it was impossible to separate mistress from friend. Each time he came to see her, they would talk about things late into the night, Edwige would drink, develop theories, give instruction, and finally, when Jan was dead tired, she would suddenly fall silent and a tranquil, blissful smile would appear on her face. Then, as if submitting to an irresistible suggestion, Jan would touch her breast, and she would stand up and start to undress.

Why does she want to make love with me? he often wondered, but could find no answer. All he knew was that their silent coitions were inescapable, just as it is inescapable that a citizen will stand at attention when he hears the national anthem, though surely neither he nor his country derives any pleasure from it.

2

During the last two hundred years the blackbird has abandoned the woods to become a city bird. First in Great Britain at the end of the eighteenth century, then several decades later in Paris and the Ruhr Valley. Throughout the nineteenth century it conquered the cities of Europe one after the other. It settled in Vienna and Prague around 1900, then spread eastward to Budapest, Belgrade, Istanbul.

From the planet's viewpoint, the blackbird's invasion of the human world is certainly more important than the Spanish invasion of South America or the return to Palestine of the Jews. A shift in the relationships among the various kinds of creation (fish, birds, humans, plants) is a shift of a higher order than changes in relations among various groups of the same kind. Whether Celts or Slavs inhabit Bohemia, whether Romanians or Russians conquer Bessarabia, is more or less the same to the earth. But when the blackbird betrayed nature to follow humans into their artificial, unnatural world, something changed in the organic structure of the planet.

And yet no one dares to interpret the last two centuries as the history of the invasion of man's cities by the blackbird. All of us are prisoners of a rigid conception of what is important and what is not, and so we fasten our anxious gaze on the important, while from a hiding place behind our backs the unimportant wages its guerrilla war, which will end in surreptitiously changing the world and pouncing on us by surprise.

If someone were to write Jan's biography, he might sum up the period I am talking about by saying something like this: His affair with Edwige marked a new stage in the life of the forty-five-year-old Jan. Renouncing at last his desultory and empty way of life, he decided to leave the town in the west of Europe and devote himself with renewed energy to important work in the United States, with which he then attained, etc., etc.

But how would Jan's imaginary biographer explain to me why Jan's favorite book just then was that novel of antiquity *Daphnis and Chloe*? The love of two young people, nearly children still, who know nothing about physical love. The bleating of a ram mingles with the sound of the sea, and a sheep grazes in the shade of an olive tree. The two young people lie naked side by side, filled with an immense, vague desire. They embrace, press against each other, are closely entwined. They stay this way for a long, long time, not knowing what more to do. They think that this embrace is the beginning and end of love's pleasures. They are aroused, their hearts are pounding, but they do not know what it is to make love.

Yes, it is this passage that fascinates Jan.

3

Hanna the actress sat with her legs crossed under her like the Buddha statues for sale in all the world's antique shops. She talked nonstop as she intently watched her thumb slowly going round and round along the edge of the pedestal table next to the couch.

It was not the mechanical gesture of a nervous person habitually tapping his foot or scratching his head. It was the conscious and deliberate, lithe and graceful gesture of tracing around herself a magic circle within which she could concentrate entirely on herself and the others could concentrate on her.

She followed the course of her thumb with delight, only occasionally looking up at Jan, who sat facing her. She was telling him she had just been through a nervous breakdown because her son, who lived with her former husband, had run away and been gone for several days. Her son's father was such a brute he telephoned her with the news half an hour before she went onstage. Hanna had come down with a temperature, headaches, and a head cold. "I had so much trouble with my nose I couldn't even blow it!" she said, fastening her big, beautiful eyes on Jan. "My nose was like a cauliflower!"

She had the smile of a woman who knows that on her, even a red nose is charming. She lived in exemplary harmony with herself. She loved her nose, and she also loved the audacity with which she called a cold a cold and a nose a cauliflower. The unconventional beauty of her red nose thus complemented her intellectual audacity, and the circular course of her thumb, mingling the two charms within its magic circumference, expressed the indivisible unity of her personality.

"I was worried about the high fever. Do you know what my doctor said? 'I have only one piece of advice for you, Hanna: Don't take your temperature!'"

Hanna laughed loud and long at her doctor's joke, and then said: "Do you know who I met? Passer!"

Passer was an old friend of Jan's. When Jan saw him last, several months before, he was about to have an operation. Everyone knew he had cancer, everyone but Passer himself, who, filled with amazing vitality and credulity, believed the doctors' lies. In any event, the operation was a very serious one, and when they were alone he said to Jan: "After that operation, you understand, I won't be a man anymore. My life as a man is over."

"I met him last week at the Clevises' country house," Hanna went on. "What a fantastic character! He's younger than any of us! I adore him!"

Jan should have been delighted to learn that his friend was adored by the beautiful actress, but it made no particular impression on him because everyone loved Passer. In recent years, his shares had risen sharply on the irrational stock exchange of social popularity. It had become almost a ritual, during desultory dinner-party conversations in town, to devote some admiring words to Passer.

"You know those beautiful woods around the Clevises' house? They're filled with mushrooms, and I adore hunting mushrooms! When I asked who wanted to go mushroom hunting with me, no one wanted to, only Passer, who said: 'I'll come with you!' Imagine that, Passer, a sick man! I tell you, he's younger than any of us!"

She looked down at her thumb, which not for an instant stopped circling along the edge of the pedestal table, and said: "So I went picking mushrooms with Passer. It was wonderful! We got lost in the woods and then we found a café. A grimy little country café. The kind I adore. In places like that you drink cheap red wine like the regulars. Passer was magnificent. I adore him!"

4

At that time the beaches in the west of Europe were covered in summer with women who wore no tops to their bathing suits, and the population was divided between partisans and adversaries of bare breasts. The Clevis family—father, mother, and fourteen-year-old daughter—sat in front of the television set, watching a debate in which representatives of every intellectual current of the day developed their arguments for and against tops. The psychoanalyst fervently defended bare breasts and spoke of the liberation from convention that has delivered us from the omnipotence of erotic fantasies. The Marxist, without giving a verdict on toplessness (the Communist Party had both puritans and libertines among its members, and it was impolitic to take either side), cleverly diverted the debate to the more basic problem of the hypocritical morality of bourgeois society, which was doomed. The representative of Christian thinking felt obliged to defend the top, but he did it very timidly, because he too could not escape the omnipresent spirit of the time; he could find only one argument in the top's favor, the innocence of children, which everyone had the duty to respect and protect. He was taken to task by an energetic woman who declared that getting rid of the hypocritical taboo against nudity should begin in childhood and recommended that parents walk around the house naked.

Jan arrived at the Clevises' just as the woman moderator was ending the debate, but the enthusiasm it had generated persisted in the apartment for quite a while. The Clevises were forward-looking people and therefore against tops. To them, the imposing gesture of millions of women throwing away that infamous piece of clothing as if on command symbolized humanity shaking off the bonds of slavery. Bare-breasted women paraded through the Clevises' apartment like an invisible battalion of liberators.

As I have said, the Clevises were forward-looking, and they held progressive ideas. There are many kinds of progressive ideas, and the Clevises always supported the best possible progressive ideas. The best progressive ideas are those that include a strong enough dose of provocation to make its supporters feel proud of being original, but at the same time attract so many adherents that the risk of being an isolated exception is immediately averted by the noisy approval of a triumphant crowd. If, for instance, the Clevises were not only against tops but against clothing in general, if they announced that people should walk the city streets naked, they would surely still be supporting a progressive idea, but certainly not the best possible one. That idea would be embarrassing because there is something excessive about it, it would take too much energy to defend (while the best possible progressive idea, so to speak, defends itself), and its supporters would never have the satisfaction of seeing their thoroughly nonconformist position suddenly become everyone's position.

Listening to them fulminate against tops, Jan remembered the small wooden instrument called a level that his grandfather, a bricklayer, would place on the top layer of a wall under construction. At the center of the instrument was a glass tube of liquid with an air bubble whose position indicated whether the row of bricks was horizontal or not. The Clevis family could serve as an intellectual air bubble. Placed on some idea or other, it would indicate precisely whether or not that was the best progressive idea possible.

When the Clevises, talking all at once, had repeated to Jan the whole of the television debate, Papa Clevis leaned over to him and said banteringly: "Don't you think that, as long as the breasts are good-looking, this is a reform one can easily approve of?"

Why did Papa Clevis express his thinking in such terms? He was a perfect host and always tried to find remarks suitable to all those present. Since Jan had the reputation of a womanizer, Clevis formulated his approval of bare breasts not in terms of its right and profound meaning, that is, as an *ethical* enthusiasm for the abolition of an age-old servitude, but in the way of a compromise (with regard for Jan's supposed tastes and contrary to his own convictions), as an *aesthetic* agreement on the beauty of breasts.

At the same time, he was trying to be as precise and prudent as a diplomat: he did not dare say straight out that ugly breasts should remain hidden. Yet, without it being said, that absolutely unacceptable idea followed all too clearly from his spoken words and was an easy target for the fourteen-year-old.

"And what about your stomachs? What about those huge bellies you're always shamelessly parading around the beaches!"

Mama Clevis burst into laughter and applauded her daughter: "Bravo!"

Papa Clevis joined in the applause. He immediately understood that his daughter was right and that he had once again fallen victim to the unfortunate propensity for compromise his wife and daughter always reproached him for. He was a man so deeply conciliatory that he defended his moderate opinions with great moderation and immediately agreed with his extremist child. Moreover, the incriminatory words expressed not his own thinking but rather Jan's supposed viewpoint; so he could readily stand by his daughter, unhesitatingly and with paternal satisfaction.

Encouraged by her parents' applause, the girl went on: "Do you think we take off our tops to give you pleasure? We do it for ourselves, because we like it, because it feels better, because it brings our bodies nearer the sun! You're only capable of seeing us as sex objects!"

Again Papa and Mama Clevis applauded, but this time their bravos had a somewhat different tone. Their daughter's words were indeed right, but also somewhat inappropriate for a fourteen-year-old. It was like an eight-year-old boy saying: "If there's a holdup, Mama, I'll defend you." Then too the parents applaud, because their son's statement is clearly praiseworthy. But since it also shows excessive self-assurance, the praise is rightly shaded by a certain smile. With such a smile the Clevis parents had tinged their second bravos, and their daughter, who had heard that smile in their voices and did not approve of it, repeated with irritated obstinacy: "That's over and done with. I'm not anybody's sex object."

Without smiling, the parents merely nodded, not wanting to incite their daughter any further.

Jan, however, could not resist saying:

"My dear girl, if you only knew how easy it is not to be a sex object."

He uttered these words softly, but with such sincere sorrow that they resounded in the room for a long while. They were words difficult to pass over in silence, but it was not possible to respond to them either. They did not deserve approval, not being progressive, but neither did they deserve an argument, because they were not obviously against progress. They were the worst words possible, because they were situated outside the debate conducted by the spirit of the time. They were words beyond good and evil, perfectly incongruous words.

There was a pause during which Jan smiled an embarrassed smile as if to apologize for what he had said, and then Papa Clevis, past master of the art of bridging gaps between his fellow creatures, started to talk about Passer, their friend in common. They were united in their admiration for Passer: it was safe terrain. Clevis praised Passer's optimism, his steadfast love of life that no medical regimen had managed to stifle. And now Passer's existence was limited to a narrow strip of life without women, without food, without alcohol, without mobility, and without a future. He had recently visited them in their country house, when the actress Hanna had been there too.

Jan was very curious to see what the Clevises' level would indicate if it was placed on the actress Hanna, in whom he saw the symptoms of a nearly unbearable egocentricity. But the air bubble indicated that Jan had guessed wrong. Clevis completely approved of the way the actress had behaved with Passer. She had devoted herself only to him. It was extremely generous of her. And yet everyone knew what a tragedy she had just been living through.

"What tragedy?" asked forgetful Jan with surprise.

How's that—hadn't Jan heard? Hanna's son had run away and been gone for several days! She had a nervous breakdown! But with Passer, who is at death's door, she no longer thought of herself at all. Trying to tear him away from his cares, she cheerfully cried out: "I'd so love to go mushroom hunting! Who wants to go with me?" Passer said he would, and the others refused to accompany them because it was thought he wanted to be alone with her. They walked around in the woods for three hours before stopping in a café to drink red wine. Passer had been forbidden both to walk and to drink. He came back exhausted but happy. The next day he had to be taken to the hospital.

"I think it's quite serious," said Papa Clevis, and then, as if in reproach, he added: "You'd better go see him."

5

Jan said to himself: At the beginning of one's erotic life, there is arousal without climax, and at the end there is climax without arousal.

Arousal without climax is Daphnis. Climax without arousal is the salesgirl at the sporting goods rental shop.

A year ago, when he first met her and invited her to his place, she made an unforgettable statement: "If we make love, I'm sure it'll be very good technically, but I'm not certain about the emotional side."

He told her that as far as he was concerned, she could be absolutely sure about the emotional side, and she accepted that assurance just as she routinely accepted deposits for ski rentals at the shop, and never breathed a word about emotions again. As for the technical side, she literally wore him out.

She was an orgasm fanatic. Orgasms were a religion to her, a goal, the highest requirement of hygiene, a symbol of health, but they were also a source of pride, a means of distinguishing her from less fortunate women, like having a yacht or a famous fiancé.

But it was not easy to give her one. She would shout "Faster, faster" at him, then, on the contrary, "Gently, gently," and then, again, "Harder, harder," like a coxswain shouting orders to the crew of a racing shell. Concentrating entirely on the sensitive areas of her skin, she would guide his hand to the right place at the right time. In a sweat, he would see the impatient expression in the young woman's eye and the feverish movements of her body, that portable apparatus for producing the little explosion which was the meaning and goal of everything.

When he was leaving her place for the very last time, Jan thought of Hertz, the opera director in the Central European city where he had spent his youth. Hertz required the women singers to perform their entire roles naked for him at special stage-business rehearsals. To check the positions of their bodies, he compelled them to insert pencils into their rectums. The pencil pointed downward as an extension of the spinal column, enabling the painstaking director to control every step and movement, the entire gait and bearing of the singer's body, with scientific precision.

One day, a young soprano got into an argument with him and denounced him to the management. Hertz defended himself by saying he had never made advances to the singers, that he had never laid a hand on any of them. That was true, but it made the pencil trick seem even more depraved, and Hertz had to leave Jan's native city in disgrace.

His misfortune became famous, and because of it, Jan began as a very young man to go to the opera. Watching the women singers' affecting gestures as they tilted their heads back and opened their mouths wide, he would imagine all of them naked. The orchestra moaned, the singers grasped their left breasts, and he would imagine the pencils sticking out of their naked rumps. His heart would pound: he was aroused by Hertz's arousal! (To this day, he is unable to see an opera in any other way, to this day, he sees it with the feelings of a very young man slipping secretly into a porn theater.)

Jan said to himself: Hertz was a sublime alchemist of vice who found the magic formula for arousal in a pencil stuck up the behind. And he felt ashamed before him: Hertz would never have let himself be constrained into the hard labor Jan had just been obediently doing on the body of the sporting goods rental shop salesgirl.

6

Just as the blackbird invasion took place on the reverse side of Europe's history, so my story takes place on the reverse side of Jan's life. I am putting it together from isolated events Jan probably did not pay particular attention to, because the obverse side of his life at the time was taken up by other events and worries: the offer of a new position in the United States, feverish professional work, preparations for departure.

Recently he ran into Barbara on the street. She asked him reproachfully why he never came to her house when she was receiving. Barbara's house is famous for its collective sex entertainments. Jan dreads malicious gossip and has rejected her invitations for years. But this time he smiles and says: "Yes, I'll be glad to come." He knows he will never return to that town again, so discretion no longer matters. He imagines Barbara's house, filled with cheerful naked people, and says to himself that it would, after all, not be such a bad way to celebrate his departure.

For Jan is about to go. In a few months he will be crossing the border. And when he thinks of that, the word "border" in its common geographical sense reminds him of another border, an intangible and immaterial border he has been thinking of more and more for some time now.

What border is that?

The woman he had loved most (he was thirty at the time) would tell him (he was nearly in despair when he heard it) that she held on to life by a thread. Yes, she did want to live, life gave her great joy, but she also knew that her "I want to live" was spun from the threads of a spiderweb. It takes so little, so infinitely little, for someone to find himself on the other side of the border, where everything—love, convictions, faith, history—no longer has meaning. The whole mystery of human life resides in the fact that it is spent in the immediate proximity of, and even in direct contact with, that border, that it is separated from it not by kilometers but by barely a millimeter.

7

Every man has two erotic biographies. The first is the one people mainly talk about, the one consisting of a list of affairs and passing amours.

The other biography is undoubtedly more interesting: the procession of women we wanted to have but who eluded us, the painful history of unrealized possibilities.

But there is also a third, a mysterious and disturbing category of women. These are women we liked and were liked by, but women we quickly saw we would never have, because in relation to them we were *on the other side of the border*.

Jan was on a train, reading. A young, beautiful woman he did not know sat down in his compartment (the only vacant seat was just opposite him) and nodded to him. He nodded back, trying to remember where he knew her from. Then he returned to his book, but could hardly read it. He felt the young woman gazing at him curiously and expectantly.

He closed his book: "Where do I know you from?"

It was no place special. They had met, she told him, five years before, in the company of mutual acquaintances. Recalling that time, he asked her some questions: what exactly had she been doing then, who had her friends been, where was she working now, was her work interesting?

He always knew how to strike a spark swiftly between himself and any woman. But this time he had the unpleasant feeling of sounding like someone in the personnel department interviewing a woman applying for a job.

He stopped talking. He reopened his book and tried to read, but felt he was being observed by an invisible board of examiners who had his complete file and were always watching him. He stared reluctantly at the pages with no idea of what was on them, knowing that the board was patiently noting the number of minutes he kept silent as part of its calculation of his final grade.

Again he closed the book and again he tried to start a conversation with the young woman, this time in a lighter manner, and again he realized that it was getting him nowhere.

Which led him to think that his failure was caused by the compartment's lack of privacy. So he invited the young woman to join him in the dining car, where they found a table for two. He talked with greater ease there; but there too he was unable to strike a spark.

They went back to the compartment. He reopened his book, but just as before, he had no idea what was in it.

For a while the young woman remained seated opposite him, then she got up and went into the corridor to look out the window.

He was terribly annoyed. He liked the young woman, and her departure was merely an unspoken summons.

At the last possible moment, he tried one more time to save the situation. He went out into the corridor and stood next to her. He told her he had probably not recognized her because she had changed her hairstyle. He pushed the hair back from her brow and gazed at her suddenly different face.

"Yes, now I recognize you," he said. Of course, he didn't recognize her. But that wasn't what mattered. What he wanted was to press his hand firmly against the top of her skull, gently push her head back, and then gaze into her eyes.

How many times in his life had he put his hand on a woman's head and said: "Let's see how you'd look like this"? That imperious touch and sovereign gaze would at once reverse an entire situation. It was as if they contained in germ (and retrieved from the future) the great scene of his full possession of her.

But this time his gesture had no effect. His own gaze was much weaker than the gaze he felt on him, the dubious gaze of the board of examiners, which knew full well that he was repeating himself and informed him that all repetition was mere imitation and all imitation was worthless. Jan suddenly saw himself through the young woman's eyes. He saw the pitiful pantomime of his gaze and gesture, that stereotyped gesticulation emptied of all meaning by years of repetition. Having lost its spontaneity, its natural, immediate meaning, his gesture suddenly made him unbearably weary, as if six-kilo weights had been attached to his wrists. The young woman's gaze created an odd field around him, increasing the weight tenfold.

He had no way of continuing. He let go of the young woman's head and looked out the window at the gardens passing by.

The train reached its destination. As they were leaving the railroad station, she told Jan she lived nearby and invited him over.

He refused.

And then he thought about it for weeks: how could he have turned down a woman he liked?

In his relation to her he was on the other side of the border.

8

The gaze of a man has often been described. It seems to fasten coldly on the woman, as if it were measuring, weighing, evaluating, choosing her, as if, in other words, it were turning her into a thing.

Less well known is that a woman is not entirely defenseless against that gaze. If she is turned into a thing, then she watches the man with the gaze of a thing. It is as if a hammer suddenly had eyes and watched the carpenter grip it to drive in a nail. Seeing the hammer's malicious gaze, the carpenter loses his self-confidence and hits his thumb.

The carpenter is the hammer's master, yet it is the hammer that has the advantage over the carpenter, because a tool knows exactly how it should be handled, while the one who handles it can only know approximately how.

The ability to gaze turns the hammer into a living being, but a good carpenter must bear its insolent gaze and, with a firm hand, turn it back into a thing. It would seem then that a woman undergoes a cosmic movement upward and then downward: the flight of a thing mutating into a creature and the fall of a creature mutating into a thing.

But it happened to Jan more and more frequently that the carpenter-hammer game was no longer playable. Women gazed badly. They spoiled the game. Was it because at this time they had begun to organize and resolve to transform women's age-old condition? Or was it because Jan was getting older and seeing women and their gaze differently? Was the world changing or was he?

It was hard to say. The fact remains that the young woman on the train looked him up and down with eyes filled with distrust and doubt, and that he let go of the hammer without taking the time even to raise it.

Recently he had run into Pascal, who complained to him about Barbara. Barbara had invited him over. He found two girls there he did not know. They chatted for a while, and then Barbara abruptly went into the kitchen and brought back a big tin-plated old alarm clock. Without a word she started to undress, and the two girls did the same.

Pascal moaned: "You have to realize they undressed nonchalantly, indifferently, as if I were just a dog or a flowerpot."

Then Barbara had ordered him to get undressed too. Not wanting to lose the opportunity to make love to two new girls, he obeyed. When he was naked, Barbara held up the alarm clock: "Look at the second hand. If you don't get a hard-on within a minute, you'll have to leave!"

"They stared at my crotch, and while the seconds ticked away, they started laughing! And then they threw me out!"

It was a case of the hammer deciding to castrate the carpenter.

"You know Pascal's a boor, and I secretly sympathized with Barbara's punitive commandos," Jan told Edwige. "Besides, Pascal and his pals have done things to girls much like what Barbara did to him. Once, a girl went to his place ready to make love, and they undressed her and tied her to the bed. She didn't mind being tied up, that was part of the game. What's scandalous is that they didn't do anything to her, didn't even touch her, they just examined her from every angle. The girl felt she had been raped."

"That's quite understandable," said Edwige.

"But I can easily imagine those two girls getting aroused by being bound up and eyed. In a similar situation, Pascal wasn't aroused. He was castrated."

It was late in the evening, they were at Edwige's, and a half-empty whisky bottle was on the coffee table in front of them. "What do you mean by that?" she asked.

"What I mean," said Jan, "is that when a man and a woman do the same thing, it's not the same thing. The man rapes, the woman castrates."

"What you mean is that it's vile to castrate a man but a fine thing to rape a woman."

"All I mean," replied Jan, "is that rape is part of eroticism, but castration is its negation."

Edwige emptied her glass in one gulp and responded angrily: "If rape is part of eroticism, then eroticism as a whole is directed against women and it's necessary to invent another kind."

Jan took a sip, was silent for a moment, and then went on: "Many years ago, in my former country, some friends and I put together an anthology of things our mistresses said while making love. Do you know what word came up most often?"

Edwige did not know.

"The word 'no.' The word 'no' repeated in succession: 'No, no, no, no, no, no, no . . .' The girl arrives to make love, but when the boy takes her in his arms, she pushes him away and says 'No,' giving the act of love the red glow of that most beautiful word and turning it into a miniature imitation rape. Even when they're approaching climax, they say 'No, no, no, no, no,' and many of them shout 'No' in the midst of it. Since then, 'no' has been a royal word for me. And what about you, were you in the habit of saying 'No'?"

Edwige replied that she never said "No." Why say something she didn't mean? "'When a woman says "No," she really means "Yes."' That male aphorism has always outraged me. It's as stupid as all human history."

"But that history is inside us, and we can't escape it," replied Jan. "A woman fleeing and defending herself. A woman giving herself, a man taking. A woman veiling herself, a man tearing off her clothes. These are age-old images we carry within us!"

"Age-old and idiotic! As idiotic as the holy images! And what if women are starting to be fed up with having to behave according to that pattern? What if that eternal repetition nauseates them? What if they want to invent other images and another game?"

"Yes, they're stupid images stupidly repeated. You're entirely right. But what if our desire for the female body depends on precisely those stupid images and on them alone? If those stupid old images were to be destroyed in us, would men still be able to make love to women?"

Edwige broke into laughter: "I don't think you need to worry."

Then she fixed her motherly look on him: "And you shouldn't imagine all men are like you. How can you know what men are like when they're alone with a woman?"

Jan really didn't know what men were like when they were alone with a woman. In the ensuing silence Edwige's face took on the blissful smile that indicated it was getting late, that the time was coming for Jan to unwind the empty film reel on her body.

After an instant's reflection, she added: "Ultimately, making love isn't that important."

Jan's ears pricked up: "You don't think making love is that important?"

She smiled at him tenderly: "No, making love is not that important."

In a moment, he completely forgot what they had been discussing, because he had just learned something that mattered much more: for Edwige, physical love was merely a sign, merely a symbolic act that confirms friendship.

That evening he dared for the first time to say he was tired. He lay down on the bed next to her like a chaste friend, letting the reel remain motionless. As he caressed her hair, he saw a reassuring rainbow of peace arching over their future together.

9

Ten years earlier, Jan had received visits from a married woman. They had known each other for years but very rarely saw each other because the woman had a job, and even when she freed herself to see him, they had no time to lose. She would first sit down in an armchair and they would chat for a moment, but only a moment. Soon Jan had to get up, come over to her, give her a kiss, and lift her into his arms.

Then he would release her from his embrace and they would separate a bit and hastily start to undress. Jan threw his jacket on a chair. She pulled off her sweater and put it over the back of the chair. He unbuttoned his trousers and let them drop. She leaned forward and began to remove her panty hose. They were in a hurry. They stood face to face, leaning forward, Jan lifting one and then the other foot out of his trousers (he would raise his legs very high, like a parading soldier), she bending to gather the panty hose at her ankles, then as she extricated her legs raising them toward the ceiling, just as he did.

It was the same each time, but one day a tiny, insignificant event occurred that he never forgot: She looked at him and was unable to hold back a smile. It was a nearly tender smile, filled with fondness and understanding, a shy smile that sought to forgive itself, but a smile unquestionably created by the glare of ridiculousness that had suddenly flooded the entire scene. He had great difficulty restraining himself from returning that smile. For he too saw, emerging from the shadow of habit, the unexpected ridiculousness of two people facing each other and with odd haste raising their legs very high. He realized he was only a hairsbreadth from bursting into laughter. But he knew that if he did, they would no longer be able to make love. Laughter was there like an enormous trap waiting patiently in the room, hidden behind a thin, invisible partition. Only a few millimeters separated physical love from laughter, and he dreaded crossing over them. Only a few millimeters separated him from the other side of the border, where things no longer have meaning.

He restrained himself. He held back the smile, dropped his trousers, and quickly moved toward his lover, to touch the body whose warmth would drive away the devil of laughter.

10

Passer's condition, he learned, had gotten worse. Only morphine injections were keeping him going, and he felt well only a few hours a day. Jan took a train to visit him at the faraway clinic, reproaching himself during the journey for having gone so seldom. It was frightening to see how Passer had aged. A few silvery strands delineated on top of his skull the same wavy curve delineated not so long ago by his thick brown hair. His face was only a memory of his former face.

Passer greeted him with his usual exuberance. He took him by the arm and energetically steered him into his room, where they sat down on either side of a table.

When Jan long ago first met him, Passer had spoken about humanity's great hopes, pounding the table with his fist as his huge eyes gleamed with endless enthusiasm. Now he spoke not about the hopes of humanity but about the hopes of his body. The doctors maintained that if he got through the next two weeks of intensive injections and great pain, he would beat the disease. As he said that, his fist pounded the table and his eyes gleamed. His enthusiastic account of the hopes of the body was a melancholy echo of his account of the hopes of humanity. Both enthusiasms were equally illusory, and Passer's gleaming eyes shed an equally magical light on both.

Then he started to talk about Hanna the actress. With shy masculine modesty, he confessed to Jan that for one last time he had gone totally mad. Mad over a madly beautiful woman, knowing all along that it was the most insane of all possible lunacies. Eyes gleaming, he talked about walking in the woods with her and hunting for mushrooms as if they were hunting for treasure, and about the café where they stopped to drink red wine.

"Hanna was incredible! You see, she didn't play the bustling nurse, she didn't give me compassionate looks to remind me of my illness and my feebleness, no, she laughed and drank with me. We downed a liter of wine! I felt eighteen again! I was in my seat on the direct line to death, and I wanted to sing!"

Passer pounded his fist on the table and looked at Jan with his gleaming eyes, above which the vanished shock of hair was delineated by three remaining silvery strands.

Jan said that we are all seated on the direct line to death. That the whole world, which is being assailed by violence, cruelty, barbarism, was seated on that line. He said it because he loved Passer and was outraged that this man so splendidly pounding his fist on the table was dying ahead of a world so undeserving of love. He was trying hard to make the end of the world seem nearer than it was in order to make Passer's death more bearable to him. But Passer refused to accept the end of the world, he pounded his fist on the table and again began to speak about the hopes of humanity. He said that we were living in a time of great changes.

Jan had never shared Passer's admiration for things changing, but he liked his desire for change, seeing it as mankind's oldest desire, humanity's most conservative conservatism. Yet even though he liked that desire, he hoped to take it away from him, now that Passer was seated on the direct line to death. He was trying to tarnish the future in his eyes, to make him regret a little less the life he was losing.

He said to him: "Everyone says we're living in a great epoch. Clevis talks about the end of the Judeo-Christian era, others about world revolution and communism, but that's all nonsense. If our epoch is a turning point, it's for an entirely different reason."

Passer stared at him with his gleaming eyes, above which the memory of his shock of hair was delineated by three remaining silvery strands.

Jan went on: "Do you know the joke about the English lord?"

Passer pounded his fist on the table and said he didn't.

"The morning after their wedding night, he says to his bride: 'I do hope, my dear, that you are now with child. I wouldn't wish to be forced to repeat those ridiculous motions.'"

Passer smiled, but without pounding his fist on the table. It was not the kind of story that kindled his enthusiasm.

Jan went on: "Talk about world revolution! We're living in the historic epoch when the sexual act is being definitively transformed into ridiculous motions."

A delicate trace of a smile appeared on Passer's face. Jan knew that smile well. It was not a joyous or an approving smile, but a smile of tolerance. They had always been far apart in their views, and in the rare moments when their differences became too visible, they would smile that smile to assure each other that their friendship was not in danger.

11

Why does the image of the border continually occur to him?

He tells himself it is because he is getting old: When things are repeated, they lose a fraction of their meaning. Or more exactly, they lose, drop by drop, the vital strength that gives them their illusory meaning. For Jan, therefore, the border is the maximum acceptable dose of repetitions.

Once, he attended a show where, right in the middle of things, a very gifted comic actor began just like that to count very slowly and with extreme concentration: "One, two, three, four . . . ," pronouncing each of the numbers with great absorption, as if they had escaped and he was engrossed in getting them back: "five, six, seven, eight . . ." At "fifteen," the audience started to laugh, and when, slowly and with greater and greater concentration, he reached "one hundred," people were falling off their seats.

At another performance, the same actor sat down at the piano and began to play a waltz rhythm with his left hand: oom-pa-pa, oom-pa-pa. His right hand hung in the air, so there was no melody, only the same oom-pa-pa, oom-pa-pa over and over again, and he looked eloquently at the audience as if that waltz accompaniment were splendid music worthy of emotion, applause, enthusiasm. He played it again and again, twenty times, thirty times, fifty times, one hundred times the same oom-pa-pa, oom-pa-pa, and the audience was choking with laughter.

Yes, when you cross the border, laughter fatefully rings out. But what if you go still farther, go *beyond* laughter?

Jan imagines that the Greek gods at first passionately participated in the adventures of humans. Then they settled in on Olympus to look down and have a good laugh. And by now they have been asleep for a long time.

In my opinion, however, Jan is mistaken in thinking that the border is a line that crosses a man's life at a specific point, that it marks a break in time, a particular second on the clock of a human life. No. I am certain, on the contrary, that the border is constantly with us, irrespective of time and our stage of life, that it is omnipresent, even though circumstances might make it more or less visible.

The woman Jan had loved most was right to say she held on to life by a spider thread. It takes so little, a tiny puff of air, for things to shift imperceptibly, and whatever it was that a man was ready to lay down his life for a few seconds earlier seems suddenly to be sheer nonsense.

Jan had friends who like him had left their old homeland and who devoted all their time to the struggle for its lost freedom. All of them had sometimes felt that the bond tying them to their country was just an illusion and that only enduring habit kept them prepared to die for something they did not care about. They all knew that feeling and at the same time were afraid of knowing it; they turned their heads away for fear of seeing the border and stumbling (lured by vertigo as by an abyss) across it to the other side, where the language of their tortured people makes a noise as trivial as the twittering of birds.

Since Jan defines the border for himself as the maximum acceptable dose of repetitions, I am obliged to correct him: the border is not a product of repetition. Repetition is only one of the ways of making the border visible. The borderline is covered with dust, and repetition is like a hand whisking away dust.

I would like to remind Jan of a striking experience from his childhood: He was about thirteen at the time. All the talk about life on other planets led him to play with the idea that nonterrestrial creatures had more erotic areas on their bodies than we terrestrials. The thirteen-year-old, secretly arousing himself in front of a stolen photo of a naked dancer, had arrived at the feeling that terrestrial women, endowed with the overly simple trinity of one sex organ and two breasts, were erotically deprived. He dreamed of a creature with a body offering ten or twenty erotic areas instead of that impoverished triangle, a body offering the eye totally inexhaustible sources of arousal.

I am trying to say that midway through his very long journey as a virgin, he already knew what it is to be bored with the female body. Even before he ever experienced climax, he had already arrived mentally at the end of arousal. He had experienced its exhaustibility.

From childhood on, therefore, he had lived within sight of that mysterious border on the other side of which female breasts were merely soft globes hanging from the chest. That border was his lot from the very beginning. At thirteen, the Jan who dreamed of other erotic areas of the female body was as aware of it as the Jan of thirty years later.

12

It was windy and muddy. The mourners stood in an uneven semicircle in front of the open grave. Jan was there and nearly all his friends, Hanna the actress, the Clevises, Barbara, and of course the Passers: the wife and son, in tears, and the dry-eyed daughter.

The ceremony seemed to have ended, and two men in threadbare clothes were lifting the ropes the coffin rested on. Just then a nervous man with a sheet of paper in his hand came up to the grave, turned around to face the gravediggers, and, raising the sheet of paper, began to read aloud from it. Looking at him, the gravediggers hesitated for a moment, wondering whether to put the coffin back down on the ground, then began to lower it slowly into the grave, as if they had decided to spare the deceased the obligation of listening to yet a fourth speech.

The coffin's sudden disappearance disconcerted the speaker. His whole speech had been written in the second person singular. Directly addressing the deceased, it made promises to him, agreed with him, reassured him, thanked him, and answered supposed questions from him. The coffin having reached bottom, the gravediggers pulled out the ropes and remained standing humbly motionless beside the open grave. And seeing that the speaker was haranguing them with so much fire, they were intimidated and lowered their heads.

The more aware the speaker became of the incongruity of the situation, the more his attention was attracted by the two doleful men, and he nearly had to tear his eyes away from them. He turned to the semicircle of mourners. But even that did not much improve his second-person speech, because it gave the impression that the dearly departed was hiding somewhere among them.

Where should the speaker have looked? In anguish he stared at his sheet of paper, and even though he knew the text by heart, he kept his eyes riveted on it.

The entire gathering gave way to a nervousness heightened by the hysterical gusts of wind. Papa Clevis had carefully pulled his hat down over his temples, but the wind was so violent it tore it off and dropped it on the ground between the open grave and the Passer family in the first row.

Initially he wanted to slip through the gathering and dart out to pick up his hat, but that, he realized, might make it appear he thought his hat more important than the solemnity of the ceremony honoring his friend. So he decided to stand still and pretend nothing had happened. But it was not a good solution. From the moment the hat landed on the vacant ground before the grave, the gathering of mourners had become still more nervous and utterly unable to follow the speaker's words. Despite its humble immobility, the hat was disturbing the ceremony much more than Clevis would have done by taking a few steps and picking it up. So he finally said "Excuse me" to the

person in front of him and stepped forward. He now
found himself on the vacant ground (as if on a small
stage) between the mourners and the grave. Bending
down, he stretched out his arm, but just then the wind
started up again, carrying the hat a little out of his
reach and dropping it at the speaker's feet.

No one now could think of anything but Papa Clevis
and his hat. Even the speaker, who was still unaware of
the hat, felt something happening to his audience. He
raised his eyes from his sheet of paper and was amazed
to see someone standing two steps away and looking at
him as if he were getting ready to pounce. He quickly
lowered his eyes back to his text, hoping that maybe by
the time he raised them again the astonishing vision
would have vanished. But when he raised them again,
the man was still there and still looking at him.

Papa Clevis could neither advance nor retreat. He
thought it unseemly to swoop down at the speaker's
feet and ridiculous to go back without his hat. So he
just stood there, nailed to the spot by indecision, trying in vain to find a solution.

He wished someone would come to help him. He
glanced at the gravediggers. They were standing
motionless on the other side of the grave, staring at the
speaker's feet.

Just then another gust of wind sent the hat sliding
slowly toward the edge of the grave. Clevis made up
his mind. He took an energetic step forward, bent
down, and stretched out his arm. The hat slipped
away, kept slipping away, he almost had it in his

grasp, when it slid along the edge and then fell into the grave.

Clevis stretched out his arm yet again, as if beckoning the hat back, but then he suddenly resolved to act as if the hat had never existed and he had found himself at the grave's edge by some trifling chance. He tried to be totally natural and relaxed, but that was difficult with everyone staring at him. He was tense; he made an effort not to look at anyone and went over to stand in the first row, where Passer's son stood sobbing.

When the menacing specter of the man who was getting ready to pounce had vanished, the man with the sheet of paper calmed down and raised his eyes to the gathering, which no longer was hearing him at all, to pronounce the last sentence of his speech. Turning to the gravediggers, he very solemnly declared: "Victor Passer, those who loved you will never forget you. May the earth rest lightly on you!"

At the grave's edge he bent over a pile of earth with a small shovel stuck in it, picked up some earth with the shovel, and then leaned over the grave. Just then all the mourners started to shake with stifled laughter. For they all knew that the speaker, looking down paralyzed with the shovel of earth in his hand, was seeing the coffin at the bottom of the grave and the hat on top of the coffin, as if the deceased, in a futile desire for dignity, had not wanted to remain bareheaded during that solemn moment.

The speaker got himself under control and shoveled earth onto the coffin, making sure none of it landed on

the hat, as if it really were covering Passer's head.
Then he handed the shovel to the widow. Yes, they all
had to drink the chalice of temptation to the dregs.
They all had to live through the horrifying battle
against laughter. They all, including the wife and the
sobbing son, had to pick up some earth with the shovel
and lean over the grave, where there was a coffin with
a hat on it, as if Passer, with his indomitable vitality
and optimism, was trying to stick his head out.

13

About twenty people had gathered at Barbara's villa.
They were sitting in the large living room, on the
couch, in armchairs, on the floor. In the middle of the
room, within a circle of not very attentive onlookers, a
girl who apparently came from a provincial town was
twisting and turning in every possible way.

Barbara sat enthroned in a huge plush armchair.
"Aren't you dragging this out too long?" she said, giving the girl a severe look.

The girl looked back at Barbara and rotated her
shoulders as if to refer to the people there and com-
plain about their indifference and inattentiveness.
But the severity of Barbara's look brooked no silent
excuses, and the girl, without interrupting her inex-

pressive, unintelligible movements, began to unbutton her blouse.

From then on Barbara no longer concerned herself with her but looked at the guests one after the other. Understanding that look, they halted their conversations and obediently turned their eyes to the girl, stripping. Then Barbara hitched up her own skirt, put her hand between her thighs, and again leveled her provocative eyes at all sides of the room. She was watching her gymnasts closely to see if they were following her demonstration.

In their own slow but sure rhythm, things were finally getting started, the girl from the provinces, now long since naked, lying in some man's arms, the others scattered in the various rooms. Barbara, however, was everywhere, always vigilant and infinitely exacting. She did not allow her guests to pair off and hide away somewhere. She flared up at a young woman whose shoulders Jan had his arm around: "Go to his place if you want him to yourself. This is a party!" Then she grabbed her by the arm and dragged her to the next room.

Jan caught the eye of a pleasant-looking bald young man who was keeping to himself and had observed Barbara's intervention. They smiled at each other. The bald man came over to Jan, who said to him: "Field Marshal Barbara."

The bald man laughed and said: "She's a coach training us for the Olympics."

Together they watched Barbara's sequence of activities:

Kneeling next to a man and woman making love, she inserted her head between their faces and pressed her mouth against the woman's lips. Out of consideration for Barbara, the man withdrew from his partner, no doubt thinking Barbara wanted her to herself. Barbara took the woman in her arms and clasped her tightly while the man stood humbly and respectfully over them. Still kissing the woman, Barbara made a circle in the air with her raised hand. The man understood that it was meant for him but did not know if she was ordering him to stay or go. He watched tensely as the hand's motion became more and more energetic and impatient. Finally Barbara removed her lips from the woman's mouth and told him what she wanted. The man nodded, slipped down to the floor again, and nestled up against the back of the woman, who was now sandwiched between him and Barbara.

"We're all characters in Barbara's dream," said Jan.

"Yes," replied the bald man. "But it never quite works. Barbara is like a clockmaker who has to keep moving the hands of his clock himself."

As soon as she had put the man in position, Barbara lost interest in the woman she had just been kissing passionately. She got up and went over to a corner of the room where a pair of very young lovers with anguished expressions were curled up against each other. They were only half undressed, and the young man was trying hard to hide the girl with his body. Like supernumeraries on an opera stage who open their mouths without emitting a sound and absurdly wave their hands to create the illusion of a lively conversation, they were struggling to make it clear that they were totally absorbed in each other, because all they wanted was to go unnoticed and thus avoid the others.

Not at all fooled by their dodge, Barbara knelt down beside them, caressing their hair and telling them something. Then she vanished into another room and came back with three naked men. Again she got down on her knees next to the two lovers, taking the young man's head in her hands and kissing it. The three naked men, guided by the silent commands of her look, bent over the girl and removed the rest of her clothes.

"When it's all over, there'll be a meeting," said the bald man. "Barbara is going to summon all of us, she's going to put us in a semicircle around her, stand in front of us, put her glasses on, analyze what we did right and what we did wrong, and praise the industrious pupils and reprimand the lazy ones."

The two shy lovers ended up sharing their bodies with others. Barbara then dropped them and headed for the two men. She gave Jan a quick smile and turned to the bald man. At about the same moment, Jan felt the delicate touch of the girl from the provinces whose strip show had set things going. Barbara's clock, he said to himself, wasn't working so badly.

The girl from the provinces took care of him with fervent zeal, but his eyes kept straying to the other side

of the room, where the bald man's member was being
worked on by Barbara's hands. Both couples were in
the same situation. Bent over, both women were making the same motions, attending to the same task; they
resembled assiduous gardeners leaning over a flower
bed. Each couple was a mirror image of the other. The
two men caught each other's eye, and Jan saw the bald
man's body shaking with laughter. And because they
were united, united like an object and its reflection in
a mirror, one of them was unable to shake without the
other shaking as well. Jan turned his head away from
the other couple so as not to offend the girl caressing
him. But his reflected image was irresistible. When he
looked over there again, the bald man's eyes were
bulging with suppressed laughter. They were united, at
a minimum, by a fivefold telepathic current. Not only
did each know what the other was thinking; they both
knew the other knew. All the comparisons they had
applied to Barbara earlier came back to mind, and
they were inventing new ones. They were at once looking at each other and avoiding each other's eyes,
because they knew that laughter was as sacrilegious
here as it is in church when the priest is elevating the
host. But from the moment that comparison passed
through both their heads, their only desire was to
laugh. They were too weak. Laughter was stronger.
Their bodies were seized by irresistible convulsions.

Barbara looked up at her partner's head. The bald
man had capitulated and was letting his laughter burst
out. As if guessing the cause of the evil, she turned to

Jan. Just then the girl from the provinces was murmuring to him: "What happened? Why are you crying?"

But Barbara was already near him, hissing through clenched teeth: "Don't think you can pull on me what happened at Passer's funeral!"

"I'm sorry," said Jan; and he laughed and the tears ran down his cheeks.

She asked him to leave.

14

Before his departure for the United States, Jan took Edwige to the seashore. It was on a forsaken island with a few tiny villages, meadows with apathetically grazing sheep, and a single hotel on a fenced-off beach. They took separate rooms.

He knocked at her door. Calling from the far end of the room, she told him to come in. Inside, he saw no one. "I'm making pee," she shouted through the half-open bathroom door.

That was familiar to him. Even with a bunch of people at her house, she would calmly announce she was going to make pee and then would chat with her guests through the partly open door. It was neither flirtatious nor shameless. Quite the contrary: it was the absolute abolition of flirtatiousness and shamelessness.

Edwige did not accept traditions that burdened mankind. She refused to acknowledge that a naked face is innocent and a naked behind shameless. She did not understand why the salty fluid that trickles from our eyes is sublimely poetic and the fluid we emit below our bellies is disgusting. It all seemed stupid, artificial, and unreasonable to her, and she treated such conventions the way a rebellious girl treats the rules of a Catholic boarding school.

Coming out of the bathroom, she smiled at Jan and let him kiss her on both cheeks: "Shall we go to the beach?"

He nodded.

"Leave your clothes here," she said, removing her bathrobe to uncover her nakedness.

Jan always found it a little strange to undress in front of others, and he almost envied Edwige the way she came and went in her nakedness as in a comfortable housecoat. She was in fact much more natural naked than dressed, as if in rejecting her clothes she was also rejecting the difficult condition of womanhood in order to become simply a human being, without sexual characteristics. As if sex resided in clothes and nakedness were a state of sexual neutrality.

They went naked down the steps to the beach, where groups of naked people were relaxing, walking around, and swimming: naked mothers and naked children, naked grandmothers and naked grandchildren, naked men young and old. There was a tremendous number of female breasts in the greatest variety of shapes: beautiful, less beautiful, ugly, huge, shriveled. Jan realized with melancholy that, next to young breasts, not only do old ones not seem younger, but, contrarily, the young breasts seem older, and all of them together were equally bizarre and meaningless.

And once again he was assailed by that vague, mysterious idea of the border. He felt he was right on the line, crossing it. And he was gripped by a strange sadness, and from that sadness as from a fog an even stranger thought emerged: it was in a crowd and naked that Jews went to the gas chambers. He neither understood just why that image kept coming back to him nor just what it meant. Maybe it meant that at that moment the Jews had also been on *the other side of the border* and thus that nakedness is the uniform worn by men and women on the other side. That nakedness is a shroud.

The sadness induced in Jan by the naked bodies scattered all over the beach became more and more unbearable. He said: "It's so peculiar, all these naked bodies here. . . ."

Edwige nodded: "Yes. And what's even more peculiar is that all the bodies are beautiful. Look, even old bodies, even sick bodies are beautiful as soon as they're only bodies, bodies without clothes. They're as beautiful as nature. An old tree is no less beautiful than a young one, and a sick lion is still king of the beasts. Human ugliness is the ugliness of clothes."

They never understood each other, Edwige and he, yet they always agreed. Each interpreted the other's words in his or her own way, and there was wonderful harmony between them. Wonderful solidarity based on lack of understanding. He was well aware of it and almost took pleasure in it.

They strolled slowly along the beach, the sand burning underfoot, the bleating of a ram mingling with the sound of the sea, a filthy sheep grazing on an islet of withered grass in the shade of an olive tree. Jan remembered Daphnis. He is lying down, spellbound by Chloe's nakedness, aroused but with no knowledge of what that arousal is summoning him to, so that the arousal is endless and unappeasable, limited and interminable. A great yearning gripped Jan's heart, a desire to go back again. Back to that boy. Back to man's beginnings, to his own beginnings, to love's beginnings. He desired desire. He desired the pounding of the heart. He desired to be lying beside Chloe unaware of fleshly love. Unaware of sexual climax. To transform himself into pure arousal, the mysterious, the incomprehensible and miraculous arousal of a man before a woman's body. And he said out loud: "Daphnis!"

The sheep was still grazing on the withered grass, and with a sigh Jan repeated: "Daphnis, Daphnis . . ."

"Are you calling to Daphnis?"

"Yes," he said, "I'm calling to Daphnis."

"That's good," said Edwige. "We need to go back to him. To go back to the time before Christianity crippled mankind. Is that what you mean?"

"Yes," said Jan, though he had meant something entirely different.

"Back then, there might still have been a bit of natural paradise left," Edwige went on. "Sheep and shepherds. People belonging to nature. Freedom of the senses. Isn't that what Daphnis means to you?"

Again he assured her that that was just what he meant, and Edwige asserted: "Yes, you're right, it's Daphnis Island!"

And because he enjoyed expanding their agreement based on misunderstanding, Jan added: "And our hotel should be called On the Other Side."

"Yes," cried Edwige enthusiastically. "On the other side of that jail, our civilization!"

Some small groups of naked people came near; Edwige introduced Jan to them. They shook his hand and proclaimed their status and their pleasure at meeting him. Then they dealt with various topics: the temperature of the water, the hypocrisy of a society that cripples body and soul, the beauties of the island.

On the latter subject, Edwige said: "Jan was just saying that it's Daphnis Island. I think he's right."

All of them were delighted by that stroke of inspiration, and a man with an extraordinary paunch developed the idea that Western civilization is going to perish and that humanity will finally be liberated from the enslaving burden of the Judeo-Christian tradition. These were phrases Jan had heard ten, twenty, thirty, a hundred, five hundred, a thousand times before, and those few meters of beach soon turned into a lecture hall. The man spoke, all the others listened with interest, and their bare genitals stared stupidly and sadly at the yellow sand.